WONDERFUL TRICKS

STORIES BY GREGORY SPATZ

Mid-List Press
Minneapolis

Published by Mid-List Press, 4324 12th Avenue South, Minneapolis, MN 55407-
3218. Visit our website at www.midlist.org.

First printing: September 2002
06 05 04 03 02   5 4 3 2 1

Manufactured in Canada.

Library of Congress Cataloging-in-Publication Data
Spatz, Gregory, 1964–
  Wonderful tricks : stories by / Gregory Spatz.
    p. cm.
"First series : short fiction."
  ISBN 0-922811-55-5 (pbk. : alk. paper)
1. Love stories, American. I. Title.
  PS3569.P377 W66 2002
  813'.54—dc21

                                        2002010874

Cover art: Marc Chagall, *Daphnis and Chloe*, 1956; photograph © Araldo de
Luca/Corbis
Cover and text design: Lane Stiles

Grateful acknowledgment is made to the following journals where these stories,
sometimes in slightly different form, first appeared: *The Journal*, "Paradise Was
This"; *The New England Review*, "Lisa Picking Cockles"; *Shenandoah*, "Walking
in My Sleep"; *Blood and Aphorisms*, "Body Imaging"; *Descant*, "Plenty of Pools
in Texas"; *The Indiana Review*, "Inversion"; *The New Yorker*, "Wonderful
Tricks"; *Epoch*, "Anyone's Venus"; *Glimmer Train Stories*, "Stone Fish"; and
Willow Springs, "Zigzag Cabinet."

For *my grandmother, Marion Spatz,*
and in memory of my grandfather,
Milton Spatz, 1914-2002

CONTENTS

PARADISE WAS THIS

———

AFTERNOONS, JASPER PLAYED CARDS WITH HIS GRANDMOTHER
because he knew she was lonely. To get to her house he walked
on the road past Comeaux's ratty farm with the tar paper
peeling off the roof, then left, up East Hill Road and past two
more houses she owned. Or, he cut through the pastures and
over the hill, ducking barbed wire and ignoring the POSTED
signs because this was his land, family land. If it was not too
muddy that was the way he preferred. He popped open the
milkweed pods and pulled on their tufts of white hair until the
unsprouted seeds came out, all in a piece; the gunk, like milk,
that dripped out of the pods and down the stalk, he didn't
touch; he knew it smelled bad and vanished once it was on you,
then stuck your fingers together. In late summer the milkweed
plants would open and the white part would blow away. One
day he would look up and there would be a galaxy of seeds
mixed in with all the bugs and birds. Now it was still spring.

———

1

The last part of the walk went along an old tractor path through pines growing next to the pond. He liked this part best. He liked the way the needles on the ground silenced his footfalls and pushed him along, making him almost buoyant, and he liked the pine smell and the way the trees made straight avenues into the sky. When he was walking this last part of the walk he would have a feeling as if he should hold his breath. He'd lower his eyelids halfway and whisper, "Thy kingdom come, Thy will be done," though he came from an unreligious family and didn't know what the words were about, had only heard them once in a while at school.

At his grandmother's, they played the games he knew— rummy, casino, and crazy-eights. They played in the den where his grandfather's reading chair was, but they didn't talk about him. It was only a year now since he'd died. He told her things that had happened at school. He didn't tell her about his mother or his sister, who rarely visited anymore. He did his new card tricks, the one with the disappearing king, the one with the ace at the bottom of the well, and the one where the deck was a house on fire. It was a matter of hiding cards behind other cards and palming them hand to hand, remarkably simple, but impressive to the adults. After a game, she would get up and go into the kitchen to refill her drink and check on something she was cooking. Then he would practice hiding cards. He'd listen to her in the next room and wait until he heard her clear her throat, then the slap of her slippers on the floor, coming back into the den, and he'd know she was all right and not out there crying, which also happened. She thought her crying frightened him; it didn't, but it made him impatient. When she was crying it was like she became another person and he had to wait for that to finish so she was herself again. "Now, here's your card," he'd say, practicing. "Isn't this your card?" He'd snap his fingers. "Magic."

———

The house was for sale. He knew about it. The house, the barns, the land, the pond, the rental houses, the trout stream, and the rundown Comeaux farm. The Comeauxs didn't care because they had no stake in whoever owned the land they worked, as long as they could go on working it. He saw Comeaux now riding up into the back field on his tractor. Comeaux had an orange cap that was splattered with manure, and a tight lipless, hairless face that reminded Jasper of a hammer. Jasper waited as he went past to see if there was anything new in the way they regarded each other.

"Hello," he yelled.

Comeaux nodded as usual, said "Hello," and kept going.

Jasper watched him all the way to the top of the hill. He shaded his eyes with one hand to see. There was the sun splintering on the tractor, jumping back off in prismatic bursts that stung his eyes; the shape of the trail and the smoke shooting up out of the tractor's exhaust; the brown top of his parents' house which he could barely see through the trees.

He climbed one of the trees in the alleyway of straight pines next to the pond where he always stopped and spun around and looked at the sky and said things to God. The first few yards were a scramble, shimmying up with nothing to hold on to. Bark came off in his hands and shattered between his legs and under his sneakers. He felt watched because of how much noise he was making, and stopped to look around. A woodpecker smashed its bill in and out of the bark of one tree farther back toward home. A propeller plane went overhead, buzzing sadly. So, these things were happening and he was not really the center of the world. He climbed a few yards higher, until there were two branches like handlebars and he could pull himself up. He pulled and sidled and swung around so he could grab another higher branch, and then he was upright, looking across the pond. There was the house, white with black shutters, fitting into the land. It didn't have a symmetrical shape and looked bigger on the outside than he thought it really was. If he closed his eyes he knew the sound of his feet in all the rooms and the way the boards popped and changed pitch, and the smells that came up in the air, room to room, and the changes in light. But anyone could live there and feel the same attachments he did, which meant his feelings were not really his own but held in objects and caused by them to exist.

When he got there, she was not in the kitchen waiting for him. "Hello!" he yelled. He saw her shoes on the mat next to the door, low boots with fur lining, the kind she got every year. He went up the step into the den. She was not there in the window seat or on the couch, reading. It didn't smell like her cigarettes. The lights were off. She might not have been in this room all day. He went through the other side of the den and out to the dining room. Here was a thick carpet and a pendulum clock in the corner. Under the table was a doorbell in the floor, which she could touch with one foot when she was "entertaining" and needed to summon Ellie, who worked for her, from the kitchen.

He continued into the hall and upstairs. "What a pleasant surprise, I wasn't expecting you," she would say, when he appeared. She said it every time. There were paintings in the upstairs hall. His uncles had done them—paintings of the streets in Europe where they lived. He checked the other rooms, tapping on half open doors and looking inside— empty, all of them. He went into the passageway leading to her room. It had a musty book smell, like her room, because she was always reading, thrillers and murder mysteries. Her door was shut. "Gran," he yelled. "What are you doing in there?"

There was no answer. He turned the doorknob and went in.

She was asleep inside on the green divan in a slip, a glass of something on the arm of the chair next to her, her head flopped to the side. "Gran," he said again. She didn't move. The twin beds were next to him with the Shetland wool blankets folded in quarters at the feet. He saw himself in the dresser mirror—his blue jeans and T-shirt, black hair; pieces of pine bark and twigs stuck to him—and saw her still lying there beside him on the divan. She was not waking up. She must be drunk. He walked over and put his hands on her bare shoulders. They were soft, the skin compressing under his fingers. He shook her and tapped the sides of her face. He smelled gin. "Get up," he said. Her eyes opened. He pulled her to her feet. "Come on, walk," he said. He put an arm around her waist and pulled her forward. "Walk," he said again. When his grandfather overdrank, he went into the bathroom and threw up so loudly everyone in the house heard it. Then his grandmother would do this. She'd hug him under one arm and say, "Walk, walk, come on, honey. You can do it. Get the alcohol out of your blood."

He tugged her along. "Jasper, dear," she said, "you don't know what you're doing." Halfway across the room her legs went out from under her. He couldn't prevent it. He looked at her on the floor with her legs twisted under her. She started to laugh. In the barn across the street, Tom, Ellie's husband, was hammering something together, then there was the zip of the table saw, cutting. Jasper waited for her to get up and watched her breathing.

———

Bankers, and people from other countries, and people representing corporations came to see. They arrived in the Realtor's long white car, which took up most of the driveway, wearing dresses and suits. They stood on the footsteps Jasper and his sister, Desiree, had left with the date scratched underneath, 7-9-66, the day men came to blacktop four years ago. Water stayed in the toes long after a rain. The real estate agent said things like, "Thirty minutes to Tanglewood. Butternut Basin, right around the corner." They walked down to the pond and the beach and probably saw how the sand was trampled and muddy, no longer white, as it had been back when his grandfather first poured it. The showers in the bathhouse next to the tennis court didn't work and the roof there sagged from a weight of pine needles. The barns across the street were in good shape because it had been years since they were used for anything. His grandfather's real business was in the city of Hartford, where he owned toy stores. Now there weren't even those. He should have put his properties up for sale long ago, people said. He should have set aside money instead of always buying things—horses, antiques, guns, wine, jewelry—then his grandmother wouldn't be left in this way. But Jasper's grandfather was a stubborn man and had liked to live as if he were king.

There were still chickens—ten of them in a coop built against the stable. Jasper got the eggs. They were there every morning as if by magic. He went in with a handful of corn to throw so the chickens would fly up out of the roost, animated bags, squawking and pecking the dirt. The corn was warm and had a sweet smell and left crumbs on his palm after he'd tossed it. In the tack room he liked leaning over the full barrel, breathing the corn smell and digging his arms up to the elbows in kernels. He tried eating some, once, but it had no taste and stuck in his back teeth, gumming them up. After the chickens were out of the roost he felt around for eggs, plinked them gingerly in a coffee can, and went back across the street for breakfast.

He helped Tom stack wood in the shed attached to the stable. It was hard for him to see what the wood was good for—if she sold the house she wouldn't stay, and didn't need wood. Still, they went at it, stacking pieces until the wood went higher than Jasper, splintery blocks reaching the shed ceiling. He played cards with his grandmother and practiced magic tricks, but not as often since it was nice out and she was busy with the Realtors. He climbed the roof of the stable and sat at the peak of it, looking down on Tom and Ellie's back yard where she sometimes lay bare-chested next to the laundry line, nursing their baby, Edgar. If she looked up and saw Jasper straddling the roof she might wave at him or make faces. Sometimes, he took off from the roof of the stable, up into the limbs of a young maple next to it. It was an easy tree to climb and had a natural seat, high up in the branches, where he could sit, almost comfortable enough to sleep. There he looked at the sky and the moving clouds and he ate a sandwich and a boiled egg, and then he got restless because it was boring to do this. The maple leaves were still light green, lighter than grass.

He went all the way down the side of the stable roof where Ellie was, to see her up close. He didn't know why he was doing this if it disturbed him.

"Hi," he said.

She smiled and giggled. "Hi, yes, I certainly am," she said. She continued laughing. She had wide teeth and loopy red blond hair that went to her shoulders.

Jasper saw the milk caught in the hairs of her nipple. He couldn't stop staring, it was so bright and blistered looking.

"Wanna try?" she asked.

"I don't think so."

"Tom says it's like peanuts today."

Tom was across the street now, cutting hedges. Jasper saw him, wet circles under his arms in the colored T-shirt he wore with the cigarettes rolled under the sleeve. It looked to Jasper like he was muttering to himself while he worked. Jasper thought Tom was very handsome; he had thin lips and shiny brown hair with a widow's peak. His sweat always smelled like the ground and grease and steel, and his chest was bone white, unlike his arms which were a dark wood color and rippled with veins and muscles. When he took his shirt off at lunch, Jasper would see grass and dirt hiding underneath, stuck to his skin.

Ellie looked at him, shading her eyes from the sun. She had said something else but he missed what it was.

"Thanks anyway," he said.

"You're very welcome, sir."

He lay flat on the roof with his arms hanging over the edge. Wasps flew around him, around his fingers and wrists, finding their paper homes in the holes under the eaves and inside the walls. He listened to their heavy droning. Wasps were awkward fliers, too easily blown off course and not able to calculate a landing. When one landed on him it was like a flick. Then his skin would tighten unwillingly from the touch of the wasp's feet, and he had to resist the urge to swat it or brush it away. That was how to get stung. There was one crawling up his forearm now, dark and obstinate, a tiny dinosaur on his pale skin, the stinger pushing and swinging up and down. He blew lightly, and it flew away.

————

His new trick was one called "The Moving Cards." He had learned it from a book called *Tommy K's ABC's of Magic*. To do it, he needed two aces of spades, one in the deck and one in his palm. The trick was moving the aces from one bunch of cards to the next so it looked as if there was only one ace flitting between cards like a cloud. "Once there was a lonely card," he said. This was the story that went with the trick—the story was meant to keep their eyes from his hands. "It wanted to be among the other cards, but couldn't find any other cards to like it." He moved his hands over the cards, turning them over at will. The ace was everywhere he wanted it to be. It went like a thread through the story and finally came out alone, rejected by all the other cards and bent up in one corner from being pressed into his palm.

"What a pretty trick," his grandmother said. They were outside in lawn chairs by the water. She had a book open in her lap. That day she wasn't drinking and it made her nervous. The ducks drifted on the water, quacking. "Do it again."

"No," he said. Sometimes there were tricks he could repeat without setting up. This was not one. He shuffled the cards, bridged them, and made them jump from hand to hand. "Pick a card," he said, and fanned them under her chin. "Don't let me see it."

"We've already done this," she said. "You do it every time we have a magic show."

"Pick a card!"

She picked one.

"Memorize your card." He watched her. "Study it. Be sure you aren't going to forget."

When her eyes were down he flipped the cards in his hand, and turned one over on the bottom of the deck. "Now put it back in the middle."

He held the deck so she wouldn't see it was upside down, cut it once, turned it over, and blew on the top of it. "Isn't this your card?" he asked, and flicked the top card so it turned over in her lap.

She almost jumped. "You devil."

He grinned. "Ha, ha." It was much too easy to fool her.

They lay back in their lawn chairs. After a while she said, "Make my sun come out," and glanced at him. "How come you can't do that?"

"Oh, I can. Abracadabra." He waved his hands in the air.

The sun stayed where it was.

At the back of Tommy K's book was a chapter on demo-litions which told how to mix soap and whisky to make an explosion; how to slice open light bulbs and glue them back together full of explosives so there would be a shower of light and glass when you flicked the switch. The book warned about the danger of such explosions in a cold, dismissive tone Jasper thought was funny. "Yes, in every house," Tommy K said, "there are enough common household items that when mixed together in the right ways and ignited will cause an explosion of such force as to level all preexisting structures. We ask that you use care and caution in the use of this material while performing acts with explosives, and never use them in such a way as to cause violence or harm." He memorized this piece of text because he thought it was so out-of-the-blue and pointless. If it was true, then who was going to pay attention to it? "Level all preexisting structures," he would say to himself sometimes at night to fall asleep. The words gave him a thrilled feeling of being alive and unsuspected, submerged in secret knowledge.

He spent most of an afternoon, one day, in the cow barn blowing apart bottles of soap and whisky. It was raining hard that day and the air was cold with blasts of wet wind. The bottles were Coke bottles, five of them, lined up in the wet straw with rags sticking out of the tops. He lit the rags and ran away, back behind a hay bale to watch. The bottles popped and burst apart and pieces of sizzling glass spun out everywhere, zinging into the walls and ringing against gutters and pieces of steel. He lay there a while after, waiting to see what came next—if anyone would run out here to see what had happened and if he was OK. But nobody came. Nobody knew he was here. It was like nothing had happened.

————

He went into the kitchen where the light was cool like the slate floor and found her crying at the big table next to the hooded barbecue flue where they used to eat on weekends. She was in a polka-dot dress, not her swimsuit. People had just been to see the house again—Indians, four of them, in pastel turbans. Only one spoke English. Jasper had watched for a while before he went to help Tom.

He got a glass of ginger ale and sat next to her at the table. Her cigarettes were out, the red leather pouch she carried them in unsnapped and one cigarette lying on top, ready to be smoked. Jasper picked it up and sniffed it and rolled it between his fingers. Such a skinny paper thing, it was hard to believe it would kill you.

His grandmother opened her eyes and took the cigarette from him.

"Are they going to buy?" he asked, though he already knew the answer. Always, it was the same.

"They said they'll let us know," she said. She shook her head. "No. They're not buying anything."

He smelled scotch on her breath and tasted the scotch taste in his mouth. Often, when she was drinking, she let him have sips of what was in her glass. Scotch was his favorite, the scorched taste of it soaked in little pieces of ice like candy. "Good," he said.

"In another few months the bank's going to come and take everything, nail boards on the windows and doors. Is that what you want?"

"No." He made his eyes go up into hers.

"Then don't say it's good."

"OK," he said, but he didn't mean it.

She sighed. "What did you have in mind to do today?" She always asked her questions in the past tense, as if the thing she asked was something he'd done or been thinking of doing for a long time already.

"Nothing at all. Pick some strawberries on the hill."

There was writing all over the kitchen table, his grand-father's letters like runes engraved in the soft wood because he had always worked here, writing his memos and letters and pressing too hard on the pen. Jasper traced his fingers over them and tipped his head to one side to see into the glare on the surface of the wood. The letters angled backward, hard wide swipes going up the backs of his *d*s and *f*s and *h*s. Jasper had always thought that one day he would sit down and really try to read them—he didn't know what he'd find, but he figured if he tried hard enough to put together sentences he'd find some. Now, for the first time, he saw it would never be possible.

The trout stream was named after an Indian chief, Konkapot, known for keeping his land from the hands of white people by signing treaties and smoking peace pipes. Jasper's grandmother had told him about it. She said his soul was in the water, so Jasper had to think about that every time he went fishing. His grandfather's soul was also in the water. After he died, and as soon as the river was thawed, they came down here and threw in the ashes. It was cold, mid-April, raining off and on, and when the ashes were gone, they stood in a circle, heads bowed, and Jasper's oldest uncle said something about bodies being used up and returned to the land. Jasper was distracted by the chatter of birds and the beaded water on the leaves on the ground at his feet. He felt the sun come out from behind the clouds and touch him on the back of the neck like a hand. Some paper-white leaves, also like hands, left in the twigs of one poplar next to the water waved back and forth.

The river was at the edge of the farthest cornfields, down behind the stable and other barns. He could hear it long before he came to it, walking the tractor trail down through the corn. Upstream was the town of Mill River, downstream was the swimming hole under the bridge on New River Road, where they went on the hottest days when the pond was too warm and still and turtles sat everywhere on the banks. He went upstream. He'd been this way, but never as far. The fields on his left were separated from the river by trees and bramble—birch, oak, maple, pine, poplar. He came to a dam, not very high. The water going over it was bent and whispering. Next to the dam was a round plot of cut grass. There was a swept trail running from the spot back up the hill to the house of whoever owned it, but the house was hidden in trees. He imagined his grandfather, A.J. Konnelly, and Chief Konkapot smoking peace pipes on the riverbed and making deals for the land, the toy salesman and the Indian chief. He lay on his back in the sun and listened for their voices through the babble of the water, and watched the clouds fly apart overhead, pieces of lint and ripped smoke.

———

"Why are you here all the time instead of home," Ellie asked. They were on the back steps. She was smoking a cigarette, snapping beans. The day was almost over and the sky was full of blond clouds brushed with red in back.

"Why not? I like it here."

"Of course," she said.

He could see down to the water, where they were sitting, the willows hanging, the rowboat up on the sand. Heat hazed everything and shimmered in the wet air.

She looked at him. "Of course you do. It's paradise."

"It is," he said. He had no way of knowing if that was

true; there was nothing for him to compare the place with. He only knew what he'd been told: paradise was this.

"How old are you?" she asked. She glanced at him. She sucked in smoke so it swirled out of the lit end of the cigarette, then blew jets through her nose. The beans went plink plink into the bowl, snapped in halves, the stems gone. She had on canvas sneakers and the bean stems were making a pile around them.

"Twelve and a half."

"The perfect age to be," she said.

"Perfect for what?"

She never answered.

———

His grandfather's swords and guns were on a rack in the deepest part of the basement, ten steps down from where the furnace and water tanks were. The swords were dull and heavy, like clubs, with corroded edges. He got them out of their scabbards and lay them next to each other. They weren't the least bit dangerous. He lifted one and swung it around him, fending off imaginary enemies. He went in and out of the light, jabbing at shadows. "En garde," he hissed. "Take that." He whirled and jabbed, cocked his wrist and made the blade jump up and down through his enemy's guts. Five reflected images of himself in the broken mirror leaning against the wall beside the file cabinets leapt up and he went at them, stabbing. The mirror crunched and shattered some more, but there he was, still fighting himself in the broken pieces. He threw the sword over his shoulder and feigned dying. He rolled on the hard floor and felt the grit going through his shirt, to the skin.

Now it was time for his last trick.

Superglue, one plastic egg glued shut with the candy taken out and a nail hole in the top, an eyedropper, and bleach—these things were not hard to find. The bleach went into the glued shut egg using the eyedropper. He filled it until there was a drop of moisture at the lip of the nail hole, then sealed the hole with superglue and let it dry. He cleaned that with a rag so no bleach was left on the outside, put it in his pocket and went up to where the furnace tank was, between the wine cellar and the extra refrigerator, slipped in behind the refrigerator in the deep brown cobwebs that peeled off on him in strings, found the cap on the tank and unscrewed it. It wasn't easy. He had to bang and pry. When it came off, he looked inside and saw from the spot of light shining back up at him that the tank was almost full. He dropped in the egg, and capped it tight. The gas would eat through the plastic in seven hours and then there would be an explosion like three sticks of dynamite followed by a gradual and devastating fire. It was five o'clock now. That meant, if Tommy K was right, somewhere around midnight the place would begin burning down. He would wake to the smell of smoke and run to her room at the end of the hall, wake her and lead her to safety.

He had to forget about it. As soon as he crossed the threshold from the cellar back into the light and shut the door behind him, he would be transformed. Down here, it was dark. Upstairs, it would be light. He'd come through in the pantry next to the washer and drier where it smelled like cleaner and detergent. He'd come into the light, lean against the door a second to catch his breath, and forget what he'd just done. He'd hold it under the surface of his thinking, a thing he knew about but did not remember.

He slept in the stable that night. The stable had a deep, horse smell—saddle soap and leather, horse sweat, sweet grain, twine and straw. He pushed the door shut and slid down in a corner under the rack of saddles. Stirrups touched his shoulders. He pulled up on them to lift himself and settle against the wall.

His grandfather used to come in on Sunday, get the lead rope and grain in a coffee can to shake up and down while he whistled for the horses. He'd go out into the grass that soaked him to the knees. "Here, Ginny," he'd yell. "Come on, Poko." He'd make squirting and clucking noises in his mouth. His grandfather's horse, Star, an Arabian stallion with long-stockinged legs and a nose nearly as sculpted as a teacup, was the hardest to catch. The struggle between them would begin the moment his grandfather set foot in the pasture with a mind to go riding, and didn't end until long after he was out of the tub, dressed in his Sunday clothes, a bright scarf tucked in the neck of his shirt, bruises and pulled muscles soaked away and a smell of menthol emollient following him everywhere. "God damn that horse," he'd say. "Damn him yourself," Jasper would whisper back.

He pulled down one of the saddle blankets and put it over his legs, then another one to put behind his head for a pillow. The blankets were stiff and coarse, like rugs, covered with horsehair. He slumped to one side, still sitting up, and tried to sleep. The flashlight in his hand kept waking him up. He dreamed it was rolling out of his fingers, then snapped his eyes open, tightening his hand, and felt it there, warm and real in his palm. He dreamed he was at the top of a steep roof and rolling down.

The chickens woke him up, squawking and flapping, making a racket outside. He flashed his light around the room, then got up and ran down the hall past the empty stalls, out the side door to the corral and the chicken coop. He flashed his light through the chicken wire and saw sawdust everywhere flying. Chickens were hopping and bawking. Two raccoons jumped down from the roost and came into the beam of his light. One froze, its red eyes reflecting light, and stood upright hissing. Then it turned around and went back into the roost. It sat there, sifting straw through its fingers and looking at Jasper, its eyes flickering and playful. The other swatted a chicken like it wanted to dance, then it too went into the roost, cooing and chattering.

He had to get Tom. Tom would come out with his gun and shoot them or scare them off. He ran around to the other side of the stable, and went full speed across the lawn. Without really remembering what it was, he felt the thing he had forgotten like a hole in his chest and the darkness down between the blades of grass he was running across. He went up onto their porch and tapped on the door. "Tom," he hissed. "Tom." No answer. He pushed on the door and it came open.

Inside, it was hot and smelled like cigarettes. In the kitchen were dishes piled in the sink, some of his grandmother's old pots and pans, some plates he recognized. He went on into the living room. Here the light was red like a film negative and there was low, deep music playing that erased outside sound. The television was on—his grandmother's old television with the rounded screen and fake wood paneling—just the picture, a man in a suit talking and raising his eyebrows in sly, self-flattering ways. The living room was full of his grandmother's old things, the tan recliner, the armchair, the lamp on the table, the couch with the flower pattern that used to be in her living room.

A door banged open and shut at the other end of the hall. "Who's there?" Tom said.

"It's me. Jasper," he said.

Tom came out of the dark. He had nothing on. His muscles swelled and rolled under his skin. Jasper wasn't embarrassed to see him naked because of the way he held himself, as if he was as comfortable dressed as undressed. It seemed only natural. His legs were all muscle, his feet splayed out on the floor.

"What are you doing here?" Tom asked. He went to the hi-fi and turned off the music. "What happened?" Before Jasper could answer he yelled down the hall, "Ellie. Ellie. It's Jasper."

There was a rustle from the other end of the hall and Ellie came out wrapped in a sheet. "Mr. Jasper. What are you doing here?"

He couldn't think of what to say. There are raccoons in the henhouse, he wanted to say. He couldn't get himself to say it.

"Are you OK?" she asked.

He shook his head.

"What's wrong?"

"Sit down."

He sat. They all sat on the couch and faced the mute man on television. He was replaced by a scene of a truck smashing into another truck. Jasper began to speak. He told them about sneaking out to sleep in the barn and waking up all of a sudden, about putting the bleach in the furnace to blow up the house earlier, then circled back around to the raccoons and trying to fall asleep in the tack room again.

Ellie touched him on the back. "Your trick won't work," she said. "It's an oil furnace, not gas. Don't worry. I don't think it would work anyway." She rubbed his shoulder and brushed something off it.

Tom sat forward suddenly and stood up. "Look, pal, you better sleep here the rest of the night." He patted the couch. He went to the closet and got down blankets. They were both moving around him now, lifting him, putting blankets on him, a pillow under his head, unlacing his shoes. Ellie brushed the hair away from his face. Her breath was sour smelling. Tom patted him roughly and squeezed his neck. "Good night," he said.

"The raccoons," Jasper said. He was so tired he could hardly speak.

"Shh," she said.

"We'll get them tomorrow," Tom said.

That was the last thing he remembered of the night.

The next day the house was still standing, stones around the foundation intact, windows blazing with the morning light, nothing wrong, nothing gone. In his mind he was working out an equation: in the world there is magic, and magic is change, but the world doesn't change. He went across the street, up the driveway, past his old footprints in the tar, and up the front steps, with three eggs the raccoons hadn't taken, and started water to cook them for breakfast.

He was in the tree when the New Yorkers returned for the third time. His grandmother said if they came this time she was pretty sure they would make an offer. The day was overcast, white, and the air was sweet with an undercurrent of cold. Wind flattened the grass in patches and gusted against the side of the stable. It went through the limbs of the tree he was in and swung him back and forth. The Realtor came out of the car first. She was in a peach dress. She always seemed to be discovering something new that excited her, her dress flaring up over her knees, her face with an expression like a question on it. The question was a lie. She didn't need answers, she wanted to pretend she was interested because it served her well to seem that way. The New Yorkers were in black and gray, a man and a woman. The man's hair was sculpted back. He had a bottle of champagne under one arm. He nodded his head once. The woman stood up straight and sniffed the air. The wind rattled the leaves. Her hard laugh came across the lawn, loud for a second, because of the way the wind took it, then gone. Their car doors chunked shut, the sound of them coming after the fact, and the Realtor led them inside.

Jasper went down the tree to the roof and up to the top of it, his feet thumping on the boards and grabbing the tar paper. Ellie was not on her lawn chair, she was inside with his grandmother. He walked at the peak of the roof to the end and back again, trying not to let his feet go off on either side. He wanted to be dead center of the ridge at the top. He walked and kept his eyes on the shingles right in front of him, counting steps and feeling the roof peak under his sneakers. He closed his eyes and did the same thing, counting. There were thirty-one steps to get across. He held his hands out to the sides and felt the wind pushing him. Seventeen, eighteen, nineteen, twenty. In his mind, he was flying—he was over the edge with nothing to hold him.

"Yoo-hoo!" It was Ellie, looking up at him, shielding her eyes. She had on a green sweatshirt and cutoffs. The skin on her legs was smooth and brown. Her legs were thin, the rest of her was not. She reminded him of a bird from this angle, her wide mouth and her bright hair and the way her stomach sloped out in front, almost hiding her legs. "Your grandma says she doesn't want you up there doing that," she said. She laughed like this was funny. "Come on down. Be a good kid and come down."

"OK."

He went down the side of the roof facing her house and jumped. The jump pushed him to his knees in the long grass for a second, but he didn't stay down.

She came and put her hand on his shoulder and they started walking. "You better not go in for a while. She has those people." She looped a finger in the air. "I'll fix you lunch."

They went to her and Tom's cottage. She told him to sit on the porch, which was glass, a greenhouse, full of plants and the smell of wet soil and fertilizer, Tom's boots piled next to the door. She went inside and came back out with tuna fish sandwiches and cranberry juice on a tray covered with trees. They ate. Edgar nursed, the top of his head tucked under her sweatshirt. Tom came in from working in the barn. His walk was a lope. He smiled at her and said hello to Jasper, then bunched up his face and bent over to nuzzle Edgar. Ellie told him to go make himself a sandwich. He came back out with the sandwich and a sweating can of beer and sat down on the step next to Jasper. The light coming through the glass was bright and warm, warmer than what was outside, making Jasper feel like it was the middle of summer, not the end of it. Tom asked them questions about the New Yorkers, who they were, what they did. "Not lawyers," Ellie said, "they're rich. She says she's from here.

Originally. He's an architect." She laughed for no reason. "Looks like they're gonna buy," she said, crooning the words and moving her eyebrows up and down.

Tom took delicate bites of his sandwich, apparently trying not to let the tips of his fingers touch anywhere he would bite. He swallowed and cleared his throat and got up to make another one. Jasper looked out through the glass at the white sky. He moved his foot on the ground and the gravel rasped. He heard the wind blow up over the top of the greenhouse. He wished this moment would not end, because whatever came after would never be more than a passing shade of what had been when he was in this world.

LISA PICKING COCKLES

————

MY FATHER CALLED ME DADDY SINCE THE TIME I WAS TWELVE, when my mother moved out and he found there was nothing else left for him but to take a more lighthearted approach to things in his life. This is not exactly what he said at the time. What he said had to do with responsibility. He said he was no longer responsible for upholding another person's system of ideas, meaning my mother's. When she had gone he moved her things out to the garage. He said this was so she could get them whenever she liked, without a scene, but she never came back for most of what had been hers. There were her winter clothes, her loom that she hadn't actually used, a cherry rocker her mother had once owned and which my father said was worth a little money, a painting of her father wearing a string tie, and other things I don't remember. These were in the garage for years, before we ever decided to do something about them.

————

He quit his job at the community college where he had taught art, and went back to painting full-time. He kept his own schedule, and there were days when I barely saw him. There were traces of his activity around the house: half-eaten bowls of soup, Henry Miller left open and face down anywhere you could imagine reading, candy wrappers on the couch, the radio left on downstairs, and so on. Sometimes he would just be waking up when I came home from school, and everything that had to be done for us was left for me to figure out. My mother might have guessed at the real depth of his irresponsibility—I would have called it his plain wish to be left alone in the world, without complications—but she couldn't have imagined what would happen when she left and he gave up the fight.

He and I traded rooms. He moved all his paints and canvases from the garage up to the attic loft, which had been mine, and let me have the downstairs room they'd shared. My mother's old office we left alone for some time, with nothing in it but the makeshift desk she'd used—an old mahogany door across two stacks of cinder blocks, and a single copy of Emily Dickinson's poems left in the wire basket that had once contained her students' papers. Eventually that room filled with dust, and old boxes and things that just didn't have a place anywhere else.

The floors in their room were varnished and bright and slipped under my feet. I felt more protected there, like I'd finally come inside after being cramped up in those rafters all my life, waiting, where it was too cold in the winter and too hot in the summer. But often I would wake up at night and not remember where I was at all. I would forget about having my own bathroom, and how I didn't have to trip down those metal spiral stairs in the middle of the night anymore, walking on the edges of my feet so they didn't get cold. Sometimes, lying there, I would let myself imagine I had no parents, and I was alone in a world exactly the size of that room, half-darkened with the shadows of the trees outside moving on the floor. I would think, "This is it," and it was as thrilling as it was terrifying. Then I'd remember my father up there asleep with all his paintings around him. I would listen for the music he played late at night, if he couldn't sleep, or try to hear him snoring, and I would tell myself how much better things were for him now. I would tell myself how much it must help him, having me there in their old room, so he didn't have to remember it as another place she was now absent from.

He re-mortgaged the house to buy back her half of it. I was told I had the choice to be with whomever I wanted, but I didn't think that was really a choice. I said I would just stick it out at home where I knew the kids in my class and the bike trails into town. And little by little, over the years, when she still hadn't come back for anything, we began to rob my mother's possessions out of the garage. If there were people visiting and we needed an extra knife, a glass, or a blanket for someone to sleep on, my father would say, "Daddy-O—check the garage. I think Leann was supposed to get some of that. She won't mind, rich woman that she is now." And then he would give whatever guests were visiting a lighthearted account of himself—what had happened, what he thought of my mother, and why it was OK to "borrow" from her in this way.

The first time he asked me to do this was not quite a year after she'd left. I was thirteen, and I think I half-expected to find her out in the garage. I was picturing her short black hair that was cropped close to her neck in the back. She would be sitting in that rocker and cursing to herself about my father, maybe holding her chin up in her hands that were always chafed-looking and pink on the sides. Of course, she wasn't there, and I stood for a long time looking around at her stuff before I remembered what I was supposed to be doing there. Wineglasses, I thought. There were boxes, and clothes I recognized draped over those boxes, one black lace-up shoe with a rounded toe that I'd seen her wear to someone's party once, a plastic spatula on top of some thick blue dishes, and other items I had already started to forget. And I thought, as long as we hung onto this stuff it was like she had died and wasn't just two states away, happily remarried to a man with money, and another kid on the way. I thought, it was no way to remember her, like she was dead, and I wondered if this might not have something to do with why she had left in the first place.

When I was fifteen my father brought me upstairs one afternoon to meet a fat woman called Linda, who was one of his models at the time. He didn't tell me, when he came downstairs to get me away from my homework, that Linda would be lying up there on his old couch with no clothes on.

"Linda Hayes, I want you to know my boy, Cary," he said. "Daddy, this is a woman that sells her body for me to paint. She calls herself Linda."

Linda sat right up on the couch and stared at me. She was a big woman, and there was a roll around her stomach that was the same tumescent white as her big breasts with their brown nipples like hoods. Her hair was thin brown and curly and she had on a few stringy gold bracelets—nothing else. She stood up and I saw shiny marks on her hips and waist like frozen rivers that did not connect, places where the skin appeared to have ruptured or trickled away from itself without healing properly. She said something to me about how we had met downstairs already—hadn't we?—and then told him that I didn't look anything like her, meaning my mother.

"Nathan," she said to my father, with her voice too full of breath for me to believe anything she would emphasize, "then again, you know, I've never really had the pleasure of her company. But isn't it just wonderful, how they come *half* out of us—like that?"

It was about the last thing I expected her to say. I was so carried away by the one fact most evident to me—her nakedness and the lack of anything in the world to prevent me from staring at it—that it was almost inconceivable to me she might be thinking about anything else. But she was unashamed, only looking back at me and thinking thoughts all her own. There was someone with a rough voice singing a folk song on my father's radio. He had gone back to his canvas and was standing there holding the end of a brush against his teeth, nodding his head in time with the music. He had on his usual, department store jeans and a gray-green T-shirt. The loft smelled like sour sheets, sweat, paint, and turpentine. Then he seemed to make up his mind about something; he added specks of color at various points of the composition in front of him—I thought it looked more like an explosion than a woman named Linda—and said, "That's exactly what I thought."

I went back to staring at Linda, who was actually repugnant in many ways—that patchy tuft of brown hair covering her crotch, curling up like a flame so it didn't quite hide the swollen V-like opening of her flesh—and yet my father was right: he knew much more than either of us. He knew how I had been thinking about these things, wondering about these models that had been going upstairs more and more often to undress for him. And it was better to see her now—sooner, rather than later—that's how he explained it to me after she had gone. He picked Linda, he said, because she was the most truly beautiful of them all.

"Sit," he said, and I sat down in the little paint-speckled chair next to his unmade bed. "No, I meant *you* sit," he said, and pointed the brush at Linda. "You can stay if you want," he said to me. "I don't care. Linda, do you care?"

"No," Linda said, and she lay back on the couch, with her arms over her head so that I could see the white powder of deodorant in her armpits.

I thought I could understand how the one circular shape underlying the explosion in my father's painting was supposed to relate to the many fat, circular shapes that were Linda on the couch, but I was not sure of this. I watched for a while and soon I thought there was certainly something unreal in the way my father saw things. It was compelling and a little sickening. His painting was like a whole secret code for sex that only he would ever see or understand—it was that complicated. Then I remembered something my mother had told me recently, when I had gone to visit her— why she said she would always both love and hate my father. She said it was because he couldn't stand anything "obvious." But he should get himself a translator, she said, because what was obvious to him was as obscure as a black night to anyone else. I could appreciate her frustration—he was never much interested in making himself directly understood. You could see that just from his painting of Linda. But the part about love she had thrown in only to make me feel better. It was supposedly my share of the injury, this absence of love between them that left me no real reason to exist. This was why she would still lie and say she loved him when really she did not. I was the only acknowledged thing left of what had been theirs together.

From that point on I understood I was free to come and go in my father's studio. Most of the time he worked from photos and had no live model, though when he had one it made no difference. We would talk a little when I went up there to see him, just after school. I would eat an apple or some graham crackers with jelly, tell him a few things about what had happened at school, and watch him work. He had long, straight brown hair that he parted on the side to cover his bald spot, heavy black plastic glasses, and a thin nose that was straight but not delicate. He often seemed unclean to me, and would wear the same clothes for days.

At times I believed my presence had begun to annoy him, but I had no confirmation. The attic loft was long and narrow, and there were many places where the ceiling was too close to stand upright. There was a little sink at one end, next to his bed, where I had always brushed my teeth at night. I remembered how I would stand there as a boy, sucking the last water out of the bristles of my toothbrush while I wondered what I would have to dream about that night. Now the sink was spattered with paint and there was a disorderly pine shelf of his painting supplies at its other side—brushes, paint tubes, palette knives, rags, coffee cans, gesso, turpentine, etc. Sometimes I didn't know for sure if he even remembered I was there, talking. And I wasn't sure which of these was more disappointing to entertain—that I was annoying, or that I was unimportant. I'd watch him suck the ends of his brushes to a point and wonder what he felt as he did this—if there were anything he anticipated, as I had once anticipated dreaming. I stared at each canvas as he was working on it, trying to imagine a solution for his silence. I saw suggestions that had to do with pain and sex, but they were never more than suggestions.

Many of my father's paintings have since been hung in unsuspecting and prestigious places all over the country—libraries, museums, and schools. This is where he has made his money. For instance, Linda's painting hung for almost a year in a bank on Avenue of the Americas in New York, until it was purchased by an unimportant movie person with a lot of money who did his banking there. Many of my father's best known paintings come from my teenage years, those years I stood watching him work while I rambled off and on about everything and nothing; "Red Hair and Clavicle," "Mindy on the Ice," "Elizabeth's Joy," "Jane," and "Once Upon a Nodding Head," are a few of these. Years after I had left home I would seek out his paintings in their new public places whenever I could, just to see if there wasn't something I had missed about them previously. But that was much later, and I never felt I had found the thing I was looking for.

There was a woman we shared. Lisa Britten. This was almost at the end of my time living with him. She showed up on a Saturday, in the middle of the day, two weeks after the opening of a group show in a SoHo gallery called Beeber, that had featured four of my father's paintings. She rode the train to Yonkers, found his name in the phone book at the station there, and asked a cabdriver to bring her to us in White Plains. She explained this later. She said she couldn't drive. I remember trying to read her expression as she stood outside our house in the street beside a pile of leaves I had raked up earlier the same day. She was wearing a khaki skirt and a denim jacket with leather trim, and the wind kept blowing strands of her long brown hair across her face, the same way it was blowing leaves off the top of that pile. I tried to guess who she was—a friend, a new model, someone with something to sell, a distant relative. I thought the way she looked over our house she was a little disappointed. She glanced up and down the street at the houses just like ours— little one-level brick houses with lofts, short lawns in front and different American-made cars in the driveways—and she seemed satisfied. She shrugged and adjusted her pocketbook, pushing it back on her shoulder, and came up the driveway with her head lowered like she was charging right at something.

"Nathan Dillard?" she said as soon as I opened the door for her. She must have been stricken by the light outside and not seeing me very clearly. She raised a hand to shade her eyes and keep the hair from blowing across her face. She was apparently anxious about something I hadn't come to understand yet—something exciting she was going to tell me, now—and for a moment I was tempted to lie, just to find out whatever it was she would tell me.

"Yes," I said, then, "that's my father." And I stood back for her to come in. There was a football game on the television that I hadn't been watching. For a moment she seemed distracted trying to see past me to it, her face showing another kind of expression that had nothing to do with the score of the game.

"Your father. Is he at home?"

"Upstairs," I said. "In the loft. That's where he works. Are you a new model?" I had had this conversation with other women, and I knew from experience that the way to set them at ease was to be as nonchalant as possible. Generally there was a kind of tired, nervous energy about those women and the stunted conversations I would have with them before they went to the back of the house and up the spiral stairs to meet my father for the first time. I would talk to those women like a person talking in his sleep, trying not to know just what they would look like undressed and lying on the couch with all their imperfections exposed while he walked around and around his paintings of them. But this exchange was different, and I felt a new kind of interest that I wasn't completely controlling.

"Model?" she asked, looking back at me. She seemed genuinely confused.

"No, I guess not," I said. "He does use live models sometimes. For his work," I added, when I thought she still wasn't following. "Models, for his artwork. He's a painter."

"Oh, not me," she said. "Really, *models!* He's such an abstract!" And I saw now she was blushing. She closed the door behind her and leaned back against it. Then she introduced herself, told me she was a reporter ("hopefully," she said) for an art magazine in the city called *New American Art* and we shook hands. She made her eyes blow up a little when she said she was glad to meet me, as if she wanted me to think she had waited for this opportunity to acknowledge me all her life. But it was a technique, badly used. Her eyes went directly into mine, dilating, looking for things and not suggesting what it was she wanted. Knowing how contrived this was did nothing to save me from its effect. I was already wishing that we would fall in love, and trying to imagine ways that might begin.

She continued to look around the house, seeing through the orange living room and into the kitchen where there were stacks of dishes in the sink, and white counters to match the white linoleum floor. She was shorter than me by a few inches. Her eyes were set close together and her face was thin, but round. The way her hair framed her face made her look younger or more innocent than I figured she probably was. There were little wrinkles around her eyes and a complexity about her skin that gave away her age. She must have been in her late twenties, and even if her expressions and her manners made me want to imagine she was just about my own age, clearly she was not someone for me to be thinking of in these ways. It didn't stop me, either, having recognized that. Her eyes were amber and took up all the light in the room. Under them were tiny veins like something spilled. A tick in one eyelid made the skin there ripple and jump until she put two fingers on it to make it stop, half-aware of how closely I was watching her.

"I can't believe it. Someone should have taken care of this—contacted him," she said. It sounded like she was reading from a script. "How unprofessional," she said, with no emphasis.

"Like I said, they may well have, but I don't know a thing about it," I said. "He never said a word."

"Well, well, what news." She shifted her pocketbook around in front of her and opened the top flap. "I only need to drop off a few forms, anyway, set a date for the interview and let him know some of the kinds of questions I'll be asking. Kind of a preliminary workover so he can think ahead. I can't believe they didn't take care of this. I knew I should have phoned—just like me to be so trustful. Miss Trustful. Probably why they never got me his address, either. Damn. Here," she said, and gave me a thin pile of yellow papers with her name stamped in script at the heading. "I'm hoping they'll make this like the feature article—depending on how it goes, of course. That's why the rush. He's a real up and coming."

I was barely listening. "Exactly," I said, turning the papers around a few times in my hands and then curling the ends together into a tube. "I'm sure he's going to love it—his big chance. The egotist."

She laughed and put a hand on my shoulder while she laughed, like she was about to fall down. "Aren't they, though," she said, and her nail caught on my sleeve—tick—as her hand fell away.

"I'll just go up and see what he's doing," I said.

"Thanks a million," she said, and cocked her head at me so sincerely, so suggestively, I couldn't see at all what she was up to.

———

My father said he was skeptical of Lisa. This was mostly his way to brace himself against what he called the hazard of self-glorification. Occasionally he talked about that. He would say, "Allow anyone that privilege, even for a minute—the privilege to entertain a judgment of you—and all your work is in vain. Vain egotism and self-glorification. Who cares how they judge, favorably, unfavorably, the point is they have all the power from that point on. You lose." But he also said, at other times, that it was impossible not to judge and know how others judged you. There was a story he would tell about this sometimes. It had to do with his first good teacher, at City College, who had once accused him of wasting time. He said to my father, "Dillard, you're wasting my time. We have a lot of smart excuses to throw around. Very, very smart and complex. That's fine, but excuses do not a painting make. That's what you're missing about your Dadaism. You want to call yourself a 'something' before you've done anything at all to see what you really are? You think there's just a lot of stupid people who can't understand you because they don't understand the nature of your fancy excuses? That's a waste of time. You should know by now."

The story was one of my father's favorite so-called moments of awakening, where he said he was suddenly able to see his whole life laid out before him, and all on account of what that one teacher had said—this judgment, which my father just then happened to need. I had heard him tell people about it many times. I'd also heard him say, many times, that nothing is worse than the scorn of a woman—meaning my mother, in particular, and all women in general. So, I knew he was thinking about Lisa Britten for days after she had left—about the questions she would ask about his life and his work, and about all the self-glorifying answers he would want to give, but probably would not.

She came to our house three more times, total. The first time she came, he stood her up. I hadn't known she would be coming, but I had known, for a week, about my father's appointment to get his teeth cleaned by a dentist in Yonkers. He was also going to use the opportunity to do many other things in town, he said, buy more supplies, shop for food, and find a new winter jacket for himself. As far as I was concerned, it was only the best opportunity for me to skip school and sleep most of the day without his knowing about it. I was a senior then, and high school was a painful place to be. Mostly, I thought it was unnecessary.

I told Lisa, when she got to our house, that I was sure it was no mistake: my father had stood her up deliberately. I said he was just being his usual difficult self. He almost never left the house, except some Friday nights, when he would go out with his art friends to get drunk or watch a movie, or both. She insisted that she had spoken to him on the phone, twice, and made absolutely certain the day she would be coming. She pointed at the date in her date book, Thursday, October 16, like that would clarify things, and told me he had said how much he was looking forward to the interview.

"He said he was thinking about it and what he wanted to say," she said. "Damn it. Are you sure?"

"Yes, I'm sure. He's not here. See for yourself." I swept one arm toward the empty living room. "You know, he's never been very good keeping his appointments."

"Well, that helps me a whole lot," she said, snapping the date book shut and putting it into her bag.

"I wouldn't take it personally."

"I'm not." She smiled fiercely. "This is just a complete waste of my day."

"There's nothing I can do about that, is there?" I said.

I knew she wouldn't be able to leave yet; she was still too fired up just to walk away. She would have to stand around a while, fuming, or maybe she would actually sit it out in the living room until he came home—or didn't come home, and she finally had somewhere else she had to go. I'd seen this before.

Then she had a new idea. "Let's get started without him. You could tell me about his background—cover the bases. This bio thing," she waved a sheet of paper at me, "it's worthless. Any way we could do that?"

By the look on her face I thought she had already decided I wouldn't be able to say anything at all interesting about my father. This was peculiar. It was like she just wanted to make herself feel more in control. Appeasing me for her previously misdirected anger was one way to do that. That would put her in charge. Then, when the things I began telling her about my father proved worthless, she could be mad, justifiably, and get that out of her system. I would have to bear it up.

"Sure," I said, and I started to rattle off the names of schools where he had gotten his training, artists he admired, galleries where he had shown paintings, and dates for all these things going back to the mid-sixties.

"Wait," she said, then got a new-looking cassette recorder with a built-in microphone out of her bag and pointed it at me. "Go on, now, I might actually use some of this."

"Oh," I said, listening to the blank tape whir through the heads in that little machine of hers. Anything I said now might easily find its way into her interview and back to him, any remark I wanted to make. "That's on?" I asked, squinting at it, and imagining how my voice would sound later, playing it back.

She nodded, holding it closer. "Speak," she said, and smiled.

"Well, he hates anything obvious. That's the place you should start. It's his philosophy in art, in life, and in general. He's a non-obvious. Completely mysterious. Paralyzed by his own mystery, I think. That's how he gets along—it's how he thrives. He drove my mother out of the house. He drove her nuts that way. The only reason I'm still here is because this is where I live, and as soon as I finish school this year I think I will probably never come back."

She clicked off the tape recorder and lowered it to her side, staring at me. I looked down at her and the only thing I could think was that she was very bowlegged—more bowlegged than any woman I had ever known. And I decided she should have on cowboy boots. I pictured her in cowboy boots and nothing else. That would become her, but she was wearing loafers. I recognized how easy it was, looking at a woman like Lisa, to imagine all these things that were not really her.

"Let's go for a walk," she said.

We walked around the neighborhood, down all the circular roads with identical houses on them—houses that were only variations on a theme, like the people who had their lives in them. We walked until we were in Bronxville. We crossed up over the freeways and kept walking. Here there were some older houses interspersed between all the new, thrown-up ones. There were lawns and little brooks, and the streets were smaller, like each one belonged to a different period in history. Most of those streets were empty and quiet, with people either at work or school, or indoors.

I told her nothing more about my father all the time we were walking. Instead, I told her about myself. I told her about an AP biology class I was taking, the one class I happened to like, and I explained the layers of life in a tree for her—cambium, pulp, phloem, xylem, bark. I knew I was seeming more interested in all of this than I actually was, only because I thought that would make me attractive to her. I told her how the sap went deep inside the cambium of deciduous trees during winter, so they could survive the colder temperatures. Leaves turned colors from the frost and fell, and all the hardwoods appeared temporarily dead, when actually they weren't. I said, "Imagine what it would look like if it didn't happen like that every year."

"May I give you some advice," she said. We were on a small dead-end street, leaning off the railing of a stone bridge that went over a still, brown brook.

I said it was fine if she did, but not to judge me too

harshly. She laughed and I noticed again how pale and thinned out her lips were from the weather, and from her age; how softly shaped she was under her clothes, and how her ears stuck out through her hair, little crescents turning pink from the cold. I had had no real friends for some time, which I blamed in part on my father's strangeness; now I felt as if I had temporarily left all that behind. I was someone else with her—anyone—and not myself, standing on this bridge with nothing familiar in sight.

She never told me how she would advise me. Instead she said, "Uh-oh, do I detect some undercurrents of 'Lisa, please let's be lovers?'" She looked hard at me. "You know what, I'll tell you—in trying to be honest—there is this funny appeal for me about being seventeen again, like you. That's the appeal. But you can't just take advantage of a person like that." The way she said this was like it belonged to some other exchange separate from the one we were having then, and she didn't quite care what it meant or how she had put it, though she also seemed a little sorry for me, or sorry I was so young. "You don't have any idea what you're getting yourself into at all, do you?"

"What?" I asked.

She nodded. "Look. No games," she said. Then, "Out with it."

Somewhere I had learned that women were not meant to be more than sexually suggestive. They were not supposed to talk like this. It was up to the men to do and say things directly—even force themselves where they weren't actually invited but felt the implication of desire in a woman's actions. I had seen this a hundred times in movies, and nothing here was going that way.

"You—what about you?" I asked, as if she hadn't just

told me.

"Come on, Cary. Let's just keep walking," she said. "I think we'd best keep walking."

I turned one way and she turned the other. It was one of those awkward moments. I was too aware of little things like the sound of a persistent jay in one of the dying trees over the brook, the color of the water in the brook and the danger of falling into that water which was no danger really except in an imaginary way, and the exact distance between the road and the ledge next to the railing where we were standing—how to make the step carefully down to the road, and why this seemed so difficult to maneuver just then. We bumped into each other—I almost knocked her down—and this unsettled all the hesitation.

"Oh, God," she said, "if you're going to make a pass at me or something, get it over with," and faced me with her arms raised to go around my shoulders.

We were still stepping on each other's feet, kissing and spinning in circles, minutes later when a long sedan went slowly past. We watched the woman driving—an old woman with glasses and blue hair—as she stopped suddenly in the middle of the street three houses away, then signaled and turned into her drive.

Lisa looked back at me. "I hear you shouldn't sleep with the person you're working on—that you'll never get to know them," she said. "That's the first thing. Intimacy is confusion. But I've never heard about sleeping with his son. What do you think? Have you?"

"I don't know. Sure," I said. It was a flip and unconvincing thing for me to say, but I couldn't imagine anything in the world that wouldn't come across like that. "Yes. Let's do it."

"You're such a good kisser," she said. "Where in hell do kids learn to kiss like that?"

I had no answer for this, except, of course, to kiss her again.

And all the way home I thought about that word—her word for it: sleep. Some part of my brain was acting as if it had gone to sleep. I was numb and shivering, like there were invisible hands stroking me and holding me up all over in ways I hadn't known about. Lisa and I would not sleep at all; we would be wide awake. But when we got home, there was my father's dented blue pickup in the driveway. Both of us stopped at the edge of the road. Once there had been an elm tree here, at the end of our driveway, until years ago when it was struck by lightning. I would often think about that tree as I came home, up the driveway. It had been so remarkably splintered and charred by the lightning, like something severed rather than struck. "The garage," I said. "We can go in the garage. He never goes there. Quick."

"What? No," she said, "we'll have to make that up another time." She smiled. "Duty calls. Really." Then she gave me a look like she thought I should take her more seriously.

"Oh. Fine," I said, as if it made no difference in the world to me. "Fine. What time is it, anyway?"

"Just about four." She glanced at her watch and I realized she wasn't going to let me delay this much longer. "Four-ten."

"If he asks you, you didn't get here until half an hour ago. OK?" I asked.

"What?" she said. "Oh, school. Oh, I see. You were skipping school." This made her smile. Then she went up to the door and pounded on it with her fist. "Now, we'll see what's what," she said with a joyous kind of anger. She turned around and quickly kissed her fingertips, then put them on my mouth like she was dying for me. This was better to believe than not to believe, regardless of how she really meant it.

"I live here," I said. "You do not have to knock."

Then there was my father in the doorway holding a glass of water, looking fuzzy behind the screen and staring down at us. He pretended to stagger backward a few steps as if it had just registered with him that this was the day he had stood Lisa up.

"I entirely forgot! I'm so sorry," he said, and winked in my direction. "Really," he said. He rolled his eyes. And as I came in after her he grabbed me suddenly and pulled me aside. He whispered, "What are you doing—weren't you at school today or what?" His breath smelled orangey and stale, like something dead or sterile had invaded his mouth— a dentist's fingers, I thought.

"You're out of line, asking me that," I said.

"I'm what?"

"You heard," I said.

———

Lisa told me, early the following week when she came to interview my father again, that she had never actually done a full-scale article before. This one she was doing all on her own, with no contract, only a few brusque words over the phone from one editor. She said she had to establish herself. No one at *New American Art* even cared what she did or who she was—not until she had something for them. She confessed this in the first few private minutes after she arrived. We were standing in the hallway with the front door closed behind us, whispering. "I screwed up *totally* with the last session," she said, "but don't dare tell him. I was all rattled."

She had dressed more formally this time, in a flowered skirt and an executive-looking white shirt with a ruffle. She was playing with one of her earrings one moment, then the next moment she had backed me against the wall and was kissing me fiercely, saying, "It's not your fault, though. I haven't been able to stop thinking about this for a second. Not for a second."

She ran her tongue back and forth over my lips and put her hand between my legs, pressed, let go, and stood away from me. "Look," she said. She shook her head like she had to clear it, and stared at something behind me. I heard my father's footsteps overhead. She looked back at me. "OK, afterward, I want to arrange something with you. Please, after this." She looked at the ceiling as if she might see my father.

"OK, OK," I said.

After her interview with my father, Lisa's mood was altered again. I watched from my room as she came circling down the stairs, looking flushed and saying things to him over her shoulder about the demarcation of so-and-so's lines. Then she saw me sitting at my desk there and seemed startled. She mouthed these words, "Have to go. Work." She made a face like she was hurt or otherwise dramatically upset, and I didn't know what that was for. She tiptoed into the room, took my pen out of my hand and wrote her number beside a picture of a hydrangea in the biology text that was open next to me. "Call," she whispered and tapped the point of the pen up and down on her number a few times, leaving little scribbly marks on the page.

Then she went out of the room. "Nathan," she called up to my father, "I'll have it for you next week. Promise. Done," she said.

"Fine," he said. Then he was halfway down the stairs. "Fine," he said again, following her out to the door.

I called her late that night and we agreed that my father had no place making things difficult for us. I told her that for all we knew he might not even disapprove—he wasn't particularly hung up about sex. We had given him a kind of significance that wasn't necessarily his. Just the same, I told her, she should be sure to bring the article for him on a Friday, late afternoon, when he would very likely be out with his friends. That way she could stay the night without his knowing. "Good deal," she said, "see you this Friday or next." But she didn't hang up. She said she wanted me to know how much I had been helping her with the article—it was like I was with her every hour of the day, she said, inside of her head and talking to her. And she asked me to describe how my life without her was, really, so she could undo some of that delusion. But before I could answer, she went right on. "No," she said, "there can be no me without you, and no you without me because we're only all the things we make of each other, right? It's the loveliest delusion of them all, too. God—and how many more times in our lives do you think we'll have to learn that one?"

I told her she was getting a little ahead of me. And, for no reason I could identify, I was suddenly able to see just how hungry for success she felt—like success was a real meal of somebody else's live flesh that you could sit down to and devour. She wanted that kind of success for herself. I didn't understand my connection with this, though, and I didn't mention it to her. I just knew I was connected.

Later that same week, I dreamed about my mother's stuff in the garage. I had had variations of this dream before, just about one every few months. In the dream I would be walking up to my father's house after months of having been gone somewhere, and I would see a giant tag sale of all my mother's leftover possessions in progress. Someone—not my father, but any number of man teachers I'd had over the years—would be in charge, and mostly he would be giving things away. "Twenty-five, give me twenty-five cents," he would say. "Twenty-five, give me twenty-five cents," and he would keep saying it, taking peoples' quarters and nickels and dimes and giving away my mother's stuff. The difference this time was that all the colors in the things my mother had once owned were exaggerated, so bright that in places they wouldn't stay still and looked like they were alive. Someone had done this to make the sale happen more quickly—to make each item look better than it was—and I wanted to know where my father was because he would have to be the one responsible. I was holding a blue, scalloped serving dish and I wanted to tell someone that this particular item was a mistake; it wasn't actually my mother's, it was my father's, but no words would come, and the more I turned the dish around to look at it the brighter blue it became until I began to see that the ink was bleeding all over my hands. I knew I had to get away, put the thing down and wash this ink off, but I could not, and that was what woke me up.

Upstairs, I heard my father's music, louder than usual— some kind of English drinking song I had heard before. It was very late, almost dawn. Then it sounded like he was pacing or doing something else rhythmically repetitive, almost in time with the music. There were some words I could make out, like "Hey," and "Whack fal da laddy-o." Maybe the music had something to do with my dream, and why I was now lying wide awake. I decided I should at least go upstairs to see what was happening, and tell him he was making too much noise.

He was lying on the floor in nothing but a pair of white boxers, looking back at one of his paintings with his head upside down and his glasses off. It was cold enough for me to see my breath; his skin must have been frozen. It was unflushed, mostly hairless, and without goose pimples. The painting was a new, dull green painting with shapes in it and one corner that was blank. For a few minutes he must not have known I was there, and I had the rare advantage of watching him as he was with himself at this hour, alone and unselfconscious. He grinned lovingly and arched his back, lay flat again, and then humped up and down a few times joyously so his ass thumped on the floor. "Ah-hahh," he said, like he was about to make an announcement, or laugh. I was embarrassed to be watching this, and to know that it was the same thing I had been hearing through the floorboards moments earlier.

"*Whack* fal the daddy-o there's whisky in the jug ..." sang the men on his radio for the fourth time. The play button at the top of the radio was depressed, so I knew this was one of his new cassette tapes and not some late night broadcast for sleepless people.

"Hey," I said. "Hey, Pop, you mind? It's a little loud."

He rolled over quickly so he was on all fours, and faced me. He was out of breath. "Mind? What?" he asked. He picked up his glasses that were open on the bed to put them on. "What?" he said, and stood up.

"It's a little loud. Do you mind?..."

"It's what?" he yelled. Then he went to the radio, tiptoeing to make light of my request, and punched "stop." There was silence. "Sorry," he said. "So sorry. Finished." He threw up his arms like a conductor and beamed at me, about to laugh again.

I nodded. "Good," I said. I could have asked him what was finished, but I didn't. He could have asked me what was good, but he didn't. And just then there was nothing else for us to say to each other. He was mostly naked and there was a whole room between us, all filled with his stuff, and nothing for us to say about any of it. I inspected his shorts, tentatively at first, to know if he had an erection from what he'd been doing before I interrupted him, but he did not. Seeing that, I was even more convinced I would never understand him.

He turned around to look at his green painting. He stood there for so long that I started to think he might have forgotten me again. Then he said, "Give me your opinion. That," he pointed at the painting, "that's your friend, Lisa." He paused. "Lisa, who is picking cockles."

"Who is what?" I asked.

"Lisa Britten, the interviewer from New York," he said, putting on an accent as he said this to let me know how he disliked her for something too prissy and organized about her nature. "It's an old Irish tune—'Picking Cockles,' I think. I guess she hasn't told you that part of her past. She's actually descended from a famous line of Irish fishermen— famous for wading out of the bog. The admiring bog." He gestured at the painting. "Thus the title."

I went closer to look, but there was nothing, I thought— only a lot of green and black confusion. "I think you're afraid of her," I announced flatly. It was a shot in the dark, but anything you wanted to make of my father's paintings was a shot in the dark. "Why are you afraid of her?"

"Don't be silly."

"Look," I said, and pointed at the canvas, "right here, it says you're scared to death of her. You think she'll find out something about you, and you don't even know what it is yet. So you paint something to make it look like it's all the other way around."

He was standing next to me, though I'd never heard him cross the room. He breathed through his nose, looking at the painting.

"Right there," I said, and moved my finger ambiguously past another section of canvas. "She's got you figured out. That's what you don't want." I was still making things up—and it occurred to me that I was relying on the little pieces of what my mother used to say to him when they were fighting. "If you act like a nobody, then that's what you are: nobody," she would say, or, "Mr. Nobody, just a grope in the dark."

I said, "She says you're all alike."

"What?" he said.

"That's her perception. That you're all alike."

Now he was leaning back, surveying things. He shook his head, having somehow regained his safe ground of discharged responsibility, only I didn't understand how he could have done that. I was just something from that life he'd taken care of long ago—that old life of his past—and nothing I could say to him would matter at all. He was alone with his painting again and all of his ideas for it, most of which he had pretty much figured out.

He said, "The amazing thing is that you seem to think I should care at all—what her perception is."

"You're right. I do."

"That's your misfortune," he said.

His eyes were shrunken and faraway behind his glasses. For a moment I thought I could see exactly what it was I had never been able to know about him before. This had to do with his death, some part of it that he wanted to prepare himself for. He wanted the same nothing that would be left after he was dead. He wanted to live with that and feel it all the time, keeping himself pure and cut off from the things in his life. This was why my mother had gone and would never come back for her stuff. She wanted him to be reminded every day of the tricky junk his life was really made of, and all the other people it included. Only, he wasn't paying any attention. He had a perfect right, I decided, not to pay attention; and ultimately he could be no less damaged by these actions than anyone else.

"She doesn't know anything," he said.

"Liar," I said.

"No, not me." He walked away from me, to the stairway. "Not me," he said again, as he went downstairs.

"Fine then," I said, but he wasn't there to hear it. I stood for a while, until I could feel what it was I really wanted there, which was only to be young again—very young—and to take up the space of a small child who has just one word for all the things in the world.

My father destroyed many of his paintings. There was a ritual for this. He would take the canvas to be destroyed outside first thing, before he'd eaten or started any new work for the day, and he would burn it in the barbecue grate in our back yard. There was always a bottle of lighter fluid under the kitchen sink just for this purpose. We never barbecued our food. He burned them, he said, because there was no other way to know you had truly gotten rid of a thing. And he had to keep all of this well outside the positive space where he did his creating. Failure was necessary, but separate, he said. He would stand over the barbecue grate, poking his crumpled canvas with a stick every now and then, to be sure it burned through completely. He burned Lisa's painting in this way two days after our early morning exchange. He said it had nothing to do with what I had said to him, and acted like he didn't want me to feel guilty for this—something I hadn't even been considering.

Lisa came over with the article Friday, the following week, while my father was gone with his friends. I read most of what she had written that afternoon, before he saw it. She said her lead had been generated by the first thing I ever told her about him. It had to do with the disarming mystery of my father's painting, which she said had previously paralyzed most critics, including herself. It went something like, "Paralyzed, and, by my own mysterious response to the painting's unruly, enigmatic power, its contrived yet randomly balanced union of nonsense and detail, forced away from any of the usual connections. A Mondrian, Deibenkorn, even Frankenthaler, this is not." I was quoted later in the article for saying he had driven my mother nuts, though I thought she phrased it in a way that made me sound small and angry, like I was only standing in the way of art.

"Lisa, Lisa," I said, and stood up in front of where she was sitting, on the edge of my bed. I had not finished the article, but there were clearly more interesting things for us at hand. "It's good," I said. She clinched her arms around my waist.

"You like it?"

"I love it. You nailed him down right," I said.

"But will he like it?"

"Oh! He'll hate it. I guarantee, he'll despise it."

She squeezed me harder. "Well, let's hope to hell it flies," she said. "I could never have gotten it done without you, either, you know."

"I doubt that very much."

"Well, maybe. Maybe I could have," she said. "But then it wouldn't have been this much fun, either—would it? God. This cannot be happening."

"But it is," I said, and I fell down on the bed over her with both of my hands on her breasts.

"You hound!" she said.

There are some things I remember about this. Mostly, it felt like I was fighting to satisfy her; that is, I had to fight to know what it was about me and the ways I was with her that would move her, physically, and this meant finding some way to control her. But she was rough to control and very strong. She had as many ideas of her own. After all, we barely knew each other. There was a piece of understanding about this which fell in place for me at the end, something I could feel in my mind but not comprehend. Bodies and bodies and bodies, was one thing I might have said about it, looking at her all spread out around me and the shapes of the muscles changing in her arms, and her bowed legs that were also full of her muscles, and the bit of loose skin on her stomach where the muscles under that were tight like a boy's.

"Christ Almighty," she said, when it was over, "tell me I

didn't just fuck your head off like I was sixteen again. Tell me that wasn't the best." Then she was on top of me, desperately kneading my chest with her strong hands, waiting and glaring at me like she would like to take me to pieces.

When he saw the article, my father hit the roof, as I had expected. There were some silly, nervous things in it that he had said about being the best at what he did, and later claimed he hadn't meant. I don't remember what else he disliked. He ripped the article into shreds, which made no difference of course. The whole thing went into print almost exactly as it had been, despite his complaints, and this was only the beginning of what was eventually to make up Lisa's relative fame, and my father's as well. I think she had, in many places, come too close to the truth for his liking. She said his paintings of women were characterized by a funny kind of non-vision that made women anything he wanted, and mostly made them nothing at all, only lovely abstractions in light and space that were impossible to excogitate. Other male artists might have turned their late twentieth-century fear of women into a garish or violent barrage of disembodied feminine details—most of which fully reaffirmed the traditional terms of gender classification, she wanted to point out—but he had chosen to let his female figures mean whatever bizarre things they meant to him and to draw from that. The argument was a little vague to me, but I blamed that mostly on my father.

She stayed that night, called a cab, and slipped out early the next afternoon while my father was still asleep in the attic. He had come in late, after we'd darkened the house, cracked some windows to air things out, and gone safely to my room. I would blame my father for driving her away with the things he said to her—the accusations and threats he made over the phone on account of that article—but I knew it was not his fault. We'd had what she came for and there was nothing else for us. Knowing how she was alive in the world somewhere, and acting like a crazy thirty-year-old teenager, was enough to keep me thinking of myself in a whole different way.

———

My father and I had the tag sale the same week I graduated from high school. It was an event that went on all day, until the sun was almost gone. I made lemon squares and Kool Aid to give away to neighbors, but this ran out early. We hadn't anticipated the numbers of people that showed up, and consequently priced things too fairly. "Everyone's a crook," my father said. "Look at the crooks," he said, "they act like they're out for a bargain. I'll tell you what. They want something for nothing—crooks. If I said, 'Here, this one's free,' she'd take it." He pointed at a woman in a tan hat who was inspecting some china figurines and nodding her head, apparently pleased. He nudged me. "Lucky for us it doesn't matter, right? What's the difference to us?"

"No difference at all," I said.

There were lamps, a dresser, the cherry rocker, the loom, some cheap jewelry, and dozens of knickknacks; records, cassettes, and typewriter ribbons; wool dresses, socks, slacks, and old misshapen shoes. He kept bringing out boxes of items and dumping them on the lawn, on the blankets we'd laid there to keep things clean. In the end I thought we would have a lot to say to each other about this day, but we did not. He took one roll of bills, several hundred and change, and put that in my hand; the other roll he put in his pocket. A few minutes later he took that out, said something like "Oh hell," took off a few twenties for himself, and gave me the rest. We both started walking then, down the driveway and into the street. "So, it doesn't turn out so badly for you, after all," he said.

"No. You know, and I think I'll buy that car like you said. Travel."

"I wish you would," he said. "I'd be happy for that."

There was only the portrait of my grandfather, standing in the empty garage for weeks, until I left. My father wouldn't explain it, but he said he didn't want to sell that painting or give it to Goodwill either, where we had taken all the other leftover items no one had wanted to buy. He said he didn't see why anyone would want it, which I knew was only an excuse, though probably he was right, too. The painting would never be sold. I bought an old Mazda with eighty thousand miles, a cracked muffler, new tires, and a rebuilt carburetor. My plans were thin. I would stop at my mother's in Ohio, stay a few weeks, and keep going west. I'd look for work, maybe, and think hard about my future. He kept saying she wouldn't want that portrait of her father, but I put it in the backseat, on top of all my stuff, just the same. I said it was better than leaving it in the garage forever, wasn't it? And it was the least we could do for her after we'd sold everything else.

He said, "If you knew how much she's going to dislike that." He was shaking his head. "You should think, seriously. Just don't say I didn't warn you."

"It's not my problem. She'll be glad," I said.

"She will not. I mean it. She won't. Don't say I didn't warn you," he said again. "That's all." He shrugged.

"Why? Did you paint it?" I asked.

He looked at it, cockeyed in the backseat. "That isn't the point," he said.

"Then you did."

He nodded. "Yes, as a matter of fact. Look—yes, I did. He died two years before I ever met her, you know. That," he said, pointing, "was a kind of a gift. She wouldn't say so. She just didn't think it did him justice. She didn't want it. What do I know? I wanted her to have it. Actually, I wanted her to *like* it. That's what I wanted, for Christ's sake, and that's what it always gets down to, isn't it? She hated me for the way I saw things."

"Partly. Yes. For you. Then there's her side of it."

He was smiling about something else now and apparently hadn't heard me. "You know, the old man never did wear a string tie, I guess. Not once," he said.

"Then why'd you paint him in one?"

"He *should* have worn a string tie, if you know what I mean. If he knew what was right." He stood back from the car then and said a few words about my promising to call him. He assured me he had no expectations—just to be told, once in a while, what was what with my life. He banged his fist on the roof of my car a few times as I backed out of the driveway, and stood there waving.

Miles later I could still hear the sound of his fist banging on my roof, and still pictured him there in the driveway, right where the old elm had been, waving.

———

Halfway across the state of Pennsylvania, in the middle of the night, at the state park where I was camping next to my car, trying to sleep but never managing to forget about the smell of the miles I'd burned off those new tires, I got up to do it. I'd seen him do this so many times, I knew exactly how to do it myself. I made the fire in the cookout grill, using the picture frame itself, some dead leaves and sticks, and lighter fluid I'd bought earlier the same night. I crumpled up the canvas that was so stiff and thick in places I thought it might cut my hands, and I took a last look. The old man's features were caved in, and I knew then just what he would look like the next time I saw him. He could never paint anyone but himself—his own state of mind—which was another fact Lisa had brought to light somehow, and it had taken me until then to see just what she meant, and how right she was about it. That was really him in the western costume, pretending he was someone's husband, not my grandfather. I dropped it into the flames, squirted more starter fluid over it to make some quick heat, and stood there looking away at the night shapes of the trees around me, poking the fire with a stick to be sure the canvas burned through all the way. I smelled mildew and smoke. When I looked back the colors in his face were blackened and smoldering. They popped into flames. Then part of his mustache and string tie were outlined in black for a moment—the many different sketched versions of his eyes, revised and layered one over the other, so they looked uncentered and screwy. I thought I would probably never want to forget that, the many ways his eyes were. Then I poked it to turn the whole thing over the other way. When there was nothing left, only a few wisps of ash and the thickest part of the frame, I got back in my sleeping bag on the ground next to my car. But I never slept. I was only as unprotected in this world as I had ever been, but that was no consolation. I was already worried about how he would take care of himself, and what would happen next in his life that I would not be there to see or help him plan for, though I hadn't done that for him anyway, only tried, and that had never made a difference.

WALKING IN MY SLEEP

BILL HENRY CALLED MY MOTHER MOLLY, NOT BECAUSE IT was her name, but because it had been his younger sister's name. His younger sister died when she was eighteen, in an automobile wreck that made her heart come halfway up her throat. Bill said there was something about my mother to make him think of Molly. Her mouth, he said, or her eyes, depending on what my mother happened to be wearing, or what kind of mood Bill was in. He slipped and called my mother Molly so many times he finally decided there must be something to it, so he made it her name—Molly. My mother's real name was Marilyn, named after Marilyn Monroe, because her parents had hoped for her to pursue a career in show business. She never did. I was always told that both of my grandparents were involved with the theater around the Albany area. This is how they met—so the story goes. They were theater people. In all the pictures I have seen of Marilyn Monroe there is little to remind me of my mother, or make me understand the exact nature of the hopes my grandparents had for her.

My mother met Bill dropping me off and picking me up for swim practice, weeknights at the YMCA. She was usually early picking me up. She would sit on one of the benches next to the pool with her crossword puzzle in her lap, counting letters and biting her lips while I swam my last laps and Bill yelled. One night, in the middle of winter, a friend of mine named Emil Hass was demonstrating something to do with kung fu when he fell into the water next to her. Emil wasn't just big, he had an unusual kind of density—he weighed more and felt thicker than he should have—and when he flopped into the water next to my mother he soaked her.

What surprised me was the look on her face. She was smiling in an unfamiliar way, like she wished to be thrilled by something, with her green eyes wide and a smudge of lipstick showing on her front teeth. Maybe she was going to giggle from the embarrassment and shock of being splashed. I couldn't tell. But I saw her as if I didn't know her, and I saw the many sexual possibilities in the ways she was always presenting herself to the world. Then Bill came to her rescue with someone's mostly dry towel. She thanked him, dabbing at her neck with a corner of the towel. He stared at the top of her head as she bent down to wipe some water off her feet. I saw that he had forgotten himself, looking at her. That the pool and the smell of chlorine and the loud echoing laughter of kids all around him were nothing in the world to him just then.

Shortly after the kung fu incident, Bill began showing up at our house Friday and Saturday nights in different colored suits. I thought the suits looked incongruous on him because I'd never seen him in anything but sweats, or a bathing suit and a whistle. Most of the time, he told us later, those suits were not actually his; he was only renting them, or borrowing from friends. You could see how the creases were in all the wrong places, belonging to actions and postures which were not really Bill's.

We had our worst season ever, that year, and never won a single meet, which I thought was Bill's fault. We would spend half of every practice out of the water, sitting on the bench and shivering, trying to visualize what Bill called "winning." He would pace back and forth, looking at us and asking things like "What's winning?" The correct response, we knew, was "Not losing," but it didn't mean much to us since all we did was lose that year. Or, "Who's your opponent?"—answer, "Myself." Sometimes he would lecture us on these points, and the relative malleability of reality—how a loss could in some way really be considered a win. It was all in your head. But we kept losing anyway, no matter how hard we tried to picture it the other way around. When Emil and a few of the best swimmers on the team quit coming to practice because they said we just never swam enough, I gave up, but I couldn't stop going to practice. By that time I was becoming obligated to Bill in other ways that had nothing to do with swim team.

In the beginning, there were always gifts: used records and books from the vintage bookstore Bill had a partnership in; inexpensive wines and liqueurs; and special passages from rare books that he wanted to read aloud for my mother. Once, he came over with a lot of rattlesnake rattles which he hid through the apartment over the course of the evening, many in places we didn't discover until days later. They were like short segments of hollow beads or hardened rice puffs stuck together, the color of skin. Finding one unexpectedly was a kind of thrill, like touching something that clearly wasn't intended to be touched. All these gifts had the effect of blurring Bill, though simultaneously reaffirming what I knew would be my most lasting impression of him in time: that his one desire in life was to be liked. He wanted to be liked boundlessly, in a way that would finally surpass all his generosity and all the things he was always trying to give away to people. It made me distrust him.

Late that spring Bill went to London to visit his living sister and shop for more books. He was gone ten days. In that time, I had hoped my mother and I would have a kind of reprieve. I wanted Bill out of my mind. I didn't dislike him, I just wanted to remember something I thought was always getting lost or muddled in his presence.

Since Bill, my mother had been like a person in a daze, but it was little better with him gone. I would meet her for her dinner break, at the pizza place across from Zack's House of Television, and we would sit there in silence, waiting for our pizza. She would smoke a cigarette, then smoke another one, and occasionally she would clear her throat, ask me something, or stare at me all of a sudden, smiling intensely as if to assure me that she was really here.

Of course, these moments never lasted. If she had to get up from our table to go to the bathroom or get another refill on her soda it always seemed to me that she was moving like a person who had another idea of her shape in mind, as though her actual shape in relation to the things around her was something she had temporarily forgotten. We talked about this once, indirectly, talking about Bill. I told her what I thought. I said he wasn't really the person he claimed he was, though I wasn't sure who he was or who he was pretending to be, either.

"I mean, what do we know about him?" I asked.

"We know the most important things," she said. She seemed impatient saying it. "He's warm and generous and thoughtful and there's the indication that he's capable of a great deal of affection. That's rare in men, these days. What else do you have to know?"

"It's rare all right. He's like Houdini—like he wants you to tie him up in some impossible situation just to see if he can twist his way out of it while you watch."

"What are you talking about? You think this is an impossible situation for him?"

I shrugged. "It will be soon enough. That's for sure."

"The world has its share of single mothers, Ted. I'm not an anomaly."

"I never said you were that. I'm just trying to guess what he's got up his sleeve."

"Not a thing. He's the sweetest man I've ever known."

"That's because you barely know him. I wish you'd wake up."

"You think I'm just walking in my sleep?" she asked.

"Yes," I said. "Yes," I said again, and hoped she would really hear this and not mistake it as some pointless insult or cry for attention.

"Well, thanks a lot," she said.

"I mean, he'll do whatever he wants with you," I said.

"I'm sure he will."

Bill's most generous gift of all came the day, just after his delayed return from Europe, when he announced his plans for us to come stay with him at his mother's house in the Berkshires for the summer while he wrote his new book. Bill often claimed to have written books—novels, biographies, and plays—though I never saw one. Certainly, nothing he wrote was ever in print. I don't think my mother was taking his offer any more seriously than I was, at first. It was only another in a series of amazingly warm and inclusive gestures from Bill. I remember her smiling and asking him several times to tell her, again, exactly what was wrong with his mother and why she wouldn't be there, whether there was really room for everyone (meaning me), and so on like that. They discussed it for almost a month before I realized this was something that would really happen.

The book was originally going to be about my mother. I got worked into it over time, probably because I was there. It was to have been based on one of Bill's favorite fairy tales, which, as he told it, is about a king and his mysterious new wife who wears out the soles of her shoes every night, dancing in a magical land that extends from the back of her closet to the other side of the world. The king is such a heavy sleeper that no matter how hard he tries he can't stay awake long enough to find out where and with whom his new wife is dancing. In every other way she is perfect for him; there is only this mystery—the shoes, worn through the soles, which he finds tucked under her pillow each morning. She claims to know nothing about them, though it's obvious from how tired she is that she's lying. In fact, she's under some kind of spell that prevents her from telling him, though she would probably like to. This is the same spell that forces her to return, night after night, to that place where she dances in the sand with a pale prince who wishes he could keep her with him forever, but can't.

Bill wanted to update this story about the king's jealousy and queen's unkept secret, though I was never sure how—

something about the queen walking around town all night in a trance, wearing out a pair of shoes the king had given her. Of course, in the updated version the king and queen were no longer royalty but ordinary working-class people, like Bill and my mother. Bill went back and forth between having me on the queen's side, walking and dancing with her in the streets—maybe getting kidnapped—or on the king's side, generating stay-awake potions, scratching his back, and playing poker with him in an adjoining room to keep him awake long enough to catch the devious queen.

He was visiting again, a few days after the day he'd told us about his plans to take us away with him for the summer, leaning against one of the counters in our kitchen and drawing things out of the air with his hands while he described my mother as she would appear in the story.

"Beautiful. People don't identify with a homely heroine," he said. "I've already said that." He paused with two of his long fingers over his lips. "Her head is balanced this particular way to make it look like she's wearing a crown, you know, even though she isn't. This is what makes you think she's a queen when you first see her—nobility in exile. There's the idea. She's a queen and yet she's not—very straight and careful, and her feet are beautiful, too. They have small, delicate arches. You wouldn't even think of them as feet, actually, if you saw them. They're more like eggs, or sugar, and her calves glow like moonbeams. She walks," he paused to let his next words gather weight, "slowly. In fact, it never seems like she's quite sure where she's going. Only when she starts to dance, then she's sure."

Listening to him, watching his hands and face, it was easy to know what he meant. He was just taking some idea he had about my mother, lifting it right out of her, and leaving behind all the ordinary, familiar things about her—her freckles, wavy stiff blond hair, big nose, and wrinkled neck. He was transported and obsessed; so was she. And I had the feeling that it was all a mistake. He didn't know when to stop himself from talking about the things he believed. She didn't know better than to believe every word he said.

He was still talking when I cut in. "Poppycock," I said to him. I thought this was the kind of word he might use, and using it against him would give me all that much more leverage. "Pure poppycock," I said.

He looked at me like he'd just rediscovered my presence in the room. My mother seemed faintly annoyed by the interruption, maybe a little endeared by what she probably misunderstood as a jealous attempt on my part to protect her from him. She was beyond protection, though. I knew this, even if she didn't. Protection was nothing at all, really. That wasn't the point. Reality was the point.

"Poppycock? Why poppycock?" Bill asked. He smiled and looked back at my mother. "Comes from the Latin, I think. *Pappa*—meaning father, food; *kakken*—to defecate. Means 'soft dung.' Something like that. The British are involved there, somewhere. They do love their anal humor."

"Well," she said, and looked at me as if she wanted to know whether I was as amused by this as she was. She coughed into her hand and stood up from her seat at the kitchen table. "More coffee?" she asked him.

"Thanks," he said, holding out his cup for her. At the time there were only a few of those cups left. They came from the set my mother had taken with us when the breakfast shop she used to run with my father went out of business, just after my father left. They were the standard diner coffee cups—cream-colored glass, with chipped green around the edges. Bill turned to me again. "Why do you say poppycock, Ted? Is there something you don't like? Something I said to upset you?"

Of course, there would be no point in my saying what I disliked if he was going to pretend to be this open-armed. He knew that. "No," I said, and I told him something else I'd been thinking about—something I'd seen on TV about a knife that could cut through anything solid, including most metals. I said there were many things in the world that were poppycock and you had to be careful. Then I apologized for the interruption and tried to seem distracted by something outside, so they would both know how unconcerned I was.

Bill was looking me over as if he had seen much more than I knew—more than he'd ever seen previously. "I understand," he said, and narrowed his eyes. "Very interesting."

The trip would require other compromises. My mother would have to quit her job at Zack's, possibly never to get it back again. I would leave all my friends in Winsted for the summer. It was nothing, I supposed, when you consider what my mother thought was in store for us, walking right into the pages of that book Bill was going to write. But it wasn't anything good, in my eyes. Bill did not know my mother. Neither my mother or I really knew Bill, and I didn't expect getting to know him better would give us any more advantages than we'd had so far from knowing him.

———

There was an afternoon, just over a week before we were supposed to have left for his mother's, when Bill and I drove out to Bradley Airport in Hartford to watch the planes land.

This was Bill's idea. My mother was at work. Bill had said, the day before, that he and I should have this time together where we could do something to get to know each other a little better.

On the way he pointed out things he thought would be of particular interest to me: an old dynamite factory where once they blew the roof off a section of buildings while they were devising explosives to use against the Germans in World War II. That factory had been converted to offices and studios now, he said, and the roofs were new. Also, he pointed out an all-girls school you could barely see through the thick trees which he said the trustees had planted there, alongside the road, in order to make the campus more private. Bill said it was a kind of sanctuary beyond those trees, and winked at me a few times. He knew because his sister, Molly, used to go. He said there was nothing but virgins in dresses, rolling lawns and old buildings back in there.

We parked on the freeway at the airport just next to the landing strip, which Bill said was a good place to watch the arriving jets descend—"Stepping down out of the sky," was how he put it. We sat on the hood of his car. I remember Bill was fairly excited when the first plane came in. "Isn't it great?" he kept yelling at me. His hair was straight back from the wind and I thought he looked like a dog running after something. I told him it was certainly great.

"The control," he said, and his eyes rolled up in his head slightly as he laughed. "Ingenuity! All that power and balance. All our human longing to be more—go faster, get farther."

I thought the burned airplane fuel smelled good, something like an electrical fire; otherwise the whole thing was mostly deafening. He pointed out the landing gear, where it was stored in flight and how it was brought down. Then he explained a few things about afterburners and wing flap, none of which interested me. The plane would wobble almost imperceptibly on the air just before it touched down, as if adjusting to the ground; then there was a roar, and the mirage of fumes and heat coming out behind would obscure its true image.

"All of a sudden it makes sense," Bill said, after we'd been watching for about half-an-hour.

"What does?"

"Oh—why I wanted to come here with you." He put his hand on my knee and squeezed, then left it there, hot and still on my bare skin. He had a look on his face like he was about to sneeze or was in some way emotionally overwhelmed.

"Why?" I asked.

He moved his hand away and shook his head. There was no noise just then, only the distant rumble of some planes preparing for takeoff on the other side of the terminal, and the cars on the highway behind us.

"I guess when I was your age—fourteen, right?—I thought I wanted to be an airplane pilot. In fact, I was so sure of it I used to make everyone call me captain. Captain Billy. That was my name. I'd even forgotten about that one until now. There was a man—a friend of my father's who had fought in World War II, and he was instrumental in that as well."

He smiled and shook his head again. Then his voice got a little deeper as he went on, as if whatever he had to say next was intended for a larger audience neither of us could see just then. He said, "And I guess this must be the subconscious part of the motivation for why I wanted to come here with you—associating you with that earlier time in my own life."

"Really. I didn't know," I said. I thought my voice sounded wrong too, like it was coming from somewhere beside me, and decided it must be the engine noise making me temporarily deaf to certain frequencies, so that my own voice sounded transformed to me. I knew I should be more interested in what Bill had to say, or at least find some way of seeming so—I didn't want to hurt his feelings. Still, I was more concerned about my ears. "Hmm," I said, and felt the bones in my head vibrating.

"God! You know, you just can't think about these things too much," he said. "Why we do the things we do—when we do things ... I mean, why do anything at all if you're always going to know the reason?" he asked. "Besides, it's very likely impossible."

He looked at me and it must have registered with him then that I wasn't really the right person for all this. "Bla, bla, bla," he said.

Then he was scraping something gray that looked like chewing gum off the hood of his car. When he looked at me again I could see he wanted me to think of him as being much more open and at risk than usual. He wanted me to think I was finally getting a straight look at something close to the center of his true personality, and I should never forget it. He must have known it was the kind of thing I had been waiting for from him all along. And because he was now going to provide it so willingly, I thoroughly disbelieved him. "Ted, I want to ask you a question," he said. "OK? And I want a real answer from you."

I nodded.

"And don't be afraid to say exactly what you think," he said.

"I won't."

"Do you think it's a good idea for your mother and me to spend as much time as we do together? Wait. Let me be more to the point. That's not a good question at all. How does your mother feel about this upcoming trip? Is it something she wants, do you think, or is she just kind of going along with it not to hurt my feelings?"

"Oh," I said. "No, she's pretty much looking forward to it. She likes it."

"I know that. What I really mean is this—how much do you think she likes me? That's it right there. I mean, does she like me at all?" He had to yell this last part at me because a plane had come in overhead and the noise hitting the ground around us was like an explosion.

I didn't answer until the plane had passed. "Delta," I said.

Bill was still waiting for my answer, nodding absently and pulling on one of his ears.

"I think my mother likes you a lot," I said, suddenly overcome by the desire to say anything he wanted to hear, anything at all that would satisfy him. He looked in so much pain sitting there, pulling on his ear, and bent over to hear me. "Probably as much as she liked my father. I'm pretty sure of it, actually. She's liked other men, you know, but not that much." I had to keep going with this—Bill wasn't saying anything. "She's never said so, but I think she definitely likes you, the way she's been acting. She likes you. She might not let on, but that's definitely the case."

He still wasn't saying anything, just staring and looking pained.

"That's what I think," I said, and shrugged like I was out of words, which in fact I was.

"No," he said. "How can you tell?"

"Ways," I said. "You have to know her. She's not every-thing you think."

"People seldom are."

"Right," I said. "You just have to get to know them."

Bill seemed struck by this for a moment, then he was laughing. "Oh, boy. Boy, oh boy," he said, and continued laughing.

I shrugged. "I don't see what's so funny about that," I said.

"But what gets in the way of knowing someone?" he asked.

"I don't know," I said. "Time. *Not* knowing them, I guess."

I thought he would laugh at this as well, but he didn't. Now he was serious. He leaned forward and cleared his throat. "Ted," he said. "You're right about that, up to a point, but the main fact is this. You get in your own way. Why? Because the only person you ever really cared about in the world is yourself. And anyone who tells you otherwise is a liar or a saint. Remember that. There are books and books about it."

"OK, I'll remember," I said.

"Good," he said.

"So, what do you think you're going to get out of my mother?" I asked.

"Hah," he said. "Hah. That's a good one!"

We watched a few more planes land, and Bill described for me what it was like being inside one. Terrible food, he said. He had that look on his face while he talked, the same lofty look he got whenever he was talking about his king-and-queen story, so I could see the two things were connect-ed in his mind, I just wasn't sure how. And I couldn't stop thinking about how his hand had been on my leg for too long—how hot and still it was there, with nothing to do. I was just letting my imagination go in the most obvious direction. I wasn't used to this kind of affection coming from a man and didn't know the right way to take it. Was it strange or was I only taking it strangely because it was unfamiliar to me? Obviously, there were hidden things governing Bill's personality in ways I would never understand. He had already said as much. We never would know each other. Still, I thought I'd like to understand what was going on with him a little better.

On the way home we stopped for ice cream, and while we were eating he started to talk about my mother again. He had a sundae with marshmallow and butterscotch, I had a plain dish of chocolate. The counter where we were sitting smelled like dishwater and warm ice cream. "Do you think—" he asked, tapping his spoon on the side of his half-empty dish, "—let me ask you something that's kind of a tough question to spring. Let me just try it out on you. Do you think it would be a good idea for your mother and me to get married?"

"Probably not a good idea," I said. "Not now."

"No, I know not now. But when, though? Never?"

"I have no idea."

"OK. Will you tell me when you think it is? I mean, if you ever—when you change your mind and you think maybe it would be a good idea, you'll tell me, right?" he asked.

I shrugged. "Sure," I said. "I'll keep on the lookout."

He held out his hand at me and we shook, grinning, with the marshmallow and chocolate stuck to our teeth, as if the whole thing were in fun, though I knew it wasn't. Bill wasn't just feeling me out or trying to get my opinion. He was genuine. I didn't know for sure what he was getting at, but it seemed to me he wanted more than approval. Whatever it was, it wasn't mine to give. I thought it was almost like he had proposed to me, not her. That was a position I'd never been in before. At times I might have wished I was able to authorize my mother's actions. Now I saw what came with it was only uncertainty and the fear that I would do everything in the world wrong and spend the rest of my life regretting it.

I don't know which part of my mother's love for Bill was strongest—her love of flattery, generally, or her love for Bill in particular, and his particular way of saying things to flatter her. The distinction was important to me. I thought understanding it would help me to predict any danger that was in store—what would eventually happen between them and whether she would be the one to cut him off, or the other way around. My father also used to want to entertain my mother when they were married. I thought he was never quite as good at this as he should have been. Certainly, he wasn't as good as Bill.

While my father baked the pies, Danishes, and pastries for their coffee shop, he would make up songs. He said making up songs was just one way to relieve the loneliness of being awake all night alone, beating eggs, measuring flour, rolling out crusts and squirting filler into pastries. Besides, he said, many customers liked hearing him sing later in the morning while he cooked—it lifted their spirits, and even made them want to come back another morning for breakfast. My mother said she had never heard a single comment to that effect, and she should know—she was the one out on the floor, serving.

Whatever she said, it didn't matter. All night he would make up his songs, and then in the morning he would stand at the grill cooking breakfasts, singing them. The one I remember best, though it may not have been his favorite, went something like, "I want to be your Mr. Right, not just another Mr. Right Now—I'll be your Mr. Good, not just another goodbye, girl." Another one was, "In the evening time, when the sun goes down, I'll be there all the time...." He had a pleasant, medium-high voice with no especially distinct characteristics. It was just a voice, I thought.

The coffee shop my parents ran for a little more than six years was across the street from the main train station in Medford, on the ground floor of an old brick building that was owned by a lawyer from Boston. We lived over it in a two-bedroom apartment that looked out on the alleyway between our building and the one next to it. The coffee shop never did a lot of business, though it wasn't often on the verge of bankruptcy either. We had a steady flow of different customers who needed to eat fast—business people, travelers, and working people. The shop might have gone on for years, generating just enough money to keep itself afloat and cover our daily expenses. Who knows?

I was too young to understand exactly what went wrong between them, and why one morning he wasn't there at the grill, flipping eggs and singing songs about my mother. My impression at the time was that he must have tried very hard to lay some part of himself at her feet, and failed. He had failed because he'd been waiting for the day she would look down and be amazed by all the marvelous and beautiful things he was always doing for her, without her ever asking. She would see, and be transformed. But the day never came. Maybe none of the things he did for her were actually beautiful to see. I don't know. I will say this: I don't think the ideas my father had for himself, and for why he wanted my mother to be in love with him, were the same ideas she, or anyone else, shared. There were other people involved, too: a friend of my mother's who I thought was always trying to convince her that men were no good (she'd already been married and divorced a few times); a Greek dishwasher who read my mother's palms and brought her Greek delicacies from a shop in town.

When I found out he had gone, I went across the street to the train station—it was the only place I knew he could have left from—and spent most of the day on the platform watching trains come and go. Of all the people I saw through train windows, standing or stepping off of trains and onto the platform, not one of them was my father. Not one of them had on the brown knit cap my mother had made and the black leather jacket he always wore, with his Levi corduroys and his dirty apron hanging out. And I wasn't sure then which thing had made him leave, his desire to do something *generally* worthwhile and his failure at that, or his desire to do something just for my mother, because being worthwhile in her eyes, alone, was somehow more important than anything in the world.

I needed to know the nature of my mother's influence; I had to know how likely it was that I would ever please her, if she had already sent away the one man we both cared most about. Questions like this troubled me for a long time after he left. They were the same questions that made me wonder which part of my mother's love for Bill came first, and whether she would eventually have to tell him to leave, or if one day he would vanish.

————

That same day Bill and I had gone to the airport, the three of us drove out to the reservoir for a swim and a cookout. It was late June and already hot. We grilled hot dogs and swam, and then sat on the trampled grass by the water to eat until the sun went down and the mosquitoes and no-see-ums were finally too bad to ignore any longer. A few bats came out of the shadows, jaggedly flying at the surface of the water and snapping up bugs. Then the sun slipped lower behind the bowl of the reservoir, and the bats were every-where at once, as thick as a flock of birds. I was hypnotized by their crazy, jerking flight pattern, which was no pattern at all and seemed on the verge of disaster. For a while I listened to Bill express his awe, trying to coordinate his opinions with my mother's, and telling her not to believe whatever myths she'd heard about bats, vampire bats or anything related.

"They're just flying mice with radar," he concluded. "Poor, misused and misunderstood creatures, long abused by mythology, out there doing us all a favor eating these damn mosquitoes." He paused. "Enormously functional and com-pletely innocent," he said. "Even beautiful, in their way."

"I had a friend, when I was a girl, who was bitten in her sleep and died from it."

"In her sleep? Not possible."

"I don't care if it isn't possible, it happened. Months after that we were afraid of attacks. We rubbed our skin with garlic and slept under the holy cross every night. Just as we were told. People actually thought, then, you could control these things—the force of evil."

"As if it wasn't right there among you already," he said, "and causing you to make up perverse untruths about a bat, just so you'd have some way to excuse yourselves—all honor and piety, I'm sure." He pressed his hands together and bowed his head, mocking prayer.

"We stank like garlic. A whole bunch of frightened eight-year-old girls stinking like garlic." She laughed at that.

"Let me guess—this is an all-girls Catholic school?" Bill asked.

My mother nodded.

"Interesting," he said. He appeared to be thinking about this—probably remembering his dead sister, Molly, and the fact she had gone to an all-girls school as well. He must have been seeing, again, how my mother and his sister were like the same person. Twins, in his mind.

My mother slapped her arm and looked up where the last rays of sun had finally come away from the clouds and the sky was fading. She slapped her neck and then clawed herself where she'd been bitten. She slapped at her cheek and shook her head so her hair whipped back and forth. "Arr," she said. "I can't stand this much more. Why are these things always biting me?"

"Would you prefer the short answer or the long one?" he answered.

"I don't care. I want to go," she said, and she stood up.

I stayed behind to watch them walk up the path to the car, which I could barely see under the trees, and noticed the way they leaned into each other, naturally keeping apace with their arms around each other and their feet sharing the path that was not meant for two. I heard my mother laugh as her head vanished for a moment under his shoulder. Bill seemed to stiffen. I heard him say something like, "Around and around." Then the car headlights were on and Bill was standing next to the driver's side with the door open, blinking, looking in the wrong direction, and calling my name into the dark.

Almost too late it came to me, the understanding that I had been the one adrift, watching, guessing, and divining things about Bill and my mother. It had become of too much importance for me—all my overblown ways of watching them, which, I was beginning to see, had probably surpassed what existed between them. The game of divining had gone beyond the things to be divined and assumed an importance all its own, enough importance so I had even forgotten myself in the process. But I had never been in love and had no way of knowing, then, this was only a part of love's special magic, the confusion, and all the attention paid to figuring out scattered, unspoken things.

There were a few sleepless nights to make me see this. Summer Friday and Saturday nights were never good for sleeping in the apartment where we lived then because of the street noise—traffic, people yelling, and motorcycle radios. I was awake most of that weekend, watching car headlights go across my walls, and the light from the street lamp outside blow in and out in the thin curtains covering my window.

On Saturday night there was an accident. Someone making a left turn onto the street we faced miscalculated the distance of an oncoming car in the other lane, or plain didn't see it, and the two collided. All of this I watched from the window above, where I was standing. I had gone to the window not because of anything I anticipated, but because I was finally a little bored not sleeping. The thing to do, I thought, would be to wait here for sleep without seeming to myself like I was waiting.

The accident happened so fast I couldn't quite be sure how it had happened. There was a terrific explosion of sound which I found gratifying in a way, because I never would have predicted it. It wasn't like the noise of two objects pounding together, it was more like one huge thing bursting apart. The bigger car, making the turn, spun around twice and ended up on the sidewalk facing in the wrong direction, with its turn signal still flashing; the other one skidded to a stop, straddling the opposite sidewalk. The smaller one was a Honda hatchback, the other was a long American sedan with tail fins. Both cars were nearly beyond my sight, where they ended up. I could see the hunched shadows of the drivers inside, and neither one was moving. I waited a few seconds, then went into the kitchen, fast, and dialed the police.

On my way back across the living room I almost ran into my mother, who was feeling her way with slow, short steps through the dark with her arms outstretched to keep from bumping anything. She was still half asleep.

"What's this about?" she asked. Her voice was thick in her throat. "What happened?" Then we were at the window together.

"An accident," I said.

"Anyone hurt?"

"I just called the police."

"And what did they say?"

"They said someone would be here right away. I was the first one to call about it."

The windowsill was cool under my fingers and my neck was already sore from leaning as far to the right as I could in order to make out the person in the Honda. He was going to be worse off than the other driver, because his car was smaller and he had hit head-on.

The next few minutes we went back and forth between the windows in my room and the windows in the living room, waiting to make out what would happen. Soon there was an ambulance and two police cars stopped on either side of the road. A pale man in uniform stood in the center of the road, directing traffic; shattered glass on the pavement surrounding him sparkled and turned blue and red in the swirling lights of the sirens, and the lights of passing cars. The driver in the sedan seemed alert and relatively uninjured, once they had gotten him out of his vehicle. He was animated with the medics, shaking his head a lot, explaining things with his hands, and helping them get him settled on a stretcher. The other driver appeared unconscious, but there was no blood that I could see. After some struggle, the medics had lifted him from his car onto a board on the ground and were now crouched over him.

"My God," my mother said. "It really puts things in perspective, doesn't it? This kind of a thing really does."

She reached out suddenly and grabbed me by the side of the head, pulling me against her neck, which smelled musty and like powder. It was an awkward pose for us both, though I didn't think she was noticing that yet. She had one finger over my lips and the others across my chin. "The world is just *full* of these perils," she said. The way she said it I knew she wanted the information to have a much greater impact than she could ever get across. It was meant to express her real awe of everything in the world that was dangerous or impermanent, and that was just too much to talk about.

"Full of hazards," she said.

"Yes," I said, and she moved her finger away from my mouth as I said it.

"You can control your life to a point, but even that—what does it matter? What does it amount to?"

"Nothing," I said.

"You're right. Nothing," she repeated. She sighed. "Ted, it's a strange time to tell you this—I've been meaning to say something about it all day." She released me then. "Bill wants to put off the trip awhile. A few days. He has things to do at the store—I don't know what. Isn't it weird how one thing makes you think of another? Now, I can't stop thinking about that. Meanwhile, these poor souls outside our window are about to be rushed off to the hospital to have their lives saved."

"I think they're all right," I said. "The one guy seems fine."

"He does."

"So, no trip with Bill?"

She shook her head. "At least not right away," she said. "We'll leave Wednesday or Thursday."

"What happened?"

"I'm not sure how to tell you. The fact is, I'm not altogether sure myself. Something I said to him, maybe."

I was looking at her forehead then, watching the movement of her eyebrows and trying to imagine all the things she withheld or just didn't know how to put in words. "He read me some of his book the other night," she said. "Just to have a taste of it, quote unquote. Anyway, I think I may have reacted the wrong way."

"I can imagine."

"No, I don't think you can. I mean, it was nothing like what I had expected."

"Huh. Was it very good?"

"Good? Yes, it certainly was. *I* thought so. A little hard to follow, maybe." Now she seemed angry, and what she wanted to say came more freely. Outside, a black man in a yellow wrecker had arrived and was leaning out of the cab of his truck to talk to the remaining policeman. I was watching the crash scene, but trying to concentrate on what my mother had to say about how Bill had always misjudged her.

"I told him, finally," she said, "on the level, you know, I'm not so innocent, if that's what you think. I'm not perfect, and I'm not a bit innocent. I've been around the block a few times, myself. I've been married, for God's sake, and I have a kid. That's the most important thing. And I've been with men, not all of them, but a few."

"True," I said.

"Yes, it's true, smart-aleck. And anyway, that didn't really go over with him. I felt I had to prove something—which is always wrong—like I had to make it back up to him, and maybe I was just too forceful about it. I don't know."

"Forceful. What did you do?"

"That's none of your business." She didn't say anything else about it for a moment. "Let's just say I'm not sure how much Bill likes being with a woman like me after all."

"What's a woman like you?" I asked.

"Middle-aged. Divorced with a kid. Lonely. You name it."

There wasn't much interesting outside to look at

anymore. The ambulance and both of the cruisers were gone, which left only the man with the wrecker. But we weren't there to look anymore. We were just talking. "You know," I said, "I can't believe neither of us has mentioned this yet—you remember how Bill's sister, Molly, died?" I looked right at her, waiting for her response.

"Yes. Molly," she said quietly, still looking out the window. "I'd forgotten about that, too."

I had in mind saying something to her about how she wasn't Molly, after all. She was herself, and she didn't need to feel bad for anything. Whether or not Bill liked her had nothing to do with her, ultimately. But that was only one way of looking at the situation, and I wasn't sure how much she would care hearing about it just then.

"I have this feeling he isn't going to be in the picture much longer," I said.

She nodded and sighed, as if she supposed I had given the correct answer to a difficult question. "We'll just see what happens," she said.

"We will."

———

The next evening Bill called three times in rapid succession. First, he called to say he was coming right then for us. His car was packed and we needed to be ready for him in ten minutes because it was already six o'clock and the drive would take a couple of hours. He didn't want us to arrive too much after dark.

"We're packing, Ted," my mother said, when she'd gotten off the phone. This is how I knew what they had talked about. She was standing in front of the closet in the front hall tossing out things behind her. "It's six o'clock now and we have to get there before dark. Come help," she said.

I picked out my duffel bag from the camping gear, hats, jackets, and pillows piling up on the floor behind her.

"Hurry," she said, and then the phone rang again.

"That'll be Bill," I said, but she didn't appear to have heard.

They were on the phone a little longer this time. When she was finished talking I thought she looked as if she were straining to see through something unpleasant that was just in front of her, trying to keep in mind some other way of seeing it. But it wasn't working. She spoke defensively, as if I had already accused her of being foolish. "He realized there's an important fair tomorrow in Springfield that he can't miss. That's all. He's got to go. *Books*," she said. She smiled. "This gives us more time to pack, anyway. He'll be here in the evening, tomorrow. Tomorrow evening."

I wanted to say something about that. It would have begun with, "He won't come, because he can't," but the phone had begun to ring again. She went straight for it.

While they talked, I went to the front window in the living room to see whatever was left of the accident the night before—skid marks, oil on the pavement, bits of glass. But there was nothing. I was impressed by this, and thinking about something else that had to do with roads and cars, how each wore the other out in ways that were invisible. Maybe the passage of time was always invisible. Things changed, and as they changed, whatever they'd been in the past was erased and gone.

There was an old man coaxing his little dog along the sidewalk then, and I thought they also looked like they'd worn each other out in some way, or else they'd been worn out by the same forces for so long that they were shaped similarly, hunching along together, occasionally looking up at something. I tried to picture them differently. The dog stopped to kick some dirt behind it. It was a red dog with black shoulders and Scottish terrier fur. The man stopped too, waiting. He glanced up and seemed to see me there in the window, but his expression never changed. He gave the dog's leash an impatient tug and kept going.

"… be here any minute," my mother was saying, behind me. She'd said something else to go with this, but I hadn't heard. "Are you just going to stand there? We're leaving now for a month. I would suggest you do something to get ready for it."

"Now we're going," I said.

"Yes, that's right. You heard."

"*Brother.* Fine," I said, and went into my room so it would seem as if I was busy packing, but I wasn't doing anything yet.

———

Bill never came. It didn't take all night for us to figure out he wasn't coming. When he was only five minutes later than he had said he would be, we knew he would never show. We gave him close to an hour, though, to be sure. My mother had a better sense of humor about it than I expected. She was making Bill jokes—maybe he'd fallen through the back of his closet to that imaginary world of his. Maybe he was off dancing in the streets somewhere. She also said this was the biggest stand-up of her life.

"What is it about *me*," she said. "That's what I have to know." She nodded her head, agreeing to some part of what she was saying. "I have to face up to that. So, Bill's a phony weirdo, OK, but what is it about *me* that makes it so I keep winding up in these situations, with flaky men? That's the question."

"Ask Bill," I said. "Call him. He'll give you lots of reasons."

"No," she said. She glanced at her watch. "Let's walk."

"Fine."

"Screw Bill."

"That's right."

We walked all around town that night. She told me for the second time about quitting her job on Friday, and what Zack had said about it. Apparently he was having other problems with the business, which she had known nothing about, and her quitting came at a particularly bad time for him. Now, even though we wouldn't be going anywhere with Bill, she didn't think she could ask Zack for her job back. She was finished with that anyway, she said, though it sounded to me like she only wished she believed that. We walked past his store and went to stand in the milkweed and mullein growing under one of the darkened side windows a few minutes, trying to see in.

"Seven years of my life," she said. "Wasted, right there, at the back booth pulling apart little wires and putting them back together."

That was when I told her the first part of what I had decided people should know about themselves, but didn't— that they fell in love too easily. They were too enthusiastic and didn't ask enough questions. "It's like you've always got to have something to be in love with," I said.

She said I was ridiculous. "Don't talk to me about love. Love is honestly the stupidest thing in the world," she said.

"And the greatest deception. Don't even talk to me about it. Let's go." She turned and started walking, a little unsurely at first, then picking up speed.

"But see how much you love to say that?" I asked, following her. "Like it's your new thing now—love is stupid."

She shook her head. "It's only the truth," she said.

"So, what about Bill's book?" I asked. "How does it turn out in the end?"

"How should I know how it turns out? He only read me a few pages."

"But which one does she end up with?"

"Which one does who end up with?"

"The queen."

She was silent a moment. "I already said I didn't know."

We were walking fast. I was out of breath and my legs were a little numb from adrenaline. "Maybe she can't end up with either of them. Sure," I said. "She's already betrayed the king, and that dancing spell is bound to wear off, eventually. Right?"

"Whatever you say," she said.

"Well, how else could it be?"

"I said I didn't know."

Back at home everything was the same. There was still no sign of Bill. Her bags were exactly as she'd left them, next to the couch, two old plastic Samsonite suitcases and the square, red vinyl bag that held all her makeup and cosmetics. It was hard not to get ideas from that. Why pack or unpack? Why stay as opposed to going somewhere, once you were packed? I knew she was thinking along these lines, and also thinking that the last place in the world she wanted to be now was home.

"Let's go," she said. "We don't need Bill to get away a

few days, do we? Let's just go. Drive all night."

"To where?" I asked.

"Anywhere. Honestly, I don't give two shits."

I shook my head. "Sounds crazy. You go if you want."

She nodded. "You're sure about that," she said, still not facing me.

"Yes," I said. I had the feeling she would agree to absolutely anything I said about this, and I glimpsed a part of what Bill must have felt for her: it was the power she gave men to make her whatever they wanted. That was why he'd liked her; he thought she would become anything he wanted. I took a deep breath and said, "I'll just stay here. Don't worry. I'll catch up on my sleep."

"OK, you do that."

She bent and picked up one of the suitcases, turned, kissed me on the ear without looking, and left. The red bag and the other suitcase were still next to the couch so I knew she wouldn't be gone long, a few hours, or a night at the most. I thought I would never have anything in the world to resist as much as I needed to resist her. I had been born into the middle of her life, which was not my own. One day things would be easier than this. I wouldn't say it was bliss, but there was something new for me that night—a quality of aloneness I'd never experienced until then, standing in the living room with the lights out just after she left, and the velvet, night-smelling air around my arms and legs. Alone. It wasn't just a promise, it was the thing itself—it was knowing I would not always have to be on the other end of my mother's adventures in life, and defined by them.

Early that morning she returned. By this time she was in the kind of emotional state I had been anticipating all along, crying and a little desperate.

"How did I ever miss this?" she asked. It was the third or fourth time she'd asked and I still hadn't answered. I was half-asleep, in pajama bottoms but no shirt. She was on the couch, speaking without looking at me. I knew how I was meant to be attached to her suffering, to know all about it, without exception and mostly without explanation. "Tell me this, how did I miss it?" she asked. "He's a *flake*. Good God Almighty, why didn't I know?"

I said, "It wasn't him, it was you. You let him."

"Let him what?" she asked. She wiped her face on her sleeve and sniffed, still crying a little. She had been crying for so long that her face was changed—her eyes sharper and narrower inside their usual shape. She smiled a little, and I knew she must be aware of her appearance.

I said, "You let him run everything—the whole thing about Molly, and the king and queen, and going to his mother's to write his book. It was all his."

It didn't seem to me like she had understood. That is, she wasn't showing any sign of new understanding on her face. She just looked at me, waiting. At first I thought this was a defense. Then I began to see that I was only telling her things she'd known all along. She wasn't surprised because she knew this already. "So what," she said. She wiped her face and smiled again, differently, without being self-conscious. "Ted. So, it was his thing. What's the problem there?"

"It's weak," I said.

She shrugged again. "So what," she said. "Weak. Maybe it is, maybe it isn't. Are there some rules for this I haven't heard about?"

I shook my head. "No," I said. I couldn't say anything else about it then. I was full of a feeling that came from looking at her like I was Bill, trying to see how she had been the one shape at the end of all his illusions. But it wasn't easy. She had on the things she'd always worn—same clothes, same hairstyle, same shoes; she was in no way different than she'd ever looked to me, except for the fact that she'd been crying. I stared at her thick collarbones, and the stretched straps of her bra in the opening of her shirt—a flower-patterned shirt she'd worn for years—and tried to imagine something desirable in what I saw. But there was nothing desirable, only familiar. I thought about the many different ways there are of looking at the same thing.

"Never mind," I said. "Where were you all night?"

"Nowhere," she said. "Driving. Now I just can't believe this … not now." She doubled over and began crying again.

"You made it home all right," I said. It was a perfectly useless thing to say, though it seemed important to me at the time.

The clock on the TV said it was four-fifteen. I was tired and I wanted to go back to bed, but I couldn't leave her. There I was, dozing on my feet for long seconds, tightening my muscles and swaying a little back and forth to stay awake and balanced. "You'll be all right. It's not like this hasn't happened before," I said. I was just saying things.

I went to stand next to her, moved her hair aside and put a hand on her shoulder. She was hot to touch, and her shoulder muscles were surprisingly tight. Her shirt was damp and she smelled damp, like wet laundry. "Come on, it'll be fine. You still have me," I said.

She burrowed at my stomach, sobbing harder, and grabbed me around the waist.

"Stop. It'll be all right," I said, and let her hold me, staring alternately at the part-line on top of her head and the blank wall with the shadow of my head on it. "It'll work out," I said, and tried to move away from her. "So, Bill's a loser."

"You're right," she managed finally, but she wouldn't let go, and she wouldn't stop crying. Then it seemed like she was trying to pull me down with her on the couch, and it was all I could do to stay on my feet.

"It's just the classic, typical thing, isn't it," I said. "He's just the classic guy who gets confused and makes someone else pay for it."

She nodded.

"Let go of me," I said.

She didn't.

"Let go," I said, again. "Please."

She stopped crying then, long enough to look up at me. Her eyes were even brighter and smaller now from crying.

"How can you say that to me?" she said, quietly.

I shrugged. I didn't even know what part of what I'd said she was referring to, but I understood I had somehow crossed an invisible line saying it. Now I might never be able to go back over again. It had happened that fast, and I hadn't even known. "I did, that's all," I said. "I said it. There's nothing wrong here. This is just typical, right? You'll be fine. In a few weeks it'll be like the whole thing never happened."

She kept staring at me. Then she said very calmly, in a tone of voice I'll never forget because it was the first time I'd ever been spoken to in that way—like the possibility of any measurement or dimension to define what was going on and what was between us was now gone. Nothing measurable mattered to her anymore. She said, "You're just getting used to this. That's what you are. The whole time, I wasn't picking that up. You'll see, though. You'll go out in the world, and you'll find there are lots of people to love. Surprisingly many people to spread yourself around on. After a while, maybe, there's so many of them, so many options, so many possibilities and so many dead ends and head-ons, nothing makes sense anymore. You want *one* thing that makes sense—that's what people want, you know, but they don't know what it is. You forget what it is to have one thing that makes more sense than anything else around."

Then she let go of me and I stumbled back a few steps to get my balance. There were pink streaks in her cheeks and forehead now, and her pupils were dilated. She was smiling and she looked a little like a painting to me, that still and distorted, with the flush flames eating parts of her face.

"Will you remember what I just told you?" she asked.

"I will."

"It's fine if you don't understand." She reached over and flicked off the light so there was only street light in the room, then she let out a long breath. "There, that's much better," she said. "Isn't it? Let's just not say anything else for a minute, and then let's go to bed and forget this whole awful night. What do you say to that?"

"Fine idea," I said.

She sighed again. "You're too accepting of me, Ted, and I'm afraid of it. We have to do something about that."

"I don't think I'm too accepting."

"Oh, you wouldn't. But you wouldn't like me very much if you did—if you knew you were too accepting."

"Why do you say that?"

"You just wouldn't. Ted, when I'm gone, will you remember me well or poorly?"

"Gone?"

"Dead."

I hesitated. "I'll probably remember the way you are," I said.

"That's very encouraging," she said.

That was the last thing we said to each other that night. Soon she fell over onto her side on the couch and was sleeping with her mouth partially open, the air making a little sucking noise as it slipped in and out. I took the light blanket from the back of the couch, spread it over her, and went back into my room to lie down.

There was the light moving in the curtains covering my windows, and once again I was awake, staring at it. I was jittery and felt my heart like it was something flipping in my chest. My breaths came too fast and close together for a person not moving. *Can't sleep, can't sleep, can't sleep,* I thought. Sleep was like a fire in my forehead. I thought about what she had said to me about liking her more because I didn't know I was too accepting of her. I wondered if she was right about that, though I was pretty sure she would never know most of the things I thought of her, good or bad. There was something to get used to in that. And I tried to imagine that if I had liked her any less than I did, then maybe I wouldn't have come between her and Bill in the ways I had, and things might have worked out for them. But there was more to it, and I knew there was more.

I pushed my head down against my pillow and tried to remember the sound of her breath going in and out. I thought that would pacify me somehow. I would even hear her out there, breathing, if I listened hard enough, and that would put me to sleep. When I closed my eyes I would see Bill's empty suits, a parade of them walking past in my sleep, without Bill inside, the empty sleeves and pant legs blowing in and out with the imagined sound that was my mother's breath. There was the pumpkin suit, the solid gray wool one like a banker's, the white seersucker with the blue bubble-gum cigars in the inside pockets, the blue-flecked one with shiny worn-out seams—each suit a night we'd spent with Bill and another aspect of his nearly submerged abnormality, coming back for me to look at it.

We'd never known who he truly was, because we couldn't. No one did. For a time, though, he was just what my mother had always hoped to find, the person who would last her the rest of her life. She was something like that to him, as well. Now he was gone and in his absence was this thing—a mood of excitement, a shape that was Bill—quickly deflating. I hated to see it go, too. Nobody likes it when the world suddenly swings back to real time and all those empty glowing things—the illusions you believed—recede back to the place they came from in your mind. Such times you may think you have the world fully unmasked, as it *actually* is, but that can never be. Meaning gets printed over meaning, with nothing under that but more made-up meanings.

The problem is what to do in those moments when you feel there's absolutely nothing worth knowing, and the whole game looks like it's about to tip over and go out of focus. Probably there's nothing at all. Probably whatever you do it makes no difference. And once you have reached that point maybe you can sleep again. At least, that's what I did that night—and I didn't dream I was Bill Henry. I don't think I dreamed about him at all after that.

BODY IMAGING

———

DEE KNEW WHAT STUART COULD DO. SHE WAS, IN FACT, THE embodiment of his worst crime, being the young thing he'd left his wife and two kids for, six years ago. Now she knew what she could do, too, and it wasn't pretty. In fact, it was so bad it made her want to give up all her ideas about love and marriage—leave them by the side of the road somewhere. You fall in love to find the clearest picture of yourself. You fall more and more in love, until one day you realize the picture you're getting back is no longer true or even necessary, and is in most ways too limiting. Then it becomes impossible to say what to do next—leave? Die? She came in and out of opinions about it, moods she couldn't explain, sudden clarity, ideas that didn't sound like her own and made her say things she had no way of knowing were true or not, they flew out of her mouth.

"It's *not* a power thing. I left because I had to. Just like you," she said to him that day, a Thursday, after their session with the counselor, the only time they dared meeting face to face anymore. They were in the lobby, standing too close and trying to decide something. He wanted to have a coffee with her at Muffin Mania, and keep talking, like they used to do three months ago, just after she'd moved out and the talk in their sessions was mainly about getting back together.

She went on, "How I see it, the only way for us," she took a breath, "for now, is to be alone." What she meant was a picture she had in her head, one of herself crouching over the frame of her bike, the sound of her chain clicking, and the wind in her ears. There weren't words to tell him about this— not ones he'd understand, anyway—only the picture.

He gave her a look that began in confusion and ended closer to righteousness. She knew what was coming—some way she must have contradicted herself—and got ready for it. "Yes, that's fine, but two days ago—" he said, his forehead bunching into wrinkles.

She wanted to touch them, to undo all that strain with her fingers like unlacing a shoe, fix him.

"Two days ago you said what we needed is to have more time *together*, to figure each other out." He paused. "I'm not criticizing, I'm just saying it's a little difficult staying current with your wishes."

Now she didn't want to touch him anymore. He opened his mouth and bit down but said nothing further. She looked away so she wouldn't laugh at him. He was so sincere sometimes it was like he was mocking sincerity, and nothing happening on his face quite corresponded with what he said. Maybe there weren't words for how he felt anymore either. Maybe he'd already used them all. She wondered if that could happen: if you could get to a point where you'd said

so much and heard so many opinions about love that finally you began caring less for what you really felt than for how
your words stacked up together as a kind of logic or love
theory. And in that case, what was he holding on to—her, or
the idea of her? She supposed that was the whole problem
right there—that she couldn't tell the difference between his
feelings and the phony words he chose to stand in for them.

There was a warped reflection of the floor in his glasses,
black and white tiles, and two young people in bright colors
at the receptionist's desk, asking for Doctor Hanes. Stuart
had on a shirt she'd given him, blue and green linen with a
button collar. His hair stuck up over his forehead like a
comb, a little oily but not unkempt. He could look like that
first thing in the morning, getting up—red hair like wire that
would endure any mistreatment and still come out essentially the same.

"That was two days ago," she said, finally looking right
into his eyes, and regretting it instantly because of how it
seemed to relieve him. "And it was on the phone. It's a whole
different matter, in person." She looked away and back
again. "You really want to know what I think?"

His hands flew up. Then, "It's all I want."

But she couldn't say it now—it was just words and ideas
anyway; more bullshit about heartbreak being a paradoxical
state, having what you can't want and wanting what you
can't have. Instead she saw the picture of herself again, riding. Now, seeing it, she realized it wasn't so much that he
wouldn't understand, if she were to tell him, it was that
telling him would be giving away too much of herself.

"I don't want to be having this conversation with you
right now, is what I think," she said.

"No one's forcing you."

"Stuart."

"Don't insult me, pretending to feel sorry. Just figure out what the hell it is you're doing."

"I'm doing what I want. You know that already." She went across the room and shoved the glass door open, watching her reflection in it swivel out, take in the day, the sky and the brick of the courtyard. Outside her sandals slapped on the cement. He would not come after her. Stuart Weydemeyer might reason with you until he was dead or blue in the face, but he never chased people. Still, she felt in a hurry to get out of here. The sun was hot and made her smell her own skin and sweat. Heat caught up under her hair like electricity.

Julia's house was three blocks back into town and five blocks east on J Street. Here was where Dee lived for now. Whenever she saw this house her heart rose and sank simultaneously—yellow and white gingerbread Victorian, shingles missing, Dead stickers in the windows, sagging wraparound porch, and a sign over the door leftover from Julia's hippy-mother days: Julia's Place. When Dee first came here, three months ago, she'd thought it would be like graduate school all over again—she'd have that mood of indecision and forgetfulness, of becoming, books all over the floor and half-finished cups of coffee and wine. Instead she was constantly on the lookout for things falling apart. The dirt bothered her. There was no mop in the house. Julia's other roommates never did their dishes. The floor in the shower stall of the upstairs bathroom sank when you stepped on it, rotten floorboards giving way. In fact, everywhere you looked was an aesthetic disappointment—ripped up tiles, mold, windows stuck half open. She wished she could stop noticing.

"Temporary. It's temporary," she told herself, and went up the porch stairs, careful to avoid the one that wasn't nailed down. She waved to Julia in the TV room, reading a book, and went upstairs to her own room—the guest room—undressed, got into her cycling clothes and sat there a while on the edge of the bed staring at the orange tree out the side window, smelling herself and thinking without really thinking. If she was honest, what she most felt like doing was going to sleep. She'd just fall over and close her eyes and be plain blank.

She fell back and looked up. The bed was in a bay of giant windows—windows on three sides with billowing dusty green curtains in a floral-tropical pattern. On the ceiling were layers of inhabited and uninhabited spider webs stuck to the frayed surface of the plaster. There was no point trying to keep up with those spiders, they rebuilt anything you knocked down with a broom in a day. She sat up again and caught her reflection in the full-length mirror across the room. The sun had made webs of age on her face, like those spider webs, only unerasable. "Yuck," she said, and stood up, still looking at herself. Her legs were getting bulbous with muscles around the thighs and she had a funny tan line just over her knee from the other shorts—the ones she wore more often. She made her kneecaps jump up and down and looked at her face again without really seeing. "I am pretty," she said out loud, and turned a little to see herself in profile. "Pretty and blond and tan." It was true, she supposed. It had been true all her life, why wouldn't it be true anymore? "And I am vain," she said. "And I am talking out loud to myself in the middle of the afternoon because I'm lonely."

She grinned.

She went downstairs, carried her bike outside, and stood in the yard a few minutes touching her toes, while Julia's red dog went in circles around her, sniffing and lashing its tail side to side. She pretended to check her brakes and seat level. Really she was just putting off going because she still felt more like being asleep. She supposed depression might be a physical as much as a mental thing, and in that case her body was probably telling her how down she was, even while her mind went on denying it. A ride would be good for that—clear her head and give her back some energy. Across the street in the neighbor's yard, sprinklers shot up an oscillating fan of water over the dead grass. Never water in the middle of the afternoon, Stuart always said. Water left standing on the grass would act like a thousand tiny mirrors, burning right through the leaf.

Today it was hot, at least a hundred, maybe a hundred and five, and the pavement would have a layer of dry hot air flowing over it. At first it would hurt—her sinuses opening to it, stiffening and drying out, her legs aching. Then after a few miles it would be better. She'd feel as if the heat were holding her upright in a solid, other dimension of reality. *This is swimming in air,* she'd think, once she was out of town, deep in the steamy tomato and spinach fields or sailing between orchards of walnut and almond trees, really cranking. She'd stay bent double most of the time, hands forward in the drops. She'd go until her groin was numb and the balls of her feet ice-cold from no circulation, hands numb, too, from leaning on them. She'd go until she was dry so far down her throat she choked on the first swallows of Cytomax. It happened every time. *I'm the damn best,* she'd think, and ride and ride until there was nothing else to think but that, her heart ballooned up and blasting inside her.

"How far today?" Julia asked, coming out onto the porch, stretching, the book dangling from her hand. Julia was pigeon-toed and had black hair cut pageboy style, winged back. Everything about her was large—long legs and arms, broad chest. She had on the same blue plaid shorts she'd been wearing for a week now, since her program at the university for at-risk teenagers finished.

"Thirty or so," she said. "The usual."

"You take it easy. Be careful in this heat."

"Sure," she said, and laughed. "You know me." She swung one leg over the saddle, clicked her foot into the pedal, and coasted out to the road.

————

Sometimes, when she was cycling, she thought over the situation with Stuart in logical, language-shaped ways, like having a conversation with herself—a conversation whose points were all caught in the heaving, repetitive rhythm of her stride. But that could be annoying once it started—she needed to repeat her ideas to herself too many times in order to know she wouldn't forget them, and then they kept changing anyway. So she avoided it. Instead she went over the past—pictures she had in her head without words—just trying to see things from as many angles as possible and not to draw conclusions. Or, she yelled curses into the wind. Fuck. Fuck you, Stuart. Fuck this, fuck that. "Fuck this life!" someone had painted on Stephenson Creek bridge, the bridge that was like a gateway linking Russell Boulevard with all the popular bike roads that were really tomato-truck roads. Cursing was part of the cyclist code. She knew from talking to other cyclists. They were always cursing, though not many of them, she guessed, yelled curses into the wind. That was a waste of breath. But she loved the scraped feeling in her throat after yelling and the overwhelming silence that followed.

"Love is not a theory," she always said. It was, ironically, the thing she'd said to Stuart that got him started with her in the first place, six years ago, bringing his first marriage to an end. They'd spent afternoons together in his office on campus, or walking through the arboretum, talking. They spent a whole winter and spring like that. It was the longest non-sexual affair she or any of her friends had ever heard of or been part of. None of them could have guessed the way it would turn out—Stuart actually leaving the woman he'd lived with half his life to marry Dee, star graduate student from his "Poets of the English Renaissance."

The way she touched him finally, she remembered, was not particularly momentous—the heel and flat of her hand covering his forearm, sliding up to his chest, removing a pen from his pocket, unbuttoning a few of his shirt buttons to feel his heart moving there under bare skin. He breathed sharply in and out. His face turned red. He took off his glasses. She pressed with her hand to be sure he really understood what she was doing, and said it: "Love is not one of your theories. It doesn't work that way." At first, she was worried about kissing him because his mouth had a funny pucker, almost a beaked shape, and she couldn't imagine how that was going to feel. But kissing him she didn't feel it at all. In fact, kissing him she lost awareness of all such things—the eggy smell of his breath, and the way lint was always getting stuck in his too-long eyelashes. Kissing him was leaving behind a whole world of physical detail.

Ahead of her were six cyclists—guys in black and yellow, the university racing colors. Summer training, she thought. They showed up ahead of her, wavering under palm trees in the heat mirage. Here was exactly the thing she needed to get herself going: guys to catch up to and pass. She checked her computer, pushed the button for speed. 20. 23. 21. If she kept it just over twenty, maybe, in a mile or two, she'd be even with them. The pavement was rough ahead, past the horse stables, then there was a break in the trees where the road turned south and the wind would hold her back. "The wind is a hill," she'd read in one cycling magazine. She liked the sound of it and often said it to herself heading into windy stretches.

Now she had a picture—one she didn't want to remember, but which she realized was always hanging somewhere at the edges of her consciousness. It was from the day Pete, her first lover, came to her and Stuart's house to say he was done sneaking around. She had, just two days before, tried to break it off with him, saying she had decided for now to keep on being married. "I want to meet the man who's ruined my happiness," Pete had said. Pete was a handsome, Armenian plumber who'd written her love songs that were as bad as he was good-looking. He had illogical beliefs in things like happiness and destiny, fate and devotion, and had never understood that she was with him primarily for the sex.

Stuart showed no emotion whatsoever until after Pete had left; then he collapsed in the green easy chair in the living room where he watched TV most nights, or graded papers. He held his sides and clawed at them, doubled up like he was laughing. She remembered him now that way, in the yellow shorts and blue shirt he ran in, tipped forward, holding his sides and, for something like the second time in all their married years, bawling. That was the picture she had. She knelt in front of him and put her arms around his shins. "Oh, I'm sorry. I'm so sorry," she kept saying. "You had no idea, did you?"

"This is about Martha, isn't it?" he'd asked, as soon as he was done weeping. Martha was his first wife. "This is about you trying to experience the same kind of illicit feelings I had for you, at first, when you and I were the ones outside the bounds of marriage."

"Shh, shh," she said. "Yes, maybe just a little. I don't know." She couldn't believe he would think of things so discursively that fast. It chilled or infuriated her, or both. Was any part of this real?

He went on, "If I tell you not to see him again you'll hate me for interceding, and that, in turn, will only fuel your desires. But I don't know what else to do in this situation. I don't want you seeing him anymore."

"No, no. I won't," she said. "Don't worry."

She didn't. She had two other lovers, but she never saw Pete again. Well, she saw him once, much later, sweating in his pickup at a stoplight. Pete had the nicest body she'd ever seen undressed—all long lines and falling angles, reddish skin like clay—and the most impenetrable facial expressions, like you would never guess the half of what he thought. That is, until you got to know him, when you realized those looks were mainly a kind of delusional arrogance, the outward show of his secret belief that he owned the world—or ought to own it, anyway, because he lost out as regularly as anyone. She did not wave at him. He either didn't see her or chose not to wave himself.

When she got even with the other cyclists it was just like she'd thought it would be. They were joking and talking because they could afford to do that, protected from the wind as they were by riding together, so slowly, all of them in low gear, presumably saving strength for some marathon hills, that or finishing a one hundred mile loop and not out to prove anything to anyone. None of them had on a helmet.

"Hey," she said matter-of-factly, and kept pedaling. She was at least five years older than the oldest one of them, but what did that matter? These days she felt more like twenty-two than thirty. "Hot as hell, isn't it," she said.

"Yup," one said.

They said nothing else, their talk suddenly seizing up, now she was here. She disliked that and didn't know what to make of it. "Hey, guys, relax," she wanted to say. "Act normal. I'm just like you." But the silence stuck. It stayed in the air whirring through their spokes and in the rhythmic rattling of chains through derailleur wheels and cogs.

The guy leading the pace-line was small and wiry, mid-twenties, and had brown eyes and pimples. Cyclists often had pimples from all the sweat and dirt constantly blowing dry on their skin. She had them herself, between her breasts and along her hairline and jaws where the straps of her helmet touched. She saw the veins in the leader's arms. His skin was white in the creases where the sweat dried. He glanced once at her and licked some new sweat off his lip. He looked confused. He looked like he wanted to say something to her but couldn't. Maybe he was just amazed to see her out here, keeping up. Maybe his brain was overwhelmed from oxygen and endorphins.

"Lady, if you want to ride with us," one guy behind her said, "find a place." He had some kind of Latino accent.

There was a long pause. Somebody chuckled. Somebody else said, "Come on back here." He dropped out slightly, making room, wheels buzzing as he stopped pedaling. He must want her to fall in in front of him so he could watch her up close and have his thoughts. She knew her shorts fit like tight velvet, and if you looked hard through the armholes of her cutoff jersey you might glimpse her jog bra, might even catch a mole or beauty mark in the soft interior light against her skin. She'd seen as much on other women. But these things weren't worn to entice. Just the opposite, in fact. She wore them to fit in.

She glanced back at them. They were hunched over, sweating, legs churning, all eyes on her.

"Lady," the man addressed her again, "if you want to ride with us...."

"I don't," she said.

She watched the numbers on her speedometer jump, 20, 21, 20 again, then 26, thumbed the right shifter knob on her handlebars for a higher gear and stood up, leaning into the pedals, blood surging through her neck and head. She heard a whoop behind her and some laughter. Then she went back down on the snout of her seat, hands forward in the drops, feet bobbing up and down until she wasn't conscious of anything but that and the wind roaring in her ears and her breath ripping in and out of her lungs—a grainy dull sound. *Fuck them,* she thought. "Fuck you all!" she yelled.

She went miles that way, hissing curses under her breath, the adrenaline slowly subsiding. Later, much later, she risked a glance back. They were still there, back in the mirage at least a mile, six flickering dots. "Hooee!" she yelled. Now she felt good.

———

"The thing to do," Julia had told her, when Dee started with cycling last year and was discouraged by how weak and slow she was, "the thing you need to do is called body imaging." Julia was an ex-triathlete. She coached soccer and track at the same high school where Dee was an advisor. Sometimes, coaching Dee, she sounded a little like she was talking to an adolescent kid. "When you see a biker out there who looks good you take her in—what she looks like, or he looks like— take that image. Hold it right here." She poked her fingers at Dee's forehead. "That's you now," she said. "That's how you look. Notice everything you like about them, the way they move, what they're wearing, whatever it is. Now it's you."

So Dee watched other cyclists and bought the things they were wearing. It helped. Really, it did—jerseys, shorts, gloves, helmet, glasses. She was careful to pick colors that weren't too obviously matched and she didn't wash things often. She loved the buildup of residual sweat in the seams of her shorts and rippling the backs of her jerseys. She was proud of that. The shirts stank. It was a rubbery sour stink, like milk and toe-jam and a little like whatever soap or perfume she used, but mostly like singed hair and flesh. Whatever it was, it was her smell, which is what mattered most, and all she really cared about—a smell she possessed completely.

"Every journey of the body," Julia had said, "is a journey of the soul, too."

Dee would think about this, sniffing herself before her rides, storing power for what was ahead.

At Seivers Creek Road she hung a right and headed for the hills. She saw the glass when she turned and tried to be careful going around it, touched the padded palm of her glove against the front wheel to knock loose any stuck pieces, then reached back and did the same with the rear wheel—holding her hand there until she felt rubber burning the leather in her palm. Then she sat back, no hands, and sucked Cytomax from her bottle, not really pedaling, nearly choked on the first swallow—it was hot as hot tea. She drank hungrily, savoring the way it slipped past her dry tonsils and soaked her throat. There were the hills ahead, brown and crumbling, and to her right was a field of cut grass with an open-sided barn at its center, hay bales stacked inside. Everything she saw now had the distorted, hyper-clarity of exhaustion and endorphin high—colors so bright and vivid they felt disconnected from her seeing them. She pushed the bottle nipple back in with her teeth, replaced it in the rear cage, and that was when she felt her tire go flat. At first it was just a wobble in her motion. Then it was a bright copper hiss, and she knew what had happened. "Shit shit shit shit," she said, squeezed the brakes, kicked her left foot out of the pedal and coasted to a stop under the nearest shade— the thin shadow of a dying, leafless walnut tree.

As always, stopping a ride in the middle of a day like this was like walking into a furnace; unbelievable how fast the heat hit. It stopped her breath and soaked into her skin so that every ounce of fluid in her body seemed to want out. "Oh my God, oh my God," she said. Sweat dripped into her eyes and stood out all over her arms. She took off her helmet and glasses, lifted the bottom of her jersey to mop her forehead and stood still a few seconds wondering if she was going to make it. Of course she would. Now her shoes made nice scuffing and rasping sounds on the pavement. She tried to concentrate on that and to remember she had other senses aside from the ones that registered how incredibly hot it was.

"No time to mess with a patch," she said out loud. Spare tube under the seat. Tire levers. She set them on the pavement. She was all economy of motion, barely moving, moving slow but fast. She pried open the quick release on the rear wheel, turned the bolt a few times on both sides and pulled the wheel from the frame, careful to remember how the chain went back on. This was the tricky part—always the tricky part with a rear flat for her—remembering how to get the chain back on. She felt around the tire's circumference for glass, lightly, barely touching. There it was, a little protruding piece of beer bottle amber embedded in the rubber. She picked it loose with a fingernail, flicked it away, felt for more, felt again, and started the annoying task of levering the tire from the rim.

The six guys came around the corner. They were a single creaking, sweating organism. Speed held them together. They took the corner hard, as one body, and came flying at her, riding much faster now. The lead guy saw her, yelled "Left," and they swerved en masse into the middle of the road. Really, it was beautiful how held within their own world they were, and what a world it was—with holes in it to let in the heat and sun and wind. Then she noticed one of them had dropped out—the leader—and was headed back toward her. He came closer, stood up over his seat with his fingertips on the handlebars and yelled, "Are you OK?" too loudly, like the heat might make her deaf or take away his voice.

"I guess so," she said softly. She was stunned, a little, by how she said it, her voice seeming to imply things she'd had no intention of implying: *Make love to me so I can forget who I am.*

He came closer. "Sure you don't need help?" He could hold his balance nearly standing still and drifted at her until they were only the width of the road apart, apparently still waiting for her to say something. Then he kicked his feet loose and stopped, straddling the frame of his bike, and rubbed the backs of his gloves through his hair and over his face. "Motherfucker. It's hot," he said.

She agreed with him. His face was so bright red now she couldn't tell where the zits were.

"You shouldn't be riding alone on a day like this," he said.

"Probably not," she said.

"It's dangerous."

"Yes, it is," she said, like danger pleased her—also like she was indifferent to its pleasure, as she was indifferent to pleasures of all kinds. And there it was: the lie she told every time and kept telling until she was so deep in it she couldn't see how to get out: *I don't feel anything. Please make me feel something.* But the opposite was true, because she felt everything and picked her lovers to make them feel things. Maybe. Actually, she had no idea what was true. Not now, in the middle of this heat, but she felt the argument coming up, a familiar knot to go over, touching it in her mind.

He squinted at her, his sight coming back a little, probably, doubled and blurred from sweat and from not going against the wind anymore.

"This is fucked," he said. He dropped his bike on that side of the road and came to stand in the shade next to her. She felt his presence like an oven working in reverse, soaking heat out of the air and into itself. Then she couldn't tell if she had only imagined that because she was so used to feeling the temperature of any body standing or lying or sitting next to hers, and feeling how it soaked up and gave off energy. Really, in all this heat, she couldn't tell whether or not he was there, which was strange because he was standing quite close. They worked together, sweat dripping on the backs of their arms and running onto everything. He got one tire lever under the bead next to the pump valve, she got another one in several inches to the left and held it. The third one went in between the first two and then she flicked her wrist back, hard, unzipping the tire from the rim. "There," she said. She yanked the tube out, her eyelashes deflecting sweat that bounced over her cheeks like tears. His breath touched her on the back of the neck and she couldn't even feel it—couldn't feel the heat in it, that is, but felt her neck hairs register a disturbance.

She uncoiled the spare tube. It had a white dust of new rubber on it and flitted through her fingers like a ribbon. She held it while he pumped in a few shots of air. How nice, it holds air, she thought. How nice to see things function as they're supposed to, according to logic and mechanics, not stupid human impulse. He held open the bead of the tire while she inserted the pump valve through the hole in the rim and then fingered the rest of the tube in snugly against the inner wall of the tire. She watched him squeeze the tire bead back up over the rim, pressing until the tips of his fingers bent backward, stippled pink and white under the nails. She was thinking a few things at once now: yes, in a way it was a matter of life or death, getting this tire on right; you could die in the heat; but in another way it was completely ridiculous—the two of them here, in the middle of spinach fields, dressed in their flashy sports clothes and fooling around with the rear wheel of a bicycle. She wondered if they would ride the rest of the afternoon together.

"OK," he said, and she popped the bead into place, up over the rim with the back of a tire lever. "Good job."

"Sure." She wiped her face and had another hit of boiling Cytomax. The man took a step away from her, holding his lower back for a second because of the way he'd been stooped forward. His hair was completely soaked through with sweat so she could see the shape of his skull. Normally, you were with a man a while before you saw his skull this intimately—say, after a shower or a bath. His teeth were bad—crooked and discolored, like rocks. And now she thought she could detect the smell of his sweat—a dank smell, like food burning. But maybe that wasn't him; maybe it was old tire rubber burning on the tarmac, or the earth and soil everywhere around them burning up. She couldn't be sure.

"Now the worst part," he said in a voice that yelped too much.

She rolled her eyes and smiled. "The worst part? Kind of like everything else in my life right now."

"Huh!" He looked hard at her, a look she imagined was meant to convey empathy but instead showed only how hard he was trying to conceal his uneasiness. "Here." He held the wheel between his knees. "You go first."

She clipped the pump head into the valve, held it there with one hand, and started pumping. The fact this motion was not unlike giving someone a hand job didn't escape her. She had to bite her lip not to laugh. The man's hand covered hers now, helping to hold the pump head tight against the valve, but she couldn't even feel it. It was just a more congealed form of heat touching her. Their legs were inches apart. She was bent double with her shoulder occasionally brushing his thigh. She could see the shaved hairs on his shins—a desert of black stumps under living sand.

"Let me," he said, and they swapped positions.

"What's your name," she said.

"Rob."

"I'm Deirdre," she said.

BODY IMAGING

113

He looked at her so he could put her face and name together, nodded once, and started pumping. It was that simple to him. It was not that simple to her. She wished it was that simple for her: face plus name equals identity. He stopped, groaned, stood up, and they traded again, then traded back.

"That should do it," he said. The tire wasn't exactly hard, but there was enough air in it to get her home, and it was becoming nearly impossible to squeeze any more in.

"Thanks so much," she said.

"Not a problem," he said, and turned away.

Already they were across the road from each other—she, clipping her helmet back on; he getting ready to clip into his pedals and head out after his friends. Had they arranged a place to meet up with him, or would the rest of the team turn back after a set time, ride until they crossed him and go from there? He wouldn't even meet eyes with her. "See you," he said. Then, "Be careful." He swung out to her side of the road, wheels whizzing, passed her and went on.

"See you," she called after him. "Thanks."

He waved one hand and stood up, pedaling hard to get cool, then went down into his seat, crouched over the handlebars. She looked longingly after him, the way his back arched over the frame of his bike, getting smaller now, the heat mirage over the road swallowing him up and making him waver like a horseman fighting through water, and she started to cry. "Oh, God," she said out loud. She knew what this was about. It was the ends of things. They left her wrecked and heartsick—ends of movies, phone calls, dinners, days. Anything that had an end. She was happy only in the middle now, and occasionally at the beginning. "Help," she howled and threw her head back. "What is going on?" The heat stung in the spaces between her teeth. There was the sun overhead and some dried, dead moss stuck to the limbs of the dying walnut tree. She concentrated on that and tried to make it the objective correlative of everything she was right then feeling.

"Get a grip," she said out loud.

Then it hit her why she hated endings. Of course. It was because she couldn't find one for herself. She couldn't find a permanent way to think of anything—a conclusive logic that didn't unravel, a final feeling to have about Stuart that didn't automatically betray her, a perspective on love that wasn't self-nullifying. In fact, the word "final" couldn't be applied to her in any way now. And every time something in her life ended, some trivial thing she had no control of, she was thrown back on seeing exactly how unformed and out of shape and in the middle of everything she was. Even the knowledge that she was looking too hard for an end (though it made her feel better, for now) wouldn't last, and some day soon she'd have to find another way of seeing it.

"Let it go," she said, and shut her eyes. "Let it go, let it go." Though what she was letting go, or holding on to, she couldn't exactly say.

She got on her bike and headed home.

Another way out of this was to make it a picture. She'd done that before: will herself into seeing what had happened—a woman, her image and shape, crying back there by the side of the road—and then she'd say, "There. See? That's me. But not anymore." Reverse body imaging. She made herself in the black shorts and the red shirt unzipped to the sternum, helmet sticking out over her forehead, dark-blond hair, and her eyes bleary from crying, the whites and blues enhanced.

"I'm leaving you!" she yelled.

The ache between her legs was coming back now, and the numbness in her hands and toes as well. These things were good, keeping her locked in the moment, right now, headed home—yet they also felt eternal, like she was part of an eternal ache that was maybe the essential thing about being human. The tips of her fingers stung from handling hot rubber and steel. They were black with chain grease so it looked as if she'd done much more than change a flat— like she'd fought off monsters of machinery in the hills with her fingernails. She sat up and sucked her first bottle dry, squeezed it so it wheezed hot mist in her mouth, then stuck it back into the rear cage. The bike whirred pleasantly under her. Everything was straight—in a straight line. Cycling forced that from you. She shut her eyes and let the wind push her. "Wind is a hill," she said. With it behind her now she could hear everything—hair rubbing the inside of her helmet, birds in the surrounding fields, road-grit under her tires. But she couldn't keep her eyes shut more than a few seconds, and soon she was bent double again, pumping her legs and watching the pavement for dangers. Here was the blandest text of all, and the one with no exceptions—rocks and pocks and oil marks. She felt it in her feet and knees, how the blandness ground up through her, erasing everything. It felt good to be so erased because it gave her a kind of tranquility. In fact, that feeling was a little like the greatest pleasure of them all, only opposite; continuous, not momentary; giving her the world back, not taking it away for a few seconds of delight.

PLENTY OF POOLS IN TEXAS

———

ONE DAY LAST JUNE I BOUGHT SOME NEW SHOES. I DIDN'T need them. I bought them because I thought that in four days I would be leaving the town I lived in, just west of Sacramento, to be with a woman I loved who was in Texas. I imagined myself wearing those shoes around Texas after it turned cool and the leaves flew. I saw my feet going up and down the steep streets of Austin where she lived. They were handsome, all-purpose shoes with a good tread and would serve me well getting around town and meeting people. And later in the winter when it was cold and I was back in business and her divorce became final, I imagined myself wearing them down to City Hall with her. After the ceremony we'd stop some stranger on the street and give him our camera: "We're just married! Take our picture!" we'd say, backing up against the wall of the old capital building. The shoes would show up at the bottom of the picture. Kayla would be leaning toward me, smiling avidly the way she did, her body twisted slightly to make contact, my upper arm between her breasts and my cheek inches from hers.

None of that ever happened. Still, I remember the day I bought those shoes—how new they were in the floor mirror, pinching my feet and giving me ideas for the future, and the saleswoman who helped me choose between blue-green and blue-black, her short bleached-white hair slipping across her chin as she kneeled in front of me to press my big toe and say, "Good fit!" The soles were thick then, and cushiony under my heels, giving me the superior feeling of a man with somewhere to be in a hurry, and the insoles had not rotted or begun twisting around between my toes.

———

When I met Kayla I had a broken nose and a patch of impetigo on my right cheek. She looked right past that to what she needed from me, which was only the opportunity to take care of things—feed me, change my bandages, wash my cheek and smear antibiotic creams on it, put me to sleep at night. I didn't see, at first, how these favors were all an attempt to forget herself. Occasionally I would have glimpses. One day at the swimming pool where we'd met—and from whose towels I'd ostensibly contracted the impetigo infection—we were sitting poolside with our feet in the water watching an amazingly seal-like man do butterfly sprints in the lap-lanes. I couldn't get over the way his legs hooked in and out behind him and his arms twirled through the water. Kayla was telling me a story about her husband and an article he'd published earlier that year to deliberately offend some of his colleagues. But the details were too convoluted, and there was a spurious outrage in the way she told them that worried me and made me sad.

"Kayla, Kayla," I said finally, facing her and taking her hands in mine.

"What?" Her eyes scoured my eyes a second, possibly intent on knowing what I wanted before I said it. She had a short, sharp chin, flipped blond hair and brilliant eyes. "What? Am I going on too much about Jeff again?"

I leaned closer, put my mouth against her neck so I could taste her skin, and imagined all the other secret smells trapped under her hair and coming up through the opening in the back of her swimsuit. My nose was still a mess from the accident, but I could already tell how much I was going to love the smell of her.

"No," I said. "Sort of." I watched the seal-man turn and start back. "Did we come here to swim or what?"

"Let me just finish first." Her eyes softened and she nodded once as if we'd agreed on something without saying what it was. "Then we'll swim. I don't want to seem like I'm totally obsessed with the past, but it's important for me that you have this as a reference point."

I should have told her to forget it. I should have dropped in the water, turned on my back and started swimming. But I'd only known her a few weeks then and, as I said, I'd never been with a woman who loved me out of panic. I didn't know the signs for that particular madness yet.

She went on, and each time her story seemed about to be coming to an end she'd spin into some other thing—Jeff's job, Jeff's parents, Jeff's daughter, the last time he locked her out of the house.

The seal-man lifted himself from the water onto the bulkhead at the other side of the pool and strutted to the deep end. He wasn't strutting, really, his muscles were constricted from exhaustion and he was having a hard time moving in the air. He waved at some lifeguards, then climbed one of the metal starting blocks next to the high-dive and crouched into position. For long seconds he hung there, arms back and leg muscles twitching, counting down to the sound of an imaginary whistle-chirp or starter's gun. Then he leaped out, body snapping back, so eager for water he was already swimming his first strokes before he was in.

I counted seven starts and short sprints across the deep end before Kayla noticed I wasn't paying attention to her. I just loved how the man hung there, locked in the moment, all his weight in his toes, waiting to pour himself through the water.

"Hey," she said. "Hank. You're a million miles away."

"No, I'm right here."

She touched two fingers to the rash on my face—mostly cured by then—and tilted my head to the other side, fingernails lightly digging at my chin, to see something about my nose. Her hand slipped down my neck to my collarbone. "Poor Henry," she said, dipped a hand in water and ran it up my thigh and took a breath. "Anyway, in the end it turns out the whole thing had nothing to do with me. It was all *him*."

She was looking at me as if I should be astonished by this information, but I was no longer sure what she was talking about. "Let's go," I said, and slipped into the water, pulling her down after me by the feet.

I swam to the middle of the pool towing her—pulled her hard so she flew through the water against me, legs wrapping around my waist, then twirled her away and pulled her against me again. "When you leave," I said, hands at her waist now, "I won't know what to do. I won't know how to take care of myself, you've spoiled me so bad." I felt better now we were in the water and embracing, not talking about her and Jeff. "Certainly, I won't want to come to this pool anymore."

"There are other pools," she said. She wiggled her eyebrows. "Pools in Texas."

"Yes," I said. "Plenty of pools in Texas."

I lay back, found some lines on the ceiling tiles to orient myself, and started kicking. I tried to imagine my feet as a single thing—a mill, a blender, a pair of bee's wings; I breathed hard through my mouth and tried to think of nothing but the moment—my breath, my feet, my hands at my sides—but I kept losing concentration. I remembered the bleach smell of chlorine soaking my skin and hair, even though I couldn't actually smell it. Now and then I'd turn my head to the side to see Kayla there, paddling sidestroke. She'd smile when I did this—a detached, matronly smile, almost disdainful, I thought.

The first time I ever saw her, before the accident, we were sharing a lane. I kept letting her get ahead of me and then catching up—underwater all the way so I could watch her legs scissor open and shut as she breaststroked and sidestroked. She kicked crookedly at the breaststroke, favoring her right leg, so she was tipped a little to the side as she swam. That day she was wearing a faded green-striped bathing suit and no goggles; I found out later she had lost them. At the end of each lap she'd stop—I'd see her there at the end-cross, legs dangling, toes touching pool-bottom a second—then turn, kick off and head back past me, eyes squinted shut underwater like she was crying and bubbles streaming from her body.

Instead of Austin, I went to Tucson. I'd already given up my bench at the shop where I worked and sold everything in my meagre collection but my wood blanks, a handful of finished bows, each with one quirk or another, and an older Italian violin given to me in the last days of my training by the master-builder I'd done my apprenticeship with, and which he had always said might be worth some money once I'd restored it. At least temporarily, I had nowhere better to go. I helped out at my sister's restaurant, Geronimoz, bartending, and cursed the heat coming and going—between my car and the chilly interior of the restaurant, my car and her old house in the foothills outside town. On my days off, despite the heat which I hated, I'd walk in the desert, carrying water for a dozen people under ordinary circumstances. Soon I'd worn off the outer edges of the heels of those walking shoes, and the toes were caked with dust and sand. I'd notice this sometimes getting into my car at the end of a hike and think it was impossible, a dirty trick, even: my shoes were wearing out and not in any of the ways I had imagined—not on the streets of Austin, or climbing the stone steps to Kayla's condo, or walking with her by the river. I climbed Mt. Lemmon from seven angles on different trails. I went to the Rose Canyon at the far side of the Sabino preservation and stuck my head under a trickle of water that had been torrent enough to wash away trees earlier in the spring. Lizards and rattlers shot off the sandy trails right in front of me and vanished under rocks. "Why don't you just kill me?" I'd ask. "Why doesn't one of you fuckers just bite me in the foot and we'll get it over with?"

The wind whistled in the Saguaro arms, pushing them

back and forth on their mile-reaching networks of thready roots and the sun hit me like knives and arrows. Kayla had gone back to Jeff. I was trying to make myself believe this every day I was out there walking—trying to bury it in my senses and instincts and walking-around muscles so I could get used to it and figure out what was next in my life.

My sister has no Indian blood, but her house was full of artifacts from the Apache and other mountain-dwelling, southwestern tribes—ancient weavings and skins, baskets, worn out rugs, bits of pottery and so on. She liked wearing beaded headbands and Indian skirts and shirts with ties rather than buttons, proving her connection with a past that wasn't even hers. Outside her door at home, between a couple of kidnapped, sagging barrel cacti was a slab of rock she'd unearthed digging her foundation and then painted with relevant Indian signs—the sign for hogan, an arrow for protection, and two arrows facing each other to ward off evil spirits. At the ends of my hikes I'd toe off my shoes by the door, slip them under the upholstered shoe-cover she claimed was charmed to ward off scorpions and spiders (she never sprayed), and head for the tiny pool in her back yard.

Underwater, I ran my fingers through my hair to rinse away the sweat and dirt, sank against the rubber side of her pool and looked up at the sunlight streaming in. I stayed down as long as I could. When I surfaced, I lay on my back so the only heat touching me was on the cheeks and eyebrows and nose. Overhead, the sky was dull violet and hazed with pollution. I thought about what it was going to be like for me to leave here. I could picture it perfectly. "Goodbye, brother-wanderer," Lucinda would say, standing next to those slumped-gutted barrel cacti and raising one hand, the other arm across her waist to hold her robe together.

"Spread my love to anyone who knows me." It would be early morning, and the sun would not be so dizzyingly bright yet. I'd draw my seat belt over my shoulder, wince and wave back to her, sweat already blistering on my forehead. Then I'd head north, maybe—back to New York where we had grown up, or Salt Lake City, where I was sure to find work; or south to Mexico, where my savings would last. Or east a thousand miles further to Kayla, in Texas, if she ever called, though I was pretty sure by then she wasn't calling.

Inside, I got a Pepsi and sat at Lucinda's kitchen table in the silence, trying to convince myself it was all for the best. Despite the ancient Indian relics and despite the fact Lucinda had lived here the last seventeen years, nothing looked set to me. Her house still seemed to me like a place someone was pretending to live. There were tracks in the living room carpet showing where she walked most often: from her couch to the short flight of stairs up to her bedroom, from the stairs to her kitchen, and from her kitchen back to the couch. Together they made an uneven triangle. Her wall plaster was cracked, puttied, and re-cracked in places from the extreme temperature shifts of the desert, and her kitchen ceiling sagged in the middle, next to the ceiling fan, dropping bits of spray-on stucco on the floor. It all looked superimposed to me—wrong, like the wear and tear on my shoes.

Some fighter planes flew by overhead, so loudly the windows rattled and a salt shaker chattered on the tabletop. Every day, at least three times a day they did this, flew over in formation, four and five at once, excoriating the stillness. Jet noise funneled after them, faded and swirled back again, the lowest bass frequencies hitting her house like an explosion and vibrating my nose bones so much they itched.

The first time Kayla and I spoke, days after my standoff with the truck driver on Highway 21, I was convalescing in the hot tub next to the swimming pool with my arms out. My elbows and shoulders were too scraped and bandaged to get underwater. The rest of me, aside from the broken nose, was sore but surprisingly unhurt—no broken bones or pulled ribs despite rolling fifty yards through the tomatoes and weeds and spinach plants. It hurt to walk and lift things, but not terribly. I could get around, breathing through my mouth, and could manage most of the basic repair work and setup to stay on top of things—cut sound-posts and bridges, carve pegs, re-hair bows, etc. I had seen Kayla a few more times since the day we shared a lane—the day I noticed her striped bathing suit and crooked frog kick—but I hadn't spoken to her. The days were getting shorter then and more and more people were showing up at the pool to swim. I just never had a reason to go up to her and say anything. I knew she was from Texas because I'd seen her getting in and out of a blue Civic with Texas plates; I knew she was either married and didn't wear jewelry swimming, or was recently unmarried, because of the line left on her ring finger where the wedding band should have been.

"What happened to you?" she asked, that day—the first day we spoke—getting into the hot tub across from me. She had on another suit over the striped one, a plain dark green one, which offset her light skin tone and hair color nicely. Her eyes were glassy and white-rimmed from the pressure of her goggles. For a second, before she was under, I noticed the air bubbles caught between her suits like blisters along her ribs and stomach.

"Bicycle accident," I said. I knew I looked much worse than I felt with that splint on my nose and the black wedges under my eyes and blood seeping across my retinas. I looked terrible. "Out on the tomato roads. Some guy in a truck ran me off the road. I mean," I breathed deeply through my mouth, glad for the moment to be in such physical discomfort because it took my mind off talking to her, distracting me from the usual worries, "I mean, it wasn't just out of the blue like that. I did a few things to probably piss him off."

She nodded, smiling as if she already understood what I was going to say next. Then, "Like what?"

"Cut him off at an intersection and give him the finger because he practically ran me off the road one time before he *actually* did it."

I'm sure there was no reflection of her in the hot tub. Still, when I think back on it I remember the water being blue and smooth, showing reflections of her all over its surface. I picture her chest bare, not strapped up in those two suits, the scoop-necked one over the V-necked one. Also, I remember her saying something she didn't actually tell me until much later—something about wood ducks and the risk of their becoming human-imprinted: "The first living thing they see, they bond to it as mother—like that. And they can never erase the image—whatever it is—badger, raccoon, person, whatever. It happens all the time to researchers. You have to be careful." She went on about some ducks who had imprinted to her, but I was more interested in her hair falling around her face and sticking to her cheeks, and her sharp, clever eyes.

She laughed. "What else do you do for fun?"

"What else?" I said. "Blow up trains and burn down houses. Kill people. Nothing much. I'd rather talk about you. What happened to you?"

Her eyes went into mine and flicked away again. She sank a little lower in the water. A man with a buzz-cut and sagging arm muscles got in next to her, wincing happily at the heat as it engulfed him. He glanced in my direction a second, nodded and looked out the window. The rest of the time Kayla and I were in the tub talking, that man was there, looking away, so the conversation had a dreamy feeling of recitation, like it was being acted for someone, though I don't think he was really listening. "Actually, I haven't been in any good accidents recently," she said. "Not since I was a kid."

"Too bad. An accident now and then, just to shake things up—it's positive energy for the soul. Like a minor earthquake."

She rolled her eyes. "Sounds like something my husband would say."

"Husband." I hung on the word a little, faking surprise.

She scooped some water and splashed her hands back under. "Yes."

"Huh. Doesn't he like to swim?" I asked.

"Oh, he loves swimming all right. He was on the Olympic team, in fact, in 1980—which is infuriating because no matter how long he goes without swimming, just sitting on his butt, he can still get in there and wipe you right out." She shook her head. "No, he'd be here if he could, probably, but he's back in Texas. We're not exactly...." She paused and looked at me with exquisite defenselessness. "Things are a little off and on right now."

"Sorry to hear it."

"More off than on, really."

"I see." There was a silence, the hot tub bubbling softly.

She lifted herself, moving away from the man and closer to one of the water jets, then sank down again, letting her eyes fall shut a second. The last few girlfriends I'd had were all married women. I knew there was something I liked in common about them—something about removing the passion and romance from any possibility of a future. For one thing, I liked how it drove me crazy for them, and vice versa. But talking to Kayla I didn't feel crazy like that. I felt crazy like I wanted her all to myself.

"Well," I said, "I think it's amazing that we have words like that at all—'off and on,' 'married,' 'single,' whatever—like the things they refer to are even the least bit comprehensible. Like you could even *begin* to name what they refer to. It's a comfort, I guess. I mean, they're so worn out you can know for sure you're not the first one using them."

"Yes." She was still looking at me, her eyes more pupil than blue. I should have gotten out of the tub and walked away. I half-wanted to—mostly because of the way I felt so held there—but I was curious, too. "Small comfort," she said. "Thank God for generalities and cliches. And thank *you* for the reminder."

———

Late July, the monsoon season came and storms blew up from the Gulf of Mexico, pounding down rain, flooding roads and ditches and washing away bridges. One afternoon on the way back from a hike I lost my car, driving into a deceptively steep-sided dip that looked only a little ruffled with surface water. At first I thought I was still going forward—soon the water would stop pouring across my windshield and I'd see the road ahead carrying me up the other side of the dip. I'd shake myself and settle back against the seat. Instead, I was swept sideways. The AC surged and whined, surged again, then died. Outside, I could hear water catching under the wheel-wells and churning through the exhaust. Then it felt like I was being sucked backward—the windshield was still streaming with water and I had nothing to orient myself against. Once or twice I caught my eyes in the rearview mirror and noticed how the panic was over-layed with a kind of thrill-seeker's amusement and disbelief, which was surprising.

When I could be pretty sure I had stopped moving I rolled down a window and looked out into the rain. But there was nothing to see from here—a rock-strewn, reddish embankment with some cholla and prickly pears on it. Water was up over the fenders of my car. I hooked my fingers into the window gutters and pulled myself through the window, onto the hood. I'd seen this often enough on TV—dumb, stranded drivers waving at the news helicopter from a ditch of rushing water. I knew it was the right way to proceed. Already I'd drifted too far from the road to see it or attract anyone's attention, though I was still fairly sure which way to face. "Hey!" I yelled, and waved my arms. The rain was steady and hard with occasional bursts of rainbowed mist and torrential sheets. It soaked my hair instantly, and turned hot running across my face and into my mouth. "Hey! Someone, help!"

When I saw water was getting inside, lapping up over the open window and submerging the floor of my car, I knew it was time to go. I slid off and let myself be bounced along until a boulder hit me in the feet and threw me against the side of one bank. I scraped my way up to dry land. By then the sun was coming out—thick, stringy yellow light that didn't seem to belong—and cacti were popping flowers and love-toads were making a noise like sick crickets in the sand. I followed the ditch back, past my ruined car, to the road where smarter drivers were backed up, ten or twenty deep, patiently waiting things out. Water turned to steam on my back and under my armpits, filling my nostrils with the ditchy stench of rainwater and desert dirt and my own body odor. As soon as I had stopped moving I could feel exactly how hot it was, and how the air was permeated with displaced ocean moisture and the sweet smells of suddenly conceived life—nearly unbreathable. Underneath that I felt how dry the earth was still—the desert sucking life from everywhere.

To the east the same storm that had taken my car sat in isolation against the red, mica-veined Tucson mountains, a massive misshapen thing like a giant's foot with crooked orange bolts of lightning flickering on and off from the cloud-head to the ground. Rain trailed down underneath it like a woman's hair raking the ground. Parts of the storm were brown and pink, catching the reflection of the mountains behind or the ground below; other parts, especially where the rain poured down, were dark gray, shimmering like the insides of a seashell. Behind the storm, where the sun went through the last rain and mist and swept fog up off the ground, there were two rainbows, one arching up inside the other. I lifted my hands together to frame it like I was taking a picture, then I went up the road looking for a ride home.

———

Hours after making love with Kayla I could still feel her with me. At times I hardly remembered what it was to be alone in my body. My tongue was her tongue going across my lips, my hand on the back of my wrist was hers, her fingers lacing between the knuckles. I smelled her perfume in my breath and all over my skin. "What is wrong with you?" I'd ask myself sometimes, looking in the mirror. "Are you crazy? She's married!" I'd imagine the impetigo on my cheek a kind of symbol for what I felt, those two red ruts, like elongated pimples oozing lymph, the physical manifestation of everything she had done to rupture my solitude and sanity. But then she'd be there at night again, talking me to sleep and smoothing things over with her high voice like the tops of trees in a wind, saying, "Come to Texas, come to Texas." All fall it was like that. The rash on my cheek faded to a smudge and the bandages came off my nose. Now it was like seeing a person I knew but didn't quite recognize in the mirror—myself, but worn out in ways I hadn't intended. The eyes and forehead were OK, but the nose hooked to the left and was bumpy at the end, making the cheeks look too narrow to support it. The scar on my cheek was shaped almost like Michigan, with a crater where the water would have stood against the land.

By winter, she had more or less moved in. We never stopped talking about the day she would leave. I still loved watching her swim. When she had a break from her work at the university she'd call. "What are you doing?" she'd ask.

"Showing bows to a guy from San Francisco," I'd say. Or, "Watching the game while I try to straighten out the varnish on that thirties Roth." I usually had one or more things going at a time. "Just setting the clamps on a couple of re-hairs and reading the paper. Why?"

"I need a swim. I can't stand it here another minute. Want to join me?"

Sometimes we met in the parking lot or the lobby; sometimes, underwater. Often we wouldn't have spoken since the night before. I liked discovering her underwater best. She had a new, metallic-blue suit that was easy to spot from a distance, and yellow-tinted goggles with a white strap. I'd get in, sink against the side of the pool to test the seal on my goggles and wait until I saw her bobbing along against the water, legs scissoring open and shut crookedly, then I'd work my way over to share her lane. I don't think she knew how much I loved watching her. I considered it a defeat if I came on deck and found her in a chair waiting, reading about ducks, or swimming sidestroke and watching for me. Then she'd wave. "Hey, I just got here!" or, "Picture meeting you here!" she might yell. Once in a while I'd see the seal-man too, swinging along next to her, his arms wide and his legs churning. He went through the water like it offered no resistance at all.

"What does it get him?" Kayla would ask sometimes. "So he can swim so beautifully, but so what?" Then she might go on about Jeff, who had quit the Olympic team two months before games to enroll in law school because, he said, he had finally realized the only way a person can have a lasting effect in the world is with his words and ideas—via the law—and not by physical exertion. "Swimming means nothing to anyone. It's all about dividing time into tenths and hundredths of seconds. So what? Who cares?" she'd say.

In the spring, she left. She was no longer teaching, and her research had left her at a point where all she needed was to write. "No reason to be here when everything I need is back home," she said.

For weeks after she'd left, I kept feeling her with me. There were little red marks in my armpits and on my thighs and neck and shoulders where she'd kissed the hell out of me the last nights we were together. My tongue was stiff for days and my ears hurt from swimming or not swimming anymore, I didn't know which, and whenever I shut my eyes I saw her over me, her hair falling around her face and her eyelids flicking open and shut, the pupils dilated from pleasure. I couldn't stop seeing that. I had a few sleeping shirts and T-shirts she'd left (Jeff's), and a copy of a book on marsupials she'd had a hand in editing, but there was no other trace of her. "Come to Texas," she'd say on the phone, if I told her how much I missed her. "We'll make a whole new life. Come!"

But sometimes she was so depressed-sounding I hardly recognized her voice. She had started back smoking again and couldn't always get herself out of bed. "What am I doing? I'm sinking, Henry. I know it. The pain is unbearable!" she'd say.

Then I'd remember what I'd known all along without really knowing: that her love for me was not really love but an attempt to forget herself. Sometimes she didn't call or answer my call until hours after an agreed-upon time, or her line was busy for hours, but she never stopped saying I should come. Not until the day in June when I bought those shoes and went walking out of the shoe store, happily picturing my future. That night she told me things weren't really on or off with Jeff, but the truth was they had been seeing each other and talking, and she just didn't think it was such a good idea for me to be moving to Texas anymore.

"And all this time you've been saying I should come?" I asked.

I heard her blow smoke into the phone. "Look, if there's been any deception in what's between us it's as much your responsibility as mine—talking to me every night and pretending we're going to have this *life* together, for God's sake, never looking at the straight truth. You think this is what I wanted?"

————

The last time Kayla and I swam together I ended up showering next to the seal-man. I'd swum hard that day and I felt good, loose in the thighs and shoulders, and my neck was like rubber. The seal-man stood under a jet of hot water, facing in with his head down and his hands behind his back, his hair a fish-fin shape against the nape of his neck and water streaming from his chin and forehead. He never turned around and never soaped himself; he just stood there letting the water hit his head and run across his muscular back. His bathing suits hung one over the other on the shower handles, sagging together, one faded to the point of disintegration, the other newer, and his goggles were on the floor at his feet. I don't know what I was expecting him to say or what I was thinking I might say to him. I'd watched him for months and tried to copy his style. I was certain he looked nothing like Kayla's Jeff—he was blond, not dark and at least ten years too young—yet in my mind the two men were one. I wanted to ask him what he thought of Kayla, really, if he'd noticed her at all, if he thought I was right to trust her. He groaned once and glanced my way without meeting eyes, then leaned forward, his hands out against the shower wall and one foot raised, toes bent to the floor. The sole of his foot was wrinkled and the skin on his heel looked swollen with water.

I got dressed and went out without combing my hair. In the lobby Kayla was waiting for me and sipping a V-8. She had on a blue dress with no sleeves and her hair was loose, wet and frayed-looking around her ears, and she wore white tennis shoes with no socks. "What took you so long?" she said, and laughed. It was almost night; the sky was brushed with pink and red in the west. We went out of the building with our fingers laced together and my arm caught between hers. I was happy because I could not imagine what was next. I couldn't picture myself in the driveway the next day, watching her back out into the road and waving one last time as the sun splintered and turned white across her hood and windshield. I wasn't imagining any of that or the silence afterward, or her hair left on my floor and stuck in my bathroom sink, or the smell of her hanging around after she was gone. There were only the seconds we were in then—heading home, talking about dinner, and getting ready to enjoy the rest of the evening together like any couple.

INVERSION

———

STEVE KRAUSS'S WIFE WORRIES ABOUT THE AIR. THEY STAND on the balcony of their one bedroom in the brick apartment complex where they just moved, watching the sunset, and she tells him so many things about the quality of that day's air he begins thinking of it as a chemical collage overhanging the land. The colors of the sunset help with this illusion—vibrant purples and blues making the crooked tops of the coastal mountains miles to their west sparkle and waver. She tells him about the inversion and how pollutants form a skin of hot air over the valley, like a pot lid, trapping bad air below and magnifying the sun's heat. She demonstrates with her hands, showing how cooler air caught outside the inversion flows straight over them, from the Pacific to the Sierras. He never tells her, but when he thinks of them trapped here on the valley floor in this smutty air, he feels a kind of comfort and relief; he feels protected, not threatened.

"They're starting the crop-burns," she says. "I saw, on the way to Vacaville this morning for my interview. The smoke was just about blotting out the sun." She leans over the wobbly railing, all her weight on one leg, her body touching his at the shoulder and along the upper arm. She has on a white tank top. He is wearing no shirt at all. He doesn't really think of the place their bare skin meets as a touch. It's more a fusion, a seam of confluent heat between them, like they are separate heads stuck on the shoulders of one body, looking in different directions. He swivels away slightly to see her, not letting his arm out of contact. She looks better from the front than in profile. In profile she's too angular—sharp nose and chin, steep forehead. From the front these angularities melt away and you can stop noticing how much it seems she has something to prove. She's prettier that way, her eyes often playful, green rimmed with gold-copper.

"Like the dry-land plowing isn't bad enough, digging up all that dust into the air, right when the inversion is at its peak and all the pollens are on a rampage, not to mention the pesticides," she continues, looking at him, almost smiling. "These huge, huge columns of smoke. I mean really huge, like the size of a football field. I felt so … violated."

He nods his head. He's seen it too, not today, but three days earlier, driving north to Winters. He says, "It's bad."

"Yes," she says, and goes on to repeat a story she heard from the woman she interviewed with that day—one about some mice found dead at the school in their cages the day after a particularly close and extensive crop-burn. "Died right there in the classroom," she says. "Think of what it must have done to those second-grader's lungs."

While she talks, he thinks through a color separation exercise he often uses with his beginning students: tape a sheet of mylar over a Brueghel print, turn it upside down, and trace out all the forms using magic markers, only primary colors. He keeps seeing how the mylar tracing ends up looking next to the print: a jumble of shapes—colorful chunks and fragments that don't add up, no matter how carefully you've traced them—hats and shoes and dancers' legs. Then you slide the mylar back over the print and see how it is truly an abstract reformulation of the original. In his mind he keeps sliding the two together and apart. He tells his students about the complexity of the human eye and says Brueghel's original is only a more exactly rendered abstraction of reality than their tracing—no more or less real. "Art is abstraction," he concludes. "There is no such thing as realism. Very possibly no such thing as reality itself."

"You're not listening," Jenny says.

"I am."

"I hear a ringing in my ears. Do you hear a ringing in your ears?"

He shakes his head. Aside from making him see things that are invisible, her suggestions also convince him, sometimes, he is feeling things he doesn't really feel. The air looks gaseous and lethal now—green-tinged currents of toxins sweeping around them. And maybe there's a faint humming somewhere in his head. His sinuses burn and there's a sour taste in the back of his throat—rice particles? He can hardly believe they're outside breathing, or that he can smell their downstairs neighbor's blooming fuchsia above all this airborne commotion. The leaves of a palm tree growing next to their deck rattle in the wind. On the lawn below, a fat woman in polyester shorts with her hair in curlers waits for her cocker spaniel to shit and coughs once into her hand, like nothing in the world is going on.

"It's supposed to make you hear a ringing in your ears if you get too much of the rice particles in your lungs," she says. She nods her head meaningfully. "All day, my ears have been ringing."

"What can you do about it?" he asks.

"You can know," she says. "You can know something terrible is happening."

———

Nearly every night they make love. Here is one way the move to California has affected them similarly: the warmer air wakes up her sex drive as much as his. She sits on him and makes herself come once or twice while he touches her all over and watches. "Now," she whispers, after what seems like hours, and they finish together. Coming isn't half as much pleasure as waiting and watching her, his heart breaking all over because of the perfect symmetry of her legs around him. He puts his hand over hers, between her legs, lightly, to feel her touching herself, moves it up her forearm, feels the tendons working, the sweat on her stomach. She is nearly inaccessible to him, but not, her eyes going through his as she comes and he sculpts her with his palms.

The first time he saw her, just over four years ago, she was naked, on the stand with two other models for his intermediate life drawing class at the college in Boston where he taught then. She was not beautiful. There was a pugnacious quality about her that he liked. Not her parts—not her sloping shoulders or small breasts or too long neck and arms; not the tufts of wiry red and yellow hair on her, two on her nipples, one trailing like a jet plume between her navel and abdomen, stopping and reappearing slightly darker between her legs—not that, exactly; not the way she moved, either; it was everything he *couldn't* see in her form that made him think he'd never understand her, and made him want to paint her.

"You," he kept saying that first day. He was terrible with remembering names. "Come forward a step more. Do something else with your hands. Yes. That's better." He stood next to her and, pointing to the air around her with a pointer, measured the number of heads from her navel to her toes, and so on. "You all should know this by now. Count: the number of heads from her chin to the end of her arm." Some students murmured along with him. He wasn't really listening to them or to himself. He was noticing the faint silvery marks on her hips and under her arms, like violin strings, the swell of her hips, watching how her narrow rib cage filled with air, in and out, her skin goose-pimpled in places. The room was too cold to let him smell her.

"OK! A series of twenty-second gesture poses," he said, walking back away from the stand, "starting," he glanced at his watch, "now!"

He wandered between students' easels. Without thinking he was still counting the seconds by her breaths in and out—still picturing her rib cage. "Nice," he said to one student. "But do his arms really move that way?" Most of the students were interested in the other models—a black man with the liquid musculature of a dancer, and another woman, heavier, with frizzy gray hair.

By the end of the twenty seconds he was at the back of the classroom. He turned and faced the stand. Jenny stood with her legs shoulder width apart, looking to one side, one hand on her right hip and the other up like a visor over her eyes, an expression on her face like a referee or a farseeing sailor.

"Change pose," he said. Pages whipped back around him. Newsprint fell on the floor. He glanced at his watch, then back to the front of the room. She faced him, hands behind her head, arms up in triangles, belly pushed out. She looked right at him, into his eyes, and didn't smile. The way she was pushing down with her hands made her chin disappear into her neck. He was going to say something to her about it, ask her to loosen the pose a little, but the way she looked right at him he couldn't say it. He glanced back at his watch. "Go," he said, and students started sketching.

He still likes looking at her, though she won't let him paint her. She doesn't model for anyone now—that ended when she finished her MAT and began teaching, about a year after they met. Nights, he sits on the side of the tub while she bathes, and they talk over the day. He watches her body, distorted under water, and forgets a lot of what he was going to say. She does more of the talking. Often, things she tells him become inextricably attached to parts of her body. There's a new friend of hers, Pauline, whose face Krauss has to think of whenever he sees Jenny's knee—some complicated story from Pauline's past—and there are the snowy egrets she saw driving back from the Bay Area one afternoon, whose long white wings whipping back and forth are her collarbones.

Before they moved to California, she got out books on the conquistadors, wineries, gold miners, and hanged outlaws. At night, he watched TV and she sat next to him on the couch in their apartment in New Hampshire, reading, every now and then repeating aloud facts about California. "There are almost no indigenous forms of vegetation left in the Central Valley, can you believe it? Except for the live oak. God. Listen to this: 'Those days'—like a hundred years ago—'a settler's journey across the valley floor from the foothills to the San Francisco Bay was made entirely in the protective shade of live oaks. Now, where once the mighty oak reigned, are over a hundred different species of grasses and less shade bearing trees, all introduced by settlers, none native to California soil. Recent agribusiness has laid its claim on the land as well.'" She closed the book on her fingers and looked at him.

He read its title: *The Changing Face of California*. "Interesting."

"It's like a whole man-made world."

The reading lamp next to her on the end table lit up her head. Individual strands of her hair were red, blond, brown, and even occasionally black, if you held one up to the light and spun it between your fingers. Together, they were a shifting weave of red-blond—the same red-blond that brushed her wrists and forearms and came in wiry tufts from her toes and navel.

"Our new home, soon to be," she said, and grinned and nudged him. "Isn't it great?"

———

Later, the heat rolls away and they sleep. The clock ticks on the nightstand next to them, and the air, coming through the open windows and sliding screen doors leading out to the balcony, is thick with smells of chemical fertilizer and pesticides; a little like the fishy smells of seashells and ocean spray and Pacific fog they're apparently missing—the ones wafting straight over them from the shore to the mountains, over the pot-lid of the inversion. Traffic on I-80, a few miles south, creates a mechanical surf sound to accompany the false oceanic smells. Maybe this is why he's slept like he's in a coma ever since they came here: he thinks he's at the beach. Or maybe it's some way the heat wipes him out at the end of the day. He can't tell. Not since he was a child, though, has he had so many consecutive nights of good sleep. His dreams are all from the deepest parts of his unconscious—gray shifting shapes, escapes and pursuits, ski lifts going nowhere. Tonight it is his ex-wife kissing him in the back of the #5 bus riding down Broadway, saying "I want you back, we can do this again," while he hangs onto the metal pole next to the rear door, bracing both their weights against the bus's rocking.

He wakes up not because of the dream, though it's disturbing enough (he hates dreaming about Kathleen—hates any reminder she's alive at all, in fact). He wakes up because Jenny is sweating. The side of him touching her is also sweating, burning up to her heat. He rolls toward her, touches her hip and feels how wet she is—soaking right through the sheets. She goes on twitching and breathing. This isn't the first time. It's been happening every second or third night since they got here. The soles of her feet touching his shins are like loaves out of the oven.

"Jen," he says, and squeezes her shoulders. "Babe, you're roasting again." He spreads her hair on the pillow behind her and blows on her neck, pulling the blanket back on her side and lifting himself on one elbow to kiss her and rub the sweat off her face. "Hey, Jenny," he says.

She told him, the last time it happened, to please, please wake her up the instant he feels it begin again. He's not sure why. He feels down the length of her arm to her hand, cups his over it, rests his cheek on her shoulder and shuts his eyes a few seconds, trying to understand whether this is really the best thing, to wake her up. He breathes with her in and out and feels her heat increasing. He tries to picture it, to give it a source inside her—a sun, a furnace—but he can't see it. Some kind of internal friction, he thinks. But what is pushing against what?

"God," he says out loud. He props himself over her again. Her mouth is open, eyes still shut. "Wake up," he says firmly, and shakes her.

She lies still a moment panting in and out, then swats him away, throws back the covers and runs for the bathroom, ripping away her nightgown as she goes, feet stomping. It looks to him, in the dark, like she's trying to pull off her own skin.

"I can't believe this!" she says. "Why?"

From the bathroom he hears her run water in the sink, hears the linen closet door open and then slam shut, the toilet seat bang down. He presses on the mattress where she was lying and feels her sweat between his fingers.

———

Whenever the inversion breaks for a day or two, as it does the following night after a brief windstorm, she is amazed to see where they live—this flat, brown, quasi-tropical desert between mountains. True, nothing much has changed. There are still the endless grids of vegetation—rice, tomatoes, sunflowers, spinach, and nut trees; there's still the hum of the freeway and the stink of cooking tomatoes from the Hunt's cannery. But somehow, in the clearer air, all of this seems inconsequential. In one book on California she read that if men were suddenly eliminated from the Central Valley ecosystem it would take just over a hundred years for most of their damages to be erased back into the sand. Whenever the air clears she is reminded of this speculation and of the general impermanence of the human race, and she is relieved.

Tonight he isn't with her—he has his night class at the university—and she's getting drunk by herself on the deck (a sweet five-dollar bottle of Pinot Noir), sitting on the cement, watching the sunset, and thinking over lines from a new poem—one she started that day. Two minutes ago she went inside to use the bathroom. Reciting to herself in the sink mirror she saw how her tongue and teeth are nearly black from wine. "Not sex I want—that collaborating urge / Summer sky aching with all that longs to loosen." She stuck out her tongue. It was still tongue-color around the sides. She grinned and clenched her teeth to inspect them. "You're drunk," she said. She cupped her hands in her face and blew out to smell her breath. "And you stink like garlic. He'll never want to kiss you." She has made the pasta dish with lemons, goat cheese, and ten cloves of garlic—the one he'll never eat. It's one of her many night-alone rituals. Drinking is another. And she isn't sure if she does these things out of spite or pleasure—if she loves the taste of garlic, or loves knowing he'll have to overcome all his dumb squeamishness about smell in order to kiss her for the next day or two.

The cement is making her legs numb. There is as much light left in the corners of the sky as there is wine in her glass. But she doesn't feel like going back inside for more—not yet. She swirls her glass so the wine leaps up its sides, leaving syrupy wine-legs. Anyway, she doesn't need more wine. She needs to get sober and go to sleep. She has another interview tomorrow, ten o'clock, at a private school in Auburn. It isn't the best job, but she'll take it—she'll take anything right now. These days of no structure and no one to talk to but Steve are making her crazy.

Images from the poem keep coming back in her head—fiddlehead ferns against the foundation of their house in New Hampshire, white birches and cedars, clouds darning the sky with moonlight. *Not sex I want,* a lie, of course, because all day she's wanted it. She presses one hand on her stomach, sighs, twitches her kneecaps and watches them move, trying to imagine them as if they're separate from the rest of her—smooth, bony animals caught under her skin. This is how Steve perceives her: knees, wrists, breasts, chest, ribs, head. Parts. He'll lie under her watching this awesome assemblage of pieces, and she won't be able to tell if she loves or hates (both probably) the power she has over him being so dismembered, incomprehensible yet adored, though she knows she's as addicted to it as he is.

She begins the poem again and goes for as many lines as she can remember, mumbling half-aloud—the back porch in New Hampshire and the wet night simmering with bug noise. She swallows the last of her wine, sets the glass on the concrete—it wobbles a second making a grating sound against the rough surface—draws her feet up under her and tilts her head back. "Failure," she says, and smiles, not actually convinced, but liking the drama of saying it.

The sky looks painted, somewhere between purple, pink, and blue, no stars yet, and there's a high skin of cirrus clouds that won't keep the heat down. Good. She tucks both hands between her legs and squeezes with her thighs. It'll be nice to sleep alone a while, sprawling. She loves that—the bed to herself. Another of her night-alone rituals: she'll wash her hair and braid it hard so the curls stay in half of the next day. She'll get in bed feeling so clean her skin stings—except for the worry, half-hidden by feeling good: what if she wakes up sweating? Maybe it's a chemical shift in her, a reaction to this landscape she can't love and the emptiness of her day-to-day life having no job—some way her loneliness turns to internal heat the same way she knows it can turn to desire. Or maybe it's the marriage itself, dying. Everything going from ripe to rotten. She knows she can't know, she can only wait and try to pay attention to what she feels.

Later, Steve will slip into bed smelling faintly like an art room—paint and turpentine. He'll touch her forehead with his lips, nudge her back over to her side of the bed, mumble something about whether or not she ate all the garlic in Gilroy and then he'll lie there breathing, waiting to sleep.

———

She wakes up sweating. She wishes she could remember the dreams that came right before her waking up; but they are not pictorial dreams, if they are dreams at all, and there are no lasting images or voices or tastes. The feeling she has, waking, is one of hauling the pieces of her mind back into place after having let them drift dangerously far into oblivion. Maybe she slept too deeply. She hopes that's all. Now she's wide awake, feeling cold air all over her and not wanting to move because of how extremely sweaty she is. There's something scary and shameful in it. How has her body done this without her knowing participation? Why? She feels around herself with her hands. The sheets touching her are soaked through to the mattress. Sweat ices her body all over. Her arms are wet and her nightgown sticks to her stomach.

She gets up, leaves the sheets on her side turned back, and goes into the bathroom for towels and a fresh nightgown. The wet nightgown she leaves hanging over the curtain rod, then she sits on the toilet and, while she pees, she works her fingers through her hair to the scalp, massaging to separate strands and help the sweat to evaporate. She mops her face and neck and hands on the clean towel, presses the towel to her stomach and crouches. Already she feels better, drier and warm again, and the whole incident seems poised on the brink of dropping back to non-memory and non-reason: a thing that happened to her but doesn't matter or make sense or bear thinking about. But she doesn't want that. She wants to remember because she wants to find some way of understanding.

She stands, dries herself all over, puts on the dry nightgown, and goes back to the bedroom. Here is the part that upsets her most: seeing the bed there in the half-light—Steve on his back, hands folded on his stomach, asleep—and feeling repelled by it. Not just repelled: she believes she has no part of this picture. The feeling is accompanied by a lot of other feelings—panic, nausea, vague anger—and an imaginary grating noise, the lines of the telephone wires shadowed on the wall over his head rocking in the breeze, blurring wide and shrinking back to their original shape. "What?" she whispers to herself, "What is this saying?" and goes to her side of the bed. She mops it dry as best as she can, spreads the towel over the wettest part and gets back in.

He rolls toward her. "Babe," he says.

She touches his foot with hers.

His hand reaches for her, pats the mattress, stops on the towel. "Maybe you need to change your pills," he says, half-asleep still, slurring his words. "A higher estrogen?"

"Could be," she says. But she's been on the same dose nearly two years and never had a problem. "Actually, I'd like to go *off* the pill altogether."

"Yes." He sighs once and yawns. "We'll make babies.

Happy white babies." His hand covers her stomach, pulls her to him. "You OK now?"

"Fine," she says. "Let's sleep."

But she doesn't sleep. Not right away. Whatever her body is trying to tell her, waking her up, she needs to pay attention. She needs to put her finger on exactly what doesn't fit with her about lying here, and make some guesses about it—like whether the feeling will last and what it comes from. She needs to think about these things—but not too directly. Direction makes her thoughts run unusefully, toward conclusions that are not conclusions really, but their parallel false ends. Like writing a poem; it can't be forced. She feels for his hand, squeezes it, and presses her forehead into his shoulder, imagining, instead, scenes of their eventual breakup. In one they are at a department store. He's heaped with bags of things she picked out already from other stores. She holds some skimpy dresses on hangers up to herself. "You like it?" she asks, "should I try it on?" waiting for his approval—the look he gives when he thinks she's being unbearably sexy, like he's starved and sated simultaneously. Then, "Be right back," she says, and ducks into a changing room. Only, she never comes back out. She vanishes somehow, out through another exit of the store. She writes him notes later, postcards and letters on torn out sheets of note paper, no return address: "I want you to take this time while we're apart to really feel what it is your world lacks without me. What is it to love a woman? What is it, to you, specifically, to love me? Why do I feel in your eyes I was imprisoned?" So on, like that.

Some nights she imagines her breakup with Steve until she can sleep. Other nights it's sex with men she used to know or wishes she'd known. She lies with her face in

Steven's shoulder, breathing the smell of his skin and sweat, and remembers, with ghosts of feeling all over her body. She loves the way men touch her, she always has—the excitement mixed with fear and attempted tenderness. It makes her feel defined and necessary, like fate destined these moments. Maybe that's all she needs: an affair—a few days of some man dying for her skin. She imagines Steve's arm another shape, attached to another hand, one that touches her roughly, grabbing maybe, and not always thinking ahead, capitulating and apologizing, knowing her too much. The night-sweats and these fantasies—one doesn't cause the other. She knows it can't be that simple. Both are symptoms of a greater dissatisfaction she can't place yet. She rolls over and stares into the dark, her skin a field of warmth now, pores all closed and glowing. She thinks over the last lines of her poem, trying to see them on the page. *Moon, bent pan bruised by shadows / Wandering bride, pill of bone converting light.* She thinks them over and over until finally she feels the peaceful opening in her mind where language dissolves and she can only fall through asleep.

———

Sunday they go out of town to escape the inversion—San Francisco, where it's windy and overcast. On a whim they leave the car in Larkspur and ride the ferry across the bay. He thinks it will be romantic—imagines them at the railing on the top deck together, wrapped around each other for warmth, maybe, kissing and watching the gulls. He gets the idea for it just after they've crossed the Richmond Bridge and are riding along a part of the freeway overpass where the pavement rolls up and down like waves. "Jen," he says.

"I have an idea...."

The ferry ride is cold, but not romantic. There are almost no other passengers. Signs all over the ferry and the ferry terminal keep reminding him this is commuter transportation, and heavily used lately, since the earthquake scrambled the Bay Bridge, forcing thousands of people to re-route their travel. He's too aware of that, the contrast between themselves as he imagines—picturesque, sweatered, windblown—and all those impatient blue-suited businessmen herding to work. He hates making a big deal of something other people consider ordinary. There's no beer for sale and no hot pretzels or hot dogs, only some vending machines with off-brand potato chips and sodas.

"Pelicans," she says, pointing. There are ten or so, flying two- and three-abreast overhead, their ridiculous beaks sorrowful grins and the slow flapping strokes of their wings incongruously majestic. "Oh what a bird is the pelican," she quotes. "His beak can hold more than his belly can." She laughs.

He watches her laugh and wishes he could believe she is as happy as she looks.

The last ferry back leaves Port Authority just past seven o'clock. They've only had a few hours and haven't gotten to see enough or walk enough. Streets leading to the Embarcadero are mostly closed, due to earthquake damage, cracked and covered with dead, drifting leaves. The Harbor freeway overpass is roped off, supported everywhere by wood scaffolding, yellow signs warning pedestrians to keep back. Next to a fountain in Market Square they watch a man perform tricks with huge gold hoops; they buy folding scissors from a woman in a wheelchair, and have dinner in an almost empty Italian restaurant near North Beach, facing the water.

On the return trip there's another couple on the top deck. They are obviously drunk, and drinking more Buds from a cooler that doubles as a footrest for the man. He's sinewy and tan with tattoos on his arms and a thin blond mustache. The woman wears bright orange jogging shorts and a blue halter top. She sits inside the man's arms to stay warm, his jacket over her shoulders. The man keeps looking at Krauss and Jenny. Every now and then he reaches inside the woman's shorts and grabs her ass or snaps her elastic. Then the woman leaps up off him, laughing and shrieking. It's hard not to watch, impossible almost, because they make so much noise.

"Asshole," the woman says, smacking the man in the head.

The man grins at her, says something Krauss can't make out and she sits close again.

"Don't watch," Jenny says. "You're encouraging them."

"I'm not watching. I'm wondering which of them is going to throw the other one overboard first." He wants to keep talking just to hear himself talk—just to shut out what the other couple is doing, because they seem so relaxed and unencumbered to him. The wind picks up suddenly as they move into the open part of the bay and the front of the ferry slaps up and down in the chop. "Tomorrow you'll hear about that job," he says. He has to speak loudly for her to hear him over the wind and the engine noise. "They'll call you back, I'm sure."

She nods and looks hopefully at him, like she'll believe anything he says, her eyes tearing from the wind. "Think if I get it we'll be all right again—I'll be all right—like before?"

"Sure," he says. "Of course. You'll be busy. You'll have friends...." He glances over his shoulder. As if on cue the man sticks his tongue in the woman's ear and she jumps off him again, laughing, wiping her ear. She yells something at him. Krauss looks back at Jenny and continues. "It'll be fine. You'll see."

She smiles weakly. Her eyes flick shut and then open. She squints at him, scanning his face. Now she's making some obscure observation about him which he'll hear later on. He knows it, and tries to convince himself that in this knowledge are his many attachments to her, all over his body, like strings in the air between them. He faces her, slides between her and the railing, and puts his arms around her waist. She puts her arms over his shoulders and starts fiddling with his hair, twirling it around one finger and letting it go. "You," he says, and kisses her. Her lips are cold. They open around his. He tastes garlic and feels her nose running onto his lip.

Later, coming down from the coastal mountains into the Central Valley, hot air blooming through the vents, she starts to cry. She cries quietly without covering her face. He watches her, feeling the air in his head—particles, pesticides, and poisons. "Jenny," he says. "You don't have to tell me. I know."

"What? What do you know?"

He shakes his head. He can't say it. Ahead the air is chocolate with fumes, running flat into the earth. She will leave him. Not right away, but eventually. She'll leave because she's bored and lonely, married to him, and for other reasons neither of them can see yet. It makes him sick to know. He puts his arm over her shoulder and draws her to him, feeling her tears soak through his shirt to the skin.

WONDERFUL TRICKS

––––––––

I DATED A WOMAN, ONCE, WHOSE TWIN SISTER WAS A FOOL. At night I'd go to their house. I'd sit on the porch and the sister who took care of the one who couldn't speak or tie her shoes, would bring out food—potatoes mainly, stuffed with tuna fish or sour cream and bacon bits; sometimes sticks of celery with salted peanut butter or baba ganouj wedged in their crevices. I drank a beer and ate the food on a porch swing, watching the women come and go. They were medium height and had sharp, Irish features, long eyelashes, and red-brown, shoulder-length hair. They were pretty. One eye opened slightly wider than the other, giving you the impression they were amused or skeptical, even when they weren't, and they used a kind of cream on their skin I loved. The cream had a smell to make you think you'd never been alone in your life and never would be alone again, it was that soothing.

The sister I dated was Marie. The one who couldn't talk or tie her shoes was Sarah. I had a thing about their feet. They were the prettiest feet I'd ever seen. Marie's toes had knuckles on them like fingers, not one digit bent out of shape or squashed into its mate, and the nails were all clean and evenly cut, creamy, like the skin of some cactus fruit. She wouldn't admit her feet were nice, though secretly, I think she knew. She never slept until she'd washed them first in the sink by her bed, dried them and put on a pair of clean, colorful socks. Every night I'd hear the taps go on and the water splashing and then I'd lift my head a little to see her there in the dim light, her eyes half lowered, her leg up in the sink basin and a towel over one shoulder, scrubbing. "Stanley. Wake up now," she'd say when she was done. "Time for you to go."

I met them making a bid to paint the outside of their house—a scabby red Victorian with porches front and back, in the oldest part of town. Right away I saw how much work it was going to be. There were loose boards all over, rotten boards, exposed wiring, and the ceiling of one of the porches was split and sagging into the middle, leaking hundred-year-old dirt and cobwebs onto the floor. That would have to be repaired before anyone went at it with a paintbrush.

I pointed out everything I saw. "Scaly," I said, touching her porch railing. She nodded her head and listened indifferently, as if she knew all this already. A pack of Camels in her front shirt pocket pulled her shirt down. The skin between her breasts looked broken out, and she had on a bra with lacy trim. I tried not to notice this or the rips in her jeans, two torn crescents just under the rear pockets that winked open and shut as she walked ahead of me.

That day Sarah was seated at a big table in the living room, construction paper spilled around her in little cut pieces, and paintbrushes in plastic cups and coffee cans. Her eyes were as blank as a blind person's and she was caressing one hand with the other, staring at something on the wall.

"Measles with encephalitis, when we were thirteen," Marie told me. "She's all right, she just can't take care of herself. I'm mom and nurse and big sister rolled into one. Like I don't get enough of taking care of people!" She went on to explain how she was a nurse, on-call every weekend for a home care/hospice agency downtown. I tried to picture Sarah's face covered with measles scars. But there were none: she was Marie, precisely, down to the spiky eyelashes and the shine in her skin.

"Home care hospice," I said. "What's that?"

"It's for people who are dying. We take care of them so they can die in their own homes, peacefully."

"Sounds stressful." My last girlfriend had been a nurse. She always talked about how hard the work was—coming home at six in the morning and dreaming all afternoon about people barking at her and urinating on the floor. It was sort of what broke us up: that I wasn't willing to move in together after a year of dating and she was tired of trying to juggle me with her schedule.

Marie frowned like she thought I was being deliberately dumb. "It's about the easiest job I've ever had. We're not trying to save anyone's life."

My bid came in at the highest. But I had purposely bid high, since her house was such a headache and wouldn't be worth my trouble unless it paid well. "I'm really sorry," she told me on the phone, a week or two later.

"Nothing to be sorry for," I said. "Happens all the time."

I heard her suck on her cigarette. "But you must have

been wondering."

"All part of the game," I said. I asked her who she'd ended up hiring and she mentioned a couple of Vietnam vets I knew from having been underbid by them before. "Very good, very good," I said. "You be sure and call again some-time if you want something painted."

I figured it was the last I'd ever hear from her, but a month later she called. "I've changed my mind again on the color for the front and back doors and those men say they can't do it. They have another job." She inhaled furiously and I imagined smoke curling around her forehead and sticking to her hair. She blew out into the phone. "Truth is I think they can't be bothered."

"Could be," I said.

"So, what do you charge for something like that?"

I told her I'd have to come out and have another look.

That time it was just before dark and she was dressed more like a regular person, shorts and a denim work shirt, no half-revealed parts of her body to avoid looking at. Her legs were stringy, muscular-seeming, and I could see the veins in her shins. I imagined those veins saturated with cigarette smoke, nicotine breaking her blood cells and making the blood thicker or thinner, I didn't know which.

I was about to start a job for an apartment complex on the other side of town and doing her doors in my spare time would be no problem at all. "I'll stop by in the morning, throw on some primer, touch up those hinges. Then on my way home I can stop off—do your first coat of enamel. Shouldn't take but a couple of nights. Two coats, maybe three." While I was talking she unbuttoned the lower buttons on her shirt, slid in one hand and began doing something—rubbing and pinching herself, I think—staring

distractedly over my shoulder. I couldn't concentrate anymore. I was conscious of my heart punching erratically. I
heard my voice drone on. "Shouldn't be too much of a
headache. I'll stay out of your way."

"Let me ask you something," she said. "You look like a
sensitive man." She blinked and smiled hard, like we had
agreed on something funny. "The type to take another person's needs," she paused seriously, "as significant."

That's when she spelled out everything she had in mind
for me. It wasn't like anything I'd ever heard before, and for
some time I didn't know what to make of it. Never in my life
had anyone come on to me like this. "A woman," I was
thinking. "A woman!"

———

After we'd eaten, Marie would take Sarah inside to help her
bathe, comb her hair, and get settled in bed. Some nights
took longer than others. I'd sit on the porch swing with my
feet on the railing, and rock, wondering if tonight was the
night Marie finally let me make love to her. I hadn't had any
sex in a year—since my last girlfriend, the nurse—and I was
at the point where I practically couldn't imagine it anymore.
Across the street were two houses just like the one the sisters
lived in—skinny, square Victorians with crooked window
trim and sagging porches. I'd see the people in the house on
the left, an older couple, sitting on their couch watching
television.

Eventually Marie slipped out onto the porch and sat next
to me, her hands smelling like soap and that lotion. "Sorry,"
she said. I'd been here almost every night for a week, but it
felt like longer than that. "Sarah wouldn't let me leave her

alone. She wants to know what you're doing here." Though Sarah couldn't speak, Marie insisted they often put questions and ideas into each other's heads. "I had to explain."

I laughed. "Good thing. At least one of us knows."

She punched me lightly in the arm. "You know," she said. "Don't pretend you don't." She fingered a cigarette from the pack in her pocket and lit up. "Mind?" she asked.

"Hell no," I said. I'd sat next to her enveloped in smoke so many nights in a row I was beginning to feel like a smoker myself.

"What can I say that will put your mind at ease?"

"Nothing. I'm at ease."

That first night, the night Marie spelled everything out for me, I didn't quite believe her. Soon enough, I figured, she'd want me to make love to her, kiss her, touch her for pleasure. "I'm a married woman," she'd said. "For the second time. And I plan on staying that way." We were inside on the couch. She sat with her legs apart, leaning forward, her elbows on her knees as if she were about to jump up. She had on white canvas Keds with pointed toes, like slippers.

"You and a lot of other people," I said. This seemed to put her off. "Where's the husband?"

"I'll tell you if you really want to know."

"Why ask if I didn't?"

She appeared to think about this. "He's a few thousand miles away, for one thing—doing what he does best. It's a long story, but basically it evolves to not being able to live together under the same roof. Happily." She pinched her nose. "With my sister included."

I scratched some paint from my left forefinger. "What does he do?"

"Doctor."

"And does he know about me?" I asked.

She shook her head. "That comes later, if at all. My offer stands. You can stay if you want, but we only touch non-sexually, and you don't sleep here. That would be too ... too much for now."

I'd always thought of people who can talk this mechanically about intimacy as uncaring or at least having no real sexual reflexes. Now I saw it wasn't a matter of caring or reflex at all, it was something else—it was a game like posing in a mirror and trying to decide which way to smile. I'd only had four other girlfriends in my life—twenty-eight years—and I felt a little out of my depth. "What's non-sexual?" I asked.

She sighed, pulled her hair back on one side. Her skin was a little shiny and greasy, glinting in the light. "I know what I want and need. Obviously, it's more than a clinical massage, or I'd go get one." She shook her head. "I want to touch and be touched." Her eyes flicked over mine and back down. "If there's an erotic content that becomes too much then I think we'll both be aware, and that's all. I trust that instinct." She paused. "And I'm willing to experiment too, in a certain way, finding the boundaries we're both comfortable with."

"Boundaries!" I said. "You really are married, aren't you?"

She nodded. "And not looking to get divorced again, either. You have to understand."

We were sitting close enough that our knees almost touched. She wasn't wearing a wedding band. I picked up her hand and held her fingers to my mouth, sniffing. "You smell so good," I said. "What is that smell? It's like fruit or flowers or something." I put my nose and mustache in her palm, sniffing.

She laughed. "It tickles," she said. "Come on." And she got up, pulling me after her, upstairs to her bedroom. While she was in the bathroom I undressed to my boxers, lay down on her bed, and let the light drain from my eyes until I could see again, anticipating the feel of her hands on my skin. I stretched, ran my hands over my bare ribs, rolled onto my stomach, and tried to stop myself from shaking.

"Mmm," she said, once she'd begun rubbing my neck and back. "What a treat." I saw weird paisleys and sparkle-patterns on the insides of my eyelids. "I thought your skin would be nice, but I had no idea it would be like this." She leaned forward and swept her forearms back and forth over my shoulder blades like wipers. "Human beings can't live without touch. It's a proven fact. You shouldn't think this is unmeaningful." Later, watching her wash her feet at the sink, I felt deceived. I could have been anyone at all.

"Stanley, wake up," she said. "Time for you to go."

———

One night we were on the porch later than usual, talking, Sarah on the floor next to us, lying on her side, playing finger games with herself. Marie had her feet on the railing and was rocking us back and forth in the porch swing. It was a perfect night. All day it had rained. The night before there had been storms and wind, now the rain had blown off, leaving the sky clean and the air sweet. I was rested, for once, not having worked that day, and a little drunk. Marie was giving me her theory of relationships. This was something she'd told me a few times already—often enough I didn't really believe her. It always sounded more like something she wanted to convince herself of. She said, "It's the person who sees how it's going to end who leaves. Don't you think?"

I told her I had no idea.

"Get dumped a few hundred times and you'll see," she said. She laughed. "I'll have to tell you all about it some day." The way she said this I knew I'd never hear another word on the subject. And for a while after that we didn't say anything, just swung and hung still, with Sarah next to us, slapping her palm on the floor unrhythmically. I wondered what things would be like if Sarah were not retarded—how I'd choose between the two women or even tell them apart, or if I'd have a choice at all. I put my feet on the railing too, one on either side of Marie's, so we looked like a person with four legs, and both of us started talking at the same time. She said, "Time to put Sarah to bed." Then quickly, like she was embarrassed for saying it, "Today I bought this new incense I want us to try—it's supposed to be relaxing or something, good for massage. See, I do think of you once in a while, when we're not together."

———

I began having the weird sensation of distances disappearing. Some nights at their house I'd look out the rear window in her bedroom, see the plants and trees under the streetlight waving in the wind across the lot from us, and I'd feel I was touching them in my eyes—like they were inside my eyes the same way a reflection sometimes sits in the bottom of a spoon. Cars passing on the street next to the front porch went into my senses and stayed there. A muffler's noise tingled in my right elbow.

"You just aren't sleeping enough," she said. I'd been

trying to explain it to her. "You're wiped out and your mind's playing tricks."

"Yeah," I said. "Wonderful tricks."

I was on my back, Marie sitting up straddling my right ankle, working my left knee and thigh with both hands. She was in a T-shirt and her underwear. The pressure of her crotch on top of my foot was almost too much, increasing and decreasing as she leaned forward and back into her hands. She was right, of course. I was exhausted. My throat stung all day and my eyes burned. Often, I couldn't feel the soles of my feet on the ladder, going up and down.

"You need a few nights off," she said. "Get some good solid nights of sleep alone." She continued rubbing my leg, fingers circling around and squeezing my thigh muscles. "I could use a few, myself." Every time she lifted my leg to get at the muscles underneath I felt a kind of slithering, from my groin to the top of my head. Then as my leg fell back against the bed and she moved around to the front muscles I'd feel myself tightening in the same places. I knew she'd go no higher than the hem of my shorts, over and under.

"Yeah," I said. It was some effort to keep this rational-seeming conversation going. "At least you can sleep in."

Again she lifted my leg and slid her fingers under, just inside the hem of my shorts, squeezing. She used her touch in ways I'd never thought people could, like she knew what I felt under my skin and when to knead, press, or let her fingers slip over me. "Except for the fact Sarah wakes up—usually about seven. Six or seven."

"Please, Marie," I said. "If you touch me any more like this I'm going to die."

"What," she said. "Like what?"

I would have rolled onto my side, but I couldn't, the way

she was sitting on me, and there was nothing else to press myself into, so I took her by the shoulders and pulled her down. "I'm going to come," I whispered. "Sorry. I just can't hold it anymore. Sorry." Her hair smelled like that lotion. Her skin was slick with it. For a few seconds, I think, she was still trying to keep up our platonic pretense, her fingers slipping around like questions (here? here?) but once my mouth found her chin, soapy-tasting, and then her mouth— an acid nose-tingling taste from her cigarettes—she stopped. "Mmm," she said. "Oh no. No, not yet." But it was too late. The moment her tongue touched mine, I let go.

Awhile later she said, "I have two things I want to tell you."

I couldn't judge how much time had passed. Her voice was dreamy so maybe we'd fallen asleep, though I hadn't been aware of sleeping, only of staring into a corner of the ceiling where I knew some cobwebs were. I couldn't see them in the dark, but I imagined them sticking to my face, the same way her hair was caught in the stubble on my cheeks.

"Yes." I waited for her to continue, moving my hands down from her shoulders to her hips, lifting her T-shirt to feel her bare waist and sliding down the elastic of her underwear. She was surprisingly soft around the hips considering how thin her legs were. My fingers sank deep into her. "Go on."

"Maybe three things."

"OK."

"First, I'm really glad to have you touch me like this. If it's what you want. And I think it is. Second—I think you know this, that old saying: beware of the man who apologizes before there's anything to apologize for—you know he has something to hide." She paused. "What's with that?"

"With what?"

"Apologizing."

"I'm not apologizing."

"You are." She dug her fingers at my ribs. "'Sorry' was the first thing you said. What are you trying to hide?"

"Nothing! I didn't know if this was what you wanted or not. Really!"

"Sure." She laughed. "This weekend I had two patients die, both men. They were exactly as skinny as you. One body I had to carry down four flights of stairs."

"So?"

"So, you should know better than to try and pull anything funny with me." She laughed again and stuck her tongue up my nostril.

"What the hell!" I jerked my head away from her.

"You don't like it?"

"It's disgusting!"

"You're young." She said nothing else, and for a few seconds I was afraid she'd ask me to leave now because I didn't feel precisely the same way about sex as she did. But then she sat up, lifted her shirt off over her head, and lay back on me.

"What was the third thing you were going to tell me?" I asked.

"That'll have to wait. Now I need you to touch me." Her tongue found mine again. "Everywhere," she said to my teeth. Her mouth was wide open, dripping saliva, like the insides of an orange.

I didn't make love to her. I couldn't. Twice I tried. She lay under me, hooked her feet on my hips and tipped her chin at me, hands on my elbows squeezing like she wanted to keep me in mind of something. But the instant I touched her, or felt myself begin slipping in, I let go. "This is so weird," I said. "I have no control. It's never happened to me in my life."

———

All the next day I couldn't tell if I was asleep or awake. This had its advantages. When I was on a roll, I was OK—slapping paint along the side of one of those apartment complex monstrosities, nothing in my way, no sweat dripping in my eyes, no bugs trying to drown themselves in my eyeballs or the sweat on my forehead, no sun directly in my face. Then I was fine. In fact, I felt more connected in a mystical way to walls and boards and the way my paint went over them. But as soon as I got stuck on something—which was often, nearly every five minutes—I felt like my head would crack. My legs suddenly broke out in a sweat and I wanted to bawl, "I can't do it anymore!" Of course I kept going.

What Marie didn't tell me that night we never made love had to do with Sarah. She told me the next morning—the only morning I woke up in her bed.

"She's possessive," I said, the moment she began explaining. It was early, five-thirty, my wake-up call. Outside, it looked chilly and wet. In ten minutes I needed to be in my truck, heading across town. "That's it, isn't it? She'll kill me if I keep coming to see you?"

Marie laughed. "If only," she said. "That would keep me out of trouble, wouldn't it?"

"You call this trouble?"

She nodded. "With a capital *T*."

"OK. So what about Sarah?"

She lay back, pulled the sheets up to her chin, and lifted her knees so the bed became a tent. "Actually, just the opposite. She's going to start having feelings for you. We're weird that way. Don't ask why. It just happens. And she doesn't have all my defenses." She was silent a second, staring at the wall behind me.

"Ah," I said, trying to move my face into her line of sight. "You mean...." But she was still staring at the wall behind me and I couldn't tell if she was listening. "Marie," I said. "You mean she might jump me? Is that what happened to the husbands?"

This made her laugh. She opened her arms, let her legs fall flat on the bed again and said, "Silly. Come here." Then a few seconds later, "I haven't seen you with no clothes. In the light, I mean. Stand up so I can see." She pushed me off her. "Stand up!'

I got up, lifted my hands over my head and turned a few circles wiggling my fingers and sashaying my hips, then flexed one arm and looked menacingly at her over my biceps.

"Oh, baby! Better than I thought," she said.

I tried a more complicated pose standing on one leg with my arms raised and hopped around a few seconds, then sat next to her again on the bed. I wanted to say it was her turn now, but I didn't. Instead, I said it was time to hit the road.

"Tonight again?" she asked. "Seven or eight?"

"You bet."

"Soon, we'll have to take a few nights off."

"Whatever." I swallowed. "Who needs sleep?"

She nodded. "There's more I have to tell you."

"Of course." I pulled my shirt on over my head.

But when I got to their house that night, no lights were on inside or out. I circled around and around, tapping on windows and yelling hello through screens, but no one answered. I went back around to the front of the house, tried the door again for no reason, and sat on their porch swing. I wanted a beer. My lips felt dry. I didn't feel panicky or nervous about being rejected yet, only confused. They were supposed to be here—Marie bringing out her microwaved potatoes on a tray with dishes of things to stuff in them, Sarah tagging behind. As long as they were moving it was hard to see any difference in them. If Marie had her hair in a twist, so did Sarah, like there was an invisible "equals" sign in the air between them, though, of course, as soon as you looked more closely—especially if Sarah was nervous or "stimming," as Marie called it, twiddling her fingers and rocking—you could see all their differences.

I thought I'd fall asleep on the swing, but I didn't. When that couple across the street got up off their couch, flicked out the lights and disappeared, something flicked off in me as well. I realized how late it was and that the sisters wouldn't be coming home. Then I had my first waves of real anxiety. I'd been betrayed. I tried to remember if Marie had given any signal to make me expect it. "Seven or eight," she'd said, and here I was. I remembered her foot sticking out from under the sheets as I left—she'd never washed or put on socks that night. They were the prettiest feet I'd ever seen, so arched and bony they looked carved.

———

More than a week I stayed away. I figured if she wanted to see me she'd call. It was up to her. She'd understand why, after one night of standing me up, I wasn't coming around on my own. I could take a hint. I've been alone most of my life. I'm not the type to make a show of my suffering. But I stewed. I talked to her in my head all the time. I was cursing her out, up and down the ladder, asking her what she thought I was, or if this was the way she treated all the men she knew. One day I spent an hour painting primer over a wall that had just been primed. "Stan!" my partner yelled. "I see!" I yelled back. "I'm not blind. You missed some spots, that's all." On my lunch, every day, I called home to check for messages. Nothing. Every day, after work, I prayed for one of those flashing red blips in the half-dark of my living room to be her—some explanation or apology recorded on the machine. But no.

I don't like thinking about how things actually ended up, the day I finally went there and caught her out back pulling weeds from her tomato patch. "Hey, Stanley," she said, like we were old pals. "What a surprise." She smiled up at me. She had on shorts, a T-shirt, and gardening gloves, and there was a smear of red dirt across her forehead. The tomatoes were coming in—big heavy red ones, like the plants had ruptured with fruit.

"Yes," I said. "One surprise deserves another, doesn't it?"

"Oh, Stan, are you going to get all bent out of shape on me about this?" She looked hard at me, shaking earth from the bottom of a clump of weeds and then tossing it. "Yup. You are. I can see that. OK. Well, let me just say first I've been meaning to call." She sniffed. "I've had it in mind for some time to write you or call and explain things, I just haven't actually *done* it. I've been kind of crazy."

"Oh, I feel so much better already."

She swiped a hand over her forehead, leaving more dirt, and then rubbed her mouth off on the back of a glove. "You think this is all about you, don't you?"

I said nothing.

"Sarah had a little episode last week and had to be in the hospital a couple nights. Nothing fun for us, believe me...."

"So why couldn't you at least let me know?"

She pulled a few more weeds, tossed them to one side, and frowned at the ground again.

"A phone call, anything to do the trick," I said.

"Oh, so I'm obligated to you now? Is that it?" She patted the earth around one plant and then moved on to the next, still squatting. I let a few seconds pass, watching her pull, shake out, and toss weeds. I was about to ask if Sarah was all right when she cleared her throat and started again. "Anyway, to continue what I was saying—while I was in the hospital with Sarah I got to thinking you and I should really cool things off anyway. Kind of stop before we get started. I mean, this was never meant to go anywhere, right? I'm a married woman and we have nothing in common to speak of. You're a nice enough man, I'm sure, but why get all mixed up hurting each other's feelings and et cetera? Since then," she sighed heavily, "since I got back, which is only like a week for Christ's sake, I just haven't had it in me, haven't been in the *mood* to call anyone. OK?"

"It's OK for you, I'm sure."

"Learn to live with it, Stan. There's nothing for you to be bitter about." The way she said this I knew we weren't finished. There was more she had to say. She continued pulling weeds, then stopped suddenly and looked at me. "You know, maybe if you hadn't always been so submissive—" I waited for her to go on, but she didn't. Her eyes were watery, blue and gray. With my old girlfriend, the nurse, toward the end, we had a lot of these fights where we'd stand in my living room, or hers, just staring at each other without speaking, not knowing what to say. This felt to me like almost the same thing, except now one corner of Marie's mouth kept turning up slightly like she was about to laugh. "Stanley. Look," she said finally. "If you came here to make love to me, why not just say so? We can skip the part where you insult me because you feel insulted. We can get right to it, if you want."

I shook my head. "That is not why I came here."

"It isn't?" She stood up, let her gardening gloves drop on the ground, then came and took both my hands in hers. "You're sure?"

"Of course I'm sure!"

"OK. It's OK." She moved closer until she was standing on my feet and I couldn't see the dirt smears on her face anymore. There was that familiar smell of her cigarettes and the lotion she used and the way her body felt against mine like she knew everything that was happening under my skin. "Isn't this better?" she said, and she started to sway like we were dancing. There was a rhythm to it. While we swayed she sang—no words, just a kind of crazy humming from the back of her throat, like she was making fun of us both. Once or twice I kissed her but she kept moving her mouth away from me and back again. I felt myself begin to loosen and stretch against the insides of my shorts, and pressed my pelvis harder against hers. "You crazy man. You want to make love to me?"

She dipped back in my arms further and further until we fell on the ground, her head halfway underneath one of the tomato plants where there were some sour smelling tomatoes, almost flat on the ground like they had been deflated, with black ants climbing over them and in and out of the tears in their skin. I wished we would move a little to the left so I didn't have to see this, but there was no time and I didn't feel right saying anything. She opened my fly, I yanked my pants down and pulled aside one leg of her shorts to reach her. She wasn't wearing anything underneath. This time I was perfectly in control. Even after I was inside her I felt myself continuing to loosen and grow. When I came she snapped her head back against the ground.

"Oh," she said, "Stanley, that was nice," and when I tried to move away from her to relieve my knees which were pressing into some rocks, she pulled me fiercely to her. "Where are you going?" she asked.

"Nowhere."

Again I tried to move a little to get the weight off my knees and she clamped her forearms around me. "Where are you going?"

She finally released me and we sat next to each other on the ground a while, knees touching. I was surprised at how happy she seemed. She scooped some of my semen from between her legs. "I've never had sex with a man in my own backyard." She laughed and wiped her hand off in the dirt vigorously, but not like she was disgusted. "Next thing you know, you'll be having me make love to you in some parking lot!"

"That's not really my taste, Marie."

"I know. It's too bad." But she sounded more amused than disappointed. "Now I have to go." She drew her legs to one side, lifted herself on her hands, and stood. "Clean up a little, check in on Sarah. She's not quite out of the woods, you know." She looked down at me a second like she thought I should be feeling sorry for her, and started walking away, her sandals slapping at her heels. "I'll call you later."

"Sure you will."

"Bad idea, Stan—now you've put it in my mind that maybe I won't, or shouldn't." She continued up the walkway to her house.

———

I should have stayed away, but I didn't. A few days later, standing across the street in her neighbor's front yard I saw what I didn't want to see—another man, the husband visiting maybe, on that porch swing, watching the women come and go. He looked relaxed and dopey, maybe a little like I had, with a beer in one hand and two sticks of celery in the other. I watched him munch and sip, munch and sip, and after the sisters went inside for their nightly routine I went a little closer for a better look. He was not a bit like me—a big suave guy with a blond mustache. He was in slacks and a dress shirt loosened at the collar. Probably he was one of the doctors who had taken care of Sarah at the hospital, if he wasn't the husband. I have no idea if he saw me. I wasn't making any great effort to hide. He wouldn't know who I was or what I wanted anyway. He swung back and forth and the chains on the porch swing creaked just like they had when I was sitting in it. My porch! I wanted to yell. My swing!

I went around to the other side of the house where I saw Marie and Sarah, in Sarah's room—Sarah in a nightgown, Marie with her hair tied back, still in the clothes she must have worn that day, a greenish, shimmery blouse open one button too far, and those ripped jeans. Behind the window screen they were hazy, like a painting. Marie sat behind Sarah and started rubbing her shoulders. Sarah's head immediately sagged forward from the pleasure of being touched.

After a while, Marie said something I couldn't hear and patted the bed beside her.

I watched until Marie had finished, brushed Sarah's hair, smeared her lips with Vaseline, kissed her, turned on a nightlight and flicked out the lights. Then I went to her window, stepped through the short pine shrubs growing there, and tapped lightly at the bottom of her screen. "Sarah," I whispered. "Sarah, come here." There was a sound of sheets being thrown back and then her feet squeaking on the floor. She was a blur behind the screen, a big white shape in a flowery gown. She shifted from foot to foot. "You're supposed to have feelings for me," I said. She went back to her bed, sank down, and pulled the covers up over her head. She didn't move. Cicadas ratcheted. A car went by on the other side of the house, radio booming higher and then lower as it shifted into the distance.

I heard their footsteps inside the house—first hers, light and uneven; then his, heavier and trudging—and seconds later the front screen snapping shut, her voice calling out just after it. For a moment I was sure he'd find me out. I crouched in the bushes until I'd seen him go by on the sidewalk, strutting, his lips pursed, whistling—happily oblivious. Even after he was gone, I stayed crouched a while, not sure if Marie would remain inside or go into the backyard for a smoke. I heard sheets moving on the other side of the screen—a faint hiss like a zipper, Sarah sighing, the bed creaking—then nothing. Soon, my back was beginning to hurt and my knees felt like they would pop from squatting, so I stepped out of the bushes and turned around.

What I saw when I looked back inside the window was so pretty—Sarah and Marie curled around each other, front to back in the bed, their hands moving over each other's arms and shoulders, one turning her face back so their cheeks were almost touching. They were like an underwater plant, the way their arms and legs moved, everything about them matching. And after a few minutes, their hands came together on the stomach of the one who lay with her back to the other, and their bodies began falling into the breathing rhythm of sleep. One sister's hair lay over the other's neck. One pair of feet were bare, the other had on blue socks. I tried to remember what it had been like when I was with Marie. I closed my eyes and all I saw was houses. I saw ladders against walls, and windows with no outside fixtures, glasses taped and ledges ready for paint. I saw Marie's house, too, newly painted—so crisp in its fresh colors you'd never guess, underneath, how scaly and worn to splinters the boards were.

ANYONE'S VENUS

———

THE LAST TIME I HAD SEX WITH MY WIFE WAS IN THE LAUNDRY room at a mutual friend's house where I was staying. We did it on the floor, between piles of things I'd taken from our apartment when I left, in the dull green light from the open drier-door because we wanted to see each other but not too clearly, and there was no moon. I didn't know it was the last time I'd make love to her. Actually, I thought we were getting back together. She was spicy-smelling and pungent, like spilled wine, and we were both excited from not having seen each other in so many days.

The next morning there were two abrasions on the end of my nose. It took me awhile, looking in the mirror, to figure out they were not pimples. I picked at the skin and pushed my face closer to the mirror. Then I remembered lying under her and the faint light from the drier-drum, and the weight of her increasing as she pushed against my face, stretching into climax; and I knew, because we had never made love this hard in all the years we were together, it had been the last time.

The woman I'm with now, Isabelle, wants to know these things—my last times with certain women, and so on. "Not the first times," she says. "That will break my heart to hear about. The last ones. They are most revealing."

So I skip ahead. I tell her about sitting on the curb outside my girlfriend Marcie's apartment in Austin after hours of lovemaking, looking at the map and getting ready to leave her, planning my way through Louisiana to Kentucky, all the way to New York. Suddenly my whole body lit up with sweat. It's never happened to me like that before or since. I watched the sweat bead and trickle and run through the hairs on my calves, and drip onto the cement. I felt it run from my face into my shirt collar and down my sides. It wasn't the kind of sweat you feel good about.

"Here come the miles and miles apart for us," I said.

We had no idea when we'd be together again, though we kept assuring each other it would happen soon.

"But the lovemaking," Isabelle says. "You're giving me afterward."

"I don't know," I say, remembering briefly. "Afterward is revealing too."

She rolls her eyes. "It's an evasion."

———

Two summers before Marcie there was another affair, this time with a woman who worked at the bar. Aileen, my wife, was gone out west at a mountain climbing school for two months and we were not on very good terms then anyway.

Nancy and I would sit at the bar and thumb wrestle and talk and sing along with our favorite songs when she wasn't waiting on people. Later we'd go to her place or mine, more or less drunk, and fall asleep wrapped around each other. Our last night together (we had no idea at the time) we were at my house. I was about to start touching her, undoing the little laces on one of my wife's nightgowns, lowering the straps, and suddenly she sat up. She coughed once and burped. The next thing I knew the bed was covered with slimy pink stuff like sea horses and confetti—strawberry daiquiri mix and shreds and chunks of half digested shrimp chimichanga. Everywhere. It was on the floor and the headboard, between the bed and the wall, even on top of the nightstand.

"What happened?" I asked. "Are you OK?"

"I'm so sorry," she said. "I didn't feel it coming." She lay still for about two seconds, then she was pulling the sheets off the bed, wiping down the walls and floor, carrying the sheets out to her car, putting new sheets on, spraying Lysol everywhere, and etc. "I'm so sorry," she kept saying. She wouldn't let me do anything to help her, either—wouldn't even let me make her tea.

Something like this happened to me once, too, just after college. I took a girl out for seafood and a few hours later threw up so violently my vomit ripped through the bottom of a paper bag, and I gave myself a hernia. It was only our third or fourth date and we were not especially close yet. I'd had no idea I was so allergic to mussels. Seconds before throwing up, lying on her couch, I held my hands on my stomach and felt the tremors and undulations through my ribs—amazing, like I'd become a mussel myself and swallowed half the ocean. "Uh-oh," I said.

"You sure you're OK?"

"No. I'm not."

"What, should I call a doctor?"

"No doctor."

The next day, getting out of the shower, I saw it and I didn't know what it was. A little lump. A little puffed-out bit of myself in my groin, like something had blown up against my abdominal wall (which in fact it had). I kept pushing it back in, sucking in my stomach, wishing it would go away. "What the hell?" I said. I pushed it in and it popped right back.

———

"Yes," Isabelle says, "but you never made love to that one. Why even tell about her?"

It's a Monday and both of us have called in sick at the agency we work for downtown.

"Why tell about who?"

She rolls her eyes. They are small, deep brown eyes in a plate-like white face. Men are always attracted to her because of her French voice and thick eyebrows and sneeringly playful mouth. She is the opposite of anyone's Venus—crass and big boned, but still delicate, like a racehorse. "The one with the mussels!" she says, affectionately pretending to be out of patience with me. "You never made love to her."

This is a lie I told her some time ago—one I can't correct for at the moment. "So?"

"So why tell about *her?*"

"Because it proves my point about the body—what I was saying before, about how we can know some things physically before we actually know that we knew them. Like Nancy vomiting—?"

"Forget Nancy! No one cares about her."

We've been in bed too long and the sun is making circles and crescents on the wall, and turning the sheets hot. This is not what we had planned. We had taken the day off to get up early and begin work on our film treatment, a modern version of the story of Percival's search for the Holy Grail. "You're right," I say. "Let's have breakfast. We'll get started."

"No, I want to know why first. Why you tell about the other one." She pins me down and moves on top of me, smiling. All that lassitude and hunger. "Are you telling it because you love her still?"

———

My first hernia operation was like going on a fishing trip. I thought so. The nurses woke me at five and wheeled back the curtains partitioning my bed from the rest of the room. "Good morning, Mr. King!" they said cheerily, and shot me in the ass with morphine. One of them was very pretty. Later, when they returned—two or three, I don't remember—my mood was unparalleled: twenty-two years old, full night's sleep, room brimming with morning light, and about to go under the knife for my first time. I was really enjoying the situation. They pulled back my hospital gown and scraped away all my pubic hair with a plastic, shell-pink razor. They squeezed my forearm and tapped on the veins until one wormed out close enough to the surface to be stuck, then lay my arm on a padded armrest with an IV-tree attached. "We're ready to roll," they said, and the next thing I knew I was going down the hall, down the elevator—a whole moving, padded room—and into the operating room.

Occasionally, throughout the operation, if I opened my eyes for too long or started fidgeting, they would drip more sedative into the IV bag. I'd feel it begin burning the insides of my veins and then my whole arm would light up and go numb and the overmastering good feelings would set in. "Mmm, I am so happy," I thought. Once or twice, waking up, I caught the doctors talking about their weekend pastimes—Frisbee and golf and a barbecue at the lake. One of them said, "You know, with enemies like that, who needs friends?" There was always the insistent tugging at my groin and abdomen (somewhere down there), like an intrusive person yanking on my belt loops. I couldn't see what they were doing. There was that raised sheet like a tent separating me from the action. I had seen, because I looked when they wheeled me in, the shiny kidney-shaped bowl where the little cut away bits of my guts would go before being tossed out, and the silver tray of gauze and scalpels and curved needles the surgeon would use to cut me and sew me up again.

I've left out the anesthesiologist—a squat, friendly Indian man with bad breath and a needle the size of a bicycle pump. He popped into the operating room just before things were getting underway. "Roll onto your side, Mr. King!" he exclaimed. "Curl like a ball. No, tighter! Pull your knees to your chin." He counted down the knuckles of my spine, delicately, pressing between the bones to differentiate. Again, he counted, this time from my ass up. Then again, back down and there was the cold swab of alcohol. "OK! You'll feel a pinch," he said, and I felt the pinch. Then there was a flash like electrical current behind my eyes and a vague grinding, tingling pressure out to the tips of my fingers. It went on too long. "Roll onto your back now," he said. He lowered the needle to his side, not quickly enough for me not to see it, and stood there looking at his watch.

"That thing was in my spinal column?" I asked.

He shook his head and went to stand at my feet, and started pinching and tugging my toes. "Feel this?" he asked. He scrubbed his thumbnails up and down my arches. "Can you feel that? We'll give it just a minute or two longer."

––––––––

"But this is not anything to do with your ex-wife, or the old girlfriend in Austin, or anything," Isabelle says. She has her feet out against the wall, legs up straight, and she's gazing contentedly at the ceiling, taking her time getting ready to say something. She wags one foot side to side. "OK. You really want to know what I think?"

"I can hardly wait."

"I think you are so silent when you care the most about something." She rolls onto her side, away from the wall, gazing at me. "It's a perversion, because you clam up when any other person would say something. And it's not that you don't care—even if that's what it looks like is happening on the outside, is that you don't care. Actually it's the other way around, which is quite ironic, because you care too much."

"Very insightful," I say.

"So you are just the same way as our hero," she says. "Look at you! Little Percival in his lover's trance at the end of the story, staring at the drops of blood in the snow and thinking about his girlfriend's mouth." She reaches and runs two fingers down my spine. "You're stuck and can think of nothing else."

Again her fingers go up and down my spine. She is the type of person who seems not to know how her touch feels.

Sometimes I imagine myself in a room of covered furniture, curtains drawn, no light, and no one around, when her hands are on me. But this is a misperception. Awkward people are no less sensitive or aware than gentle ones, they just don't necessarily know the world by touch—that is, their knowledge isn't necessarily given back to you in their touch. I've learned this at least a dozen times in my life. Isabelle is right here. She just doesn't feel, in her fingers, what it is to be me.

———

I was not a good patient. When Katrina, the woman I'd eaten the mussels with (it was months ago, by then), came to visit me in the hospital we closed the curtains and lay on my bed together. It must have been lunch hour. No one was around.

"We can't be doing this," she kept saying. "No sex. Remember? The doctor said. No sex, no heavy lifting, no exercise. You're going to strain yourself, and then you'll have to get corrective surgery."

"Right," I said. "But we can just stop before I come." I smelled horrible—that morphine was like burnt plastic and putrefied onions on its way back out through my pores. I couldn't believe she was willing to be this near me.

"I love you so so so much," she said.

I watched her hand skim up and down on me. It was a beautiful, blond hand. The incision next to it was scab-puckered and painted over with pink sterilizing agent, and the sutures were like an elephant's ingrown hairs. But the hand was pretty. I was mesmerized, watching it.

"Oh, Kat, wait," I said. "You'd better stop." She didn't stop. "Kat! Sss." Too late. It was like ripping myself open from the inside. She leaned forward to lick me out of her hand and rub me clean with the sheets.

"You didn't stop," I said. "Why didn't you?"

She sighed and lay back next to me, grinning. "Ahh. I love it that you have no control with me."

———

"Tell me again," Isabelle says from inside the shower. There's the sound of water shattering on porcelain, then soap and shampoo. "I don't understand. How do you know for sure it's really the last time?"

"Only in retrospect," I say. "There's a way you can tell. Everything feels like it was heightened. I already said that."

"But supposing you meet again years later and you decide then that you still have feelings? Are you saying it can't happen?"

"Not for me. Things have a definite period in my life, and they're over when they're over."

I pull the shower curtain open partway. Her head is back, fingers raised to her temples, and her legs are streaming with soap. "Such a hard ass," she says. Her eyes are closed and her lips slightly pursed. Then she's looking at me and blinking away water. "Get in!" she says, and I step up into the tub, pulling the curtain back behind me, and backing her up so we're both under the shower head. Her skin is hot and the tips of her fingers on my hips and waist feel the same as the water but with a more deliberate pressure. Water sprays off the top of her head and turns to mist.

"Let's fuck like it's for the last time," she says, close to my ear. She pushes me against the wall and springs forward, arms around my neck.

"Hey, stop," I say. "It's not like that."

"Yes. We'll pretend, and then we can know it means nothing whatsoever."

————

That week, my first week out of the hospital, it was hot and I could do nothing but lie around on Katrina's couch, sweating and drinking fruit juice and scratching myself. My sweat was oily from inactivity. My eyes burned. I had two weeks of sick leave from my job at the university we'd just graduated from. She was writing a book-length poem about her dead brother, Christopher, and she would come into the room where I was lying, periodically, to test her lines on me. I had never spent so much time alone in one place with a woman.

"Listen to this," she might say.

I'd flip off the volume on the TV. "Go ahead."

The poem was about truth and valor, in addition to being about her brother, and had a number of different little sections I could never keep straight—ones where he was alive and then dead, then alive again in another form. It was confusing. Her sentences were all punched up for display and full of high diction, but still innocent. She wanted her brother back. That was the point. She wanted him back and he was dead. What could be more earnest?

"I like the part where he tells you to return to the land of the living," I said, one afternoon. "I like that, because it means he has to find his own ideas of valor and truth and stop relying on the mother so much."

She was on the arm of the couch. Sunlight poured down the wall from the skylight behind her and made individual strands of her hair stand out. A nest of my dirty clothes sat on the linoleum at her feet. She kicked it away and moved her leg so I could see inside her skirt.

"OK, but don't you think the pine tree imagery is getting a little flat?"

I shook my head. "I think you should come lie here next to me, is what I think." I patted the couch and then slid my fingers between the folds of her skirt.

"No, no," she said. She stood up.

Her hymen was as thick as a quarter and no one would be inside her until it was cut out. I don't think she minded at the time: she wanted us at this distance. She wanted her brother resurrected. If I made love to her then it would no longer be like that, a triangle; it would be the two of us, alone.

She went to the other end of the couch, let her clothes fall off and lay down facing me. "You watch," she said. "Then we'll see about you."

It hurt, watching her, and afterwards, too, when I broke into her mouth.

What did she look like? Pretty. The kind of girl models are always posing to be—wide green eyes, corn-silk hair, impeccable teeth, narrow waist and torso, etc. You didn't get much from looking at her. You looked at her and the thoughts ran straight out of your head.

———

Two years after the incident with the shrimp chimichangas, I saw Nancy for the first time, alone at the mall with a pink and white triplet stroller. Her hair was lighter and fluffed out on the sides and she looked a little heavy. Washed out. She had on baggy dungaree overalls, so it was hard to be sure about the weight. Also, I might have misremembered her. As soon as she saw me she started waving. There was something apologetic and too enthusiastic about the gesture that brought me back in time—right away I was feeling shameful and sad and too judgmental, liking and not liking her simultaneously.

"Burt!"

"Nancy!" I said. "Is that you?"

We didn't embrace. The stroller stood in between us. There was the smell of messy babies and sweat and baby powder pouring off her, not patchouli and cigarettes anymore. "My God, all these years! Just look at you. And those are yours?" I asked, pointing. The babies were asleep in their blankets, puffy and crustacean-like with identical faces, and one of them had on a little white cap with a tassel.

She nodded. "Can you believe it? Six months old."

"No!" There were a few rings and stones on her ring finger—gaudy, inexpensive ones—so I could fill in the rest of what must have happened. Someone in the police force or the army or some other branch of civil service. I'd always noticed that type of man staring at her when we were at the bar. Her father was a cop. It was where she'd been destined from the start: babies and diapers and a big man with a crew cut at the kitchen table in his T-shirt and a shoulder holster, drinking coffee. She'd just needed a few guys like me to ruin her ideas about what-might-have-been before she got on with the rest of her life. All those pointless drunken nights at the bar with her, singing and talking and killing away the awful time....

ANYONE'S VENUS

187

"But I want to know more about the pretty girl in the hospital room, since you like her so much," says Isabelle. We're in the kitchen, having breakfast—maple-flavored, ten-grain cereal with bananas, rice cakes, and coffee. There's a bowl of fruit on the table and a vase of wilted tiger lilies I bought for her days ago. Her head is wound around with a white towel and she is still in her bathrobe.

"I don't like her."

She continues chewing and looks blankly into her cereal bowl. She hasn't heard. She doesn't have very good hearing and occasionally there are these meaningless pauses in our conversation. Her eyesight is also peculiarly unreliable. In the middle of the night sometimes, or just after waking up in the morning, her eyes will refuse to focus in one direction. The left pupil wanders to the edge of its orbit and she looks stir crazy. Such times it's hard to believe she is the child of a super-model and a celebrity-tycoon, and was once much sought-after as a child model, herself—her twelve- and thirteen-year-old face blown up and replicated in magazines and on billboards all over the world.

She stops chewing. "Did you say something, Burt?" she asks.

"Yes. I said you're wrong about that. I don't like her. The girl you were asking about."

She chews some more and swallows. "That's so lame," she says. "You are so lame. You love her. How can you say you don't? Lame, lame." She spoons more cereal into her mouth and chews, still staring at me. "You shouldn't worry, you know. I only want to know why." Two drops of milk fly out and land on her chin. I lean forward to wipe them away, and she closes her eyes the instant I touch her, her jaw muscles relaxing. When I'm done she says, "With you I don't even have to worry about getting food on myself, you take such good care of me. Like a parent."

"I thought I was lame."

She laughs. "That was before. Do you find your opinion of someone changes radically every few seconds when you're with them all the time?"

"No," I say. "Not really."

"I do. Mine changes continually. I can't help it. May I have the sugar, please?"

———

At the end of my summer with Katrina we were on Cape Cod for three days. When we returned home she would have one day to pack, one last night with her parents in New Jersey, and then off to Prague to begin a course of study in philosophy. Maybe we would see each other some time the following summer.

The Cape was overcast and wintry those three days, like fall, though it was only August. We went for cold hikes in the dunes, paddled on one of the freshwater lakes outside Wellfleet, and, at night, we swam in the frigid ocean water just steps from our cabin door. We built snapping, driftwood fires in the cabin and lay on blankets and pillows, trying to slow the time by doing and saying absolutely nothing, just lying there staring at each other.

"We can do it ourselves," she said.

"Do what?" It was our last night and we were getting settled by the fire. Her wet hair was pinned at the nape of her neck. My skin was still numb and prickling, tight with saltwater residue, and I was beginning to feel a little light-headed from the fire.

"Remove my hymen."

"Seriously, Kat?"

She crossed her arms and stared at me.

"You mean cut it?" I asked.

She nodded. "Probably."

"I don't think so."

"Yes. I almost did it myself, once before." She shrugged. "A few years ago. It's not such a big deal."

"I thought it was."

"It is, but it isn't." She went into the kitchen-dinette part of the cabin and came back with two full glasses of wine. "So," she said. There was a silence. She drained one wine glass, staring at me, and put it on the table beside her. Her head looked smaller, with her hair pulled back, and her skin was shining.

"No, I don't think we should," I said. "I think it's a bad idea. Maybe dangerous."

She swirled the second glass of wine. "Want it?" she asked. The glass was smeared with hard-water stains around the sides, and looked chipped and crusted from use.

"No. Kat?"

She drank that one too and set it on the table, then came and lay down next to me. "Wait until the wine kicks in a little," she said, and pushed and pulled some pillows behind her so her torso was slightly elevated.

"You're not really going to," I said.

Her hands were crossed on her chest. She breathed in and out a few times. "Stay close to me," she said. "Like this." She pulled me to her so my arm was under her neck and my face was directly over hers. "Much better," she said.

The whole time I was like that. I watched her face and occasionally touched her shoulder or her forehead, or kissed her and asked if she was all right. I tried not to see or to imagine what she was doing. There was a bumping sound and the sound of her bare feet slipping against the floorboards, then a twitch across her eyebrows like a wire pulling under the skin, and then the same thing again. "I got it," she said. And a few seconds later, "Yes, I got it." She rolled me on top of her and locked her fingers through mine. They were slick and tacky with blood. Her cheeks were wet but she wasn't making any sound of crying. "Make love to me," she said. "Please now." Our teeth cracked together. I could feel her gums against my incisors, her tongue under my tongue, and her humid breath and her groans vibrating in my larynx.

———

"My God. You will never have this again, what you had with that girl," Isabelle says. She puts a fist to her mouth but doesn't burp or hiccup or laugh.

"Who wants it? It's silly."

She shakes her head. "First you say how you never made love to her, now you're giving me this bloody sex story. Am I supposed to believe it? Am I supposed to care?" She pauses. "You make no sense."

"*Sense,* Isabelle? Sense is all bullshit!" I'm not sure why I'm yelling. It's not like I'm angry, and I don't have anything to prove. "Don't you know by now? For Christ's sake. Sense is nothing. Sense is what you *make up* about things." Then just as suddenly, I'm laughing and a kind of light bursts into my head. "Look at this. I'm laughing, I'm crying, and I don't even know what it's about." I wipe my cheeks with the sleeves of my T-shirt and try to pull the shirt off over my head but it's stuck in my belt.

"Poor baby," Isabelle says. I hear her stand and push her chair back. Then she's beside me with her numb hands moving on my shoulders and up and down my neck—the same little pattern of movement, up my neck and back down to my shoulder muscles, and up again. "Poor baby, I'm so sorry," she says. She pulls me into her stomach and for a second I can smell myself on her so clearly—my smells running through the soap and citrus lotion and powder on her skin and in her hair, and the leftover smell of prior mornings caught in the threads of her bathrobe.

———

When it was light enough, Kat and I went for a last walk on the beach. The sky was pink and white, layered with low clouds and dully iridescent. The sand was cold and hard and the tide was just coming in. We walked to the end of the land where the beach gave way to stiff marsh grasses and the air became so putrid with the stink of petrifying algae and swamp life that we couldn't breathe comfortably. Neither of us said anything about it. We turned together and started back. Little bayside waves lapped at the stony shore and I thought of telling her some story from my childhood, but there was no point in any more narrations. We were passed by a couple of joggers and a group of early morning beachcombers. By the time we got back to our cabin the air was warming up and it felt to me like we needed to leave right away. We didn't belong here anymore. I had a funny kind of happy, nervous excitement about this—almost like I was looking forward to saying goodbye to her, though I knew that truly I wasn't.

All the way home we were touching. Our skin couldn't

be out of contact. That was how it felt to me. Even when we weren't touching, the air between us seemed packed with contact. As we drove inland the weather improved, turning warmer and brilliantly sunny. We didn't talk much. We rolled the windows down and let the air blow through the car, deafening us.

Just before leaving the beach, Kat flew out to the water one last time. She had an old mayonnaise jar with the label stripped off. At the water's edge she knelt, spun the top off and scooped in a few handfuls of rocks and sand. "For my parents," she said, coming back up the steps into the sloppily abandoned cabin—blankets and bloody towels and couch cushions on the floor. She smiled at me and held the jar up. "My mom said bring her back the beach." This is what I remember when I think of that last day. I remember her coming up the back steps and the wind lifting her hair around her face and blowing her shirt out in front, one hand lifted to her throat, and the sad, sad sound of her feet hitting the back plank steps. The way I remember it: I'm still standing there and she keeps coming up the steps. She never gets there, she just keeps coming.

STONE FISH

ONE DAY WHEN I WAS THIRTEEN MY FATHER AND I WERE stacking wood in the shed behind our house. He had on a black-and-white wool plaid jacket he'd worn for years— one my mother had given him and which her father had worn as a young man. The collar and elbows were shaggy with burst threads. I'd been talking so much I could hardly stand the sound of my voice. Often when I was with him I'd get like that, talking to fill in the silence until the things I said were ridiculous and childish-sounding. I was in love with a girl then because of her eyes. More than anything, I wanted her to ride her bicycle past our house when I was outside with my shirt off, splitting wood. But we lived miles from the rest of the world, on a dirt road where the only cars that passed were neighbors' cars and friends of neighbors. It would take a long time being lost on a bicycle for anyone to wind up out here.

Talking to him I lost track of what I'd said and what I hadn't. I couldn't remember if I'd told him about her eyes, or having my shirt off when she rode by on her bicycle, or only about trying to work up the courage to ask her to the Ice Capades. I hated myself for having said this much, though, at the same time, I knew if I were to stop talking I would only feel in the silence as if he were reading my mind.

"Jeremy," he said, finally, an exasperated tone like he'd held out as long as he could not speaking. "Why fixate on her appearance? For God's sake, you don't even know her. Girls aren't just what they *look* like."

I knew this was essentially true, though I also knew it was the sort of truth no one paid attention to, including him. My mother was a beautiful woman. I still remembered the way she would lift me to her when I was small—her wide, crooked eyes and the widow's peak in her hair that was so sharp it looked carved. Before she left, she'd stood in front of me, squeezing her hands together like she wanted to keep something in them from escaping. "You have a wonderful father," she said. "Never forget that. He'll take care of you and some day, when you feel like it, you can find me, wherever I am, and we'll go on just like before. What do you say?" I was about five years old. I knew I shouldn't cry or cling or do any of the things she wasn't doing. "Yes," I said, and let her lift me to her one last time to kiss me before she left.

My father said, "You'll be unhappy for a very long time if you think I'm wrong about that."

We went on stacking wood. The calming logic of it, finding spaces and filling them with pieces of wood lain horizontally made what we said seem unimportant—like we were only trying our ideas and didn't mean them. What really mattered was stacking wood. Still, I wished my mother were there. I wished she were inside—like mothers on TV shows, and the mothers of my friends—heating up soup and getting ready to say, when we walked in the door, "You two must be freezing," or "Here are my men!" Instead there would be the usual. My father would stir-fry chicken or tofu in the wok. Then he'd head off to the basement, to his workbench, where he spent his evenings carving fish from blocks of marble and wood. I'd sit in my room reading ski magazines and bad novels until I was too bored to keep reading; then I'd go downstairs, sit on the couch, and play chords on his guitar or deal myself a hand of solitaire.

———

A few years after she left, I was sick for weeks with mumps and a high fever that made me hallucinate. My hallucinations were all in my ears and fingertips. I'd hear things louder than they were—my hair on the pillow crackling like a forest fire, my father yelling and stamping when, in fact, he was being his quietest. And without warning the sensation in my fingertips would become reversed and exaggerated so I couldn't feel the thing I was touching, only the pressure of my bones inside my skin and the prickly weight of my blood circulating.

One night my fever went over 105. My father said I woke him up crying and talking. Nothing I said made sense. I don't remember that. I do remember lying on the bath mat at his feet, naked and unbelievably cold, his face distorted above me. I was on my stomach and could only see him from the corners of my eyes. He held a yellow enema bag, and I was vaguely aware of a pressure building against the inner walls of my abdomen, also something icy trickling between my legs. "Be calm," he said, and put one foot lightly on the small of my back to keep me still. "I'm right here," he said. I could feel the tiles under my cheek, through the bath mat, and when I spread my arms I could feel them with my fingers—smooth, even grids of acrylic. I kept pressing and pressing in order to remember what real sensation felt like in case the finger hallucinations started.

He sat me on the toilet while the bathtub filled, then plunged me in freezing water. "Be calm," he kept saying. "This is what we have to do." Later he told me it was a cure he'd learned from a book of holistic medicine my mother had left us. He shook out the thermometer and tried to stick it in my mouth but I wouldn't let him. "Come on, Jeremy, cooperate. If we don't get this under control I'll have to take you to the hospital. Is that what you want?" My skin felt like it might break and my heart was choking me. I felt his hands on my shoulders, holding me down, and smelled water everywhere, heard my feet kicking in and out of it. "Please," I was yelling. He told me this later. "Please, please!" He said I was in the water for just about five minutes before he gave up. He dried me, carried me back to bed, and sat next to me the rest of the night, rubbing my back with alcohol until the fever broke.

When I woke up, I only vaguely remembered the enema, the tile floor, and the cold water. He was still next to me in the chair, a look on his face that was both stern and frightened. I smelled rubbing alcohol and sweat soaked into my sheets. I knew then I had almost died, but I didn't know what had stopped me. The humidifier behind him chugged out a thin stream of fog. He leaned forward and the chair creaked. It was a kitchen chair he had brought up weeks ago in order to sit next to me reading books aloud and playing card games. On the floor at his feet were my sick things—

games and sketchbooks, pill bottles, crumpled pj's, a tea-cup, Kleenex.

"How old are you?" he asked. His voice was steady.

"Eight," I answered.

"What's your name?"

"Jemmy," I said. It was my childhood name, the one he still called me by occasionally, though more and more, and always at school, I was Jeremy.

He breathed deeply in and out and rubbed his fingertips under his eyes. Then he asked me a few more simple questions—the president of the United States, how many quarters in a dollar, the name of the high school where he taught math. He got into the bed with me and held my head to his chest and said, "OK. You're OK." I knew I should feel close to him, but I didn't. I wondered why, in all the years that had passed, we'd never touched like this.

For days afterward, even after the hallucinations stopped, I went on pretending there were things in my ears and under my fingertips he couldn't know about, just so he'd remember what it had been like to believe he was losing me. And later, when I was fully recovered and back in school, if I tried to bring up the night I'd almost died he'd shake his head or look sideways at me and raise one eyebrow, and say, "Died? I don't think so, Jem. You were pretty sick."

———

When the snow came, I kept track of it. If it came after dark I'd turn on the porch light outside and watch it swirl through the skirt of yellow light. The best snow in my opinion was a fast heavy snow of small flakes. I could watch for hours, the way it whipped down, quick as static, always telling the same stories. The smaller the flakes the longer the snow was likely to last. Fat plummy flakes, though dazzling, meant clearing skies and no accumulation; they represented a false hope since I wanted snow so thick it wiped out the world. If a snowfall came during the day and I wasn't at school, I'd stand at the kitchen window and measure it according to how well I could make out the trees on the far side of the neighbor's field. Best of all were mornings after a snowfall I hadn't known about—how the light would have lifted and brightened, making everything inside appear to me like I was seeing it for the first time.

The winter I turned fourteen the snow didn't come until February. There were squalls and flurries and storms that lasted an evening before blowing off or turning to rain, but no accumulation. I thought the ground looked tired and disgraced from being exposed all this time. My father never shared my interest in snow and I was trying hard then to seem more like him—quiet and standoffish, with slight, practical answers ready for any question he might ask. I kept my disappointments to myself. After school I'd walk a mile or so into the woods along old tractor paths, to an abandoned Boys Club camp where there was a quarry, a watchtower, and a locked, decrepit bunk. I carried my skates around my neck, the laces knotted together, and a sandwich in my coat pocket for later. The skates banged each other every few steps and the laces cut at the back of my neck so I'd have a sore feeling in my shoulders by the time I arrived, like I'd been staring for too long in one direction.

At the edge of the ice I'd stand a few seconds, appreciating the look of things, letting my feet settle against the cold insoles of my skates and feeling the heat trapped in the layers of my clothes continually seeping out and renewing itself.

From where I was you couldn't really see the quarry or any-thing of the abandoned Boys Club. Too many trees were in the way. Dead cattails and dry yellow humps of grass came up through the ice, and tree branches hung down at face level, like any swamp. But as you pushed out further the swamp gave way to frozen water stretching hundreds of feet in all directions. Sometimes at the end of an afternoon skating I'd have a hard time finding the inlet where my boots were and the trail home again. I'd circle around watching stars come out—past the rocky beach where the boys used to swim, and around the bend to the watchtower and the pine trees covering the upward slope to the top of Mt. Pisqua, and further out to a point that always made my heart race, where the ice and boulders ran into each other along the shore, and back again to another slope of pines stretching up.

―――――

One day there was a woman on a log next to the beach where the boys would have swum. She was in a bright pur-ple coat, sitting forward with her hands on her knees. I stopped in the middle of the ice, dizzy for a second because I wasn't moving anymore. The flatness of ice in contrast with the surrounding hills made the land seem to swell up subtly. There was a boom like gunshot from the other side of the quarry, some pressure far under the ice releasing, and then silence. I saw my skate tracks scratched all over the surface of the ice, wavering lines interrupted here and there by the patches of frost-barbed ice that were impossible to skate across, and trapped oxygen bubbles where my skate blades crumbled the surface. In a few months all those tracks would be gone and if I were standing here then I would be dead.

Another reason for my dizziness.

"Hey," I yelled. I raised one arm and let it fall back at my side. "Hey!"

She didn't move or acknowledge me. From where I was I couldn't even tell if she was looking in my direction. The wind went through the trees, and something—an empty plastic grocery bag, it looked like—blew past her, skittering and ballooning over the ice. Still, she didn't move.

I skated the long way around, past the watchtower and the slopes of pine trees going to the top of Mt. Pisqua. Now and then I'd glance up to be sure she was still there, the ends of her coat moving in the wind, her face pointed away from me. The last time I looked she was finally watching me. I thought she was pretty in a familiar way, with a pert, chiseled nose and wide mouth. Her eyebrows were thick and dark, almost joining over the bridge of her nose.

I stopped in front of her. "I saw you across the water," I said. I stood on the toes of my skates. I was out of breath. She smiled but said nothing, the edges of her smile compressing skin all the way back to her ears. There were no buttons on her coat and she had a long, dirty white scarf that looked like drapery around her neck. I couldn't tell if she was Indian or Spanish. Her eyes were brown and green, like looking at the ground through ferns. Miranda, the girl I'd been in love with most of that year, had sapphire eyes that were so pretty I wanted to lick them. To me they were *things* not eyes. This woman's eyes were not like that. "How come you didn't answer?"

"Did I have to?" Her voice was deep without being gravelly, almost delicate.

I thought back to the specific seconds when I was standing in the middle of the water. "I guess not."

"I came out here yesterday too. I saw you then." She looked at my feet. "Those are some nice skates. Are they your sister's?"

"Mother's," I said. "Just because they're white doesn't mean they're a girl's. Skates are all the same." These were my father's words coming through me.

"Yes, I see," she said. "I think they're fine. And does your mother know you're out here by yourself?" Before I could answer she went right on, "Of course. You don't look ill-cared for." She smiled again. "What's your name?"

"Jeremy."

"Mine's Lucy Sanders." She cleared her throat. "Can you do something for me now, Jeremy?"

"What's that?"

She stretched her legs out straight in front of her and shut her eyes a second before going on. Her gloves were two different colors, one green, one tan, both of them ragged at the fingertips so I could see skin underneath and the smooth edges of her nails. "Skate one more time around the ice for me? I love to watch. It looks so liberating."

"Sure." I pushed off with one foot and squiggled back a few yards from her.

"I never could do that," she said.

"It's easy."

She blinked at me and fake-smiled so I thought for a moment I must have said something to offend her. Then she seemed refreshed by a new thought. "How thick do you think the ice is?"

"Only a few feet, ten at the most," I said. "The water's over a mile deep—no one knows, really. A man drowned here a few years ago and they never found him. Scary, isn't it?"

"Not to me," she said.

I skated away from her full speed, heading back the way I'd come, crouched forward and swinging my arms. I dug as hard as I could with my toes and the edges of my skates, keeping my head up straight so I wouldn't lose balance. As I came out of my second turn and started heading for the trees I looked over my shoulder to get a glimpse of Lucy watching me, but the shore was a blur and my eyes were tearing. I couldn't pick her out. Not until I finished my final turn and started back toward the Boys Club did I realize she had gone. I straightened up and stopped skating then, let the wind push me. I listened to the sound my skates made on the ice. "Hey!" I yelled. I considered possible paths she'd taken, following them with my eyes, up from the log across the clearing to the rotten bunk, and past that into the woods. Next to the bunk was an old foundation with most of a chimney left standing from a house that had burned down years ago. Her purple coat should have been easy enough to spot even at this distance, but she was nowhere.

I spent the rest of that afternoon circling the quarry, feeling watched and alone. A few times I thought I sensed her behind me on the shoreline somewhere; I'd stop and turn suddenly, hoping to see her. Always, the shore was blank— no one, just the bare trees and dead leaves and sticks covering the ground, some patches of ice and rocks showing through silver and white. When the sun started going down and the sky over the hills turned the same brown as the ground only luminous, I found my boots and jacket and skated with them to the other side of the quarry where I had last seen her. I sat on the log where she'd been sitting and ate half the sandwich while I untied my skates, the other half while I slid into my boots. Some swirly, dense clouds at the top of Mt. Pisqua caught the last light of the sun, making it look like the mountain was on fire. The wind had died down by now and the woods were almost utterly silent.

I inhaled until my lungs were tight and shouted, "Lucy Sanders! I'm going home! If you're here, you should probably come with me or you'll freeze to death!" My voice faded off and echoed at the other side of the quarry. I heard a stick snap somewhere to my right and looked quickly, but there was nothing. Again, it was silent. "OK," I said. I pulled my jacket around me and zipped up, left my skates on the ice next to the log, and headed across the clearing to the bunk. My arms in the jacket made a quiet hissing noise against my sides. As I walked, I kept looking left and right but nothing moved anywhere in the woods. The bunk was locked as always, with nothing new inside—the same shadows and carved graffiti, bottles, broken windows, and bits of glass on the floor. Everywhere I looked things were undisturbed. I went back across the clearing to the foundation, took a few steps into the bushes behind the old chimney and kicked over some milk bottles and half a ruined dresser drawer left from the fire, its plastic liner fluttering in the breeze. I cupped my hands around my mouth. "Lucy!" I called. I waited a few more seconds and when nothing happened I headed down to the ice, picked up my skates and went back across the quarry just as the stars were coming out.

———

At home I found my father in the basement under the flood-lights dabbing black paint around the eyes of an elegant, two-foot-long spruce salmon and touching up the outlines of his gills and scales. Another fish he was working on, only half exhumed from a chunk of marble, lay next to him on the carving block surrounded by his different sized chisels and gouges. I loved watching him carve—his hammer taps at the back of a chisel making its point slip and jump over the form of a fish, back and forth, up and down, hacking away bits of stone or wood to find the fish's shape. He always seemed happiest to me then. He'd stand on the balls of his feet and arch his back and move around the block of stone patiently, like he was slow dancing.

"Hey, Jeremy," he said. "I was just starting to wonder where you were." He looked at me a moment, maybe waiting for me to say something about skating. "Hungry?" he asked.

"Not really yet." The smell of his oil paint came across the room at me. He had on his old plaid wool jacket and a denim work apron underneath, covering most of his thighs. Behind him the space heater suddenly came on, lit up and started rattling, turning the floor around him orange.

"How's school?"

Always the same questions. Behind them he wanted more, I just didn't know what. Sometimes it seemed he could as easily have poked me in the chest to see if I had a response as ask these redundant questions. "OK, I guess. Boring."

He stood up straight and looked at me a second, screwing the cap back on the tube of black paint. Then he went to the sink to rinse his brush. I knew he was trying to think of other things to ask me now—a test he'd known I was preparing for, a paper, a girl, a teacher whose anecdotes were worth repeating. He had been late after school for a staff meeting that day and we hadn't seen each other since morning. "Let's go up," he said. "I'm hungry even if you aren't." He pulled the plug on the floodlights and heater, unknotted his work apron, slid it from around his neck, and draped it over the half-made stone fish.

I indicated with my chin. "He's looking good," I said.

"It's a she. Maybe two of them. I can't tell yet." I knew if I looked more closely I'd see his faint pencil marks scratched around the sides of the stone—meaningless, indecipherable notes to himself about where the fish might lie in the stone.

"Who's it for?"

He passed me and headed up the stairs. "No one. I thought it'd look nice on the front porch, maybe." Our feet shuffled over the grit and made the wood stairs ring. "Or maybe I'll give it to your grandparents for their anniversary in May." He laughed. "Should be done by then. Wipe your feet," he said and waited to let me pass before switching off the lights and closing the basement door. I don't know when, exactly, but sometime between seeing him down there outlining the details on his salmon and arriving back at the top of the stairs, I had decided not to tell him about Lucy. I saw my skates lying together on their sides on the mat next to the front door and heard her voice in my head and I knew I wouldn't say anything.

"Hey," he said, as I stepped around him. "You have good color today." He put his hand on my cheek.

"It's the wind."

After dinner I sat at the kitchen table and he coached me through math problems, gently scolding me for having so little interest in his subject. The sour smell of his breath and his heat coming through the back of my shirt as he leaned over me vigorously scratching out numbers and theorems in pencil, left-handed, kept waking me up and putting me to sleep. "See how this changes the fraction, so the unknown, x, comes out on the top and then you can use your law of inequality to simplify it further...." Always, things worked out for him in this rational, speechless, pencil landscape. I hated it. I pictured us like dogs, me chasing after him while he went around barking and digging up piles of leaves to show me where the secret numbers were and how to locate them later on without him. At the end I wrung my forehead in my hands. "OK, OK, I understand, I just don't get how you *did* it. Now can I go to bed?"

QED, he printed at the bottom of the page, and laughed. "See you in the morning."

The next day was warm and overcast. After school I walked across the fields separating the middle school from the senior high where my father taught. Cross-country skiers in tights and wool hats were running the periphery of the school grounds, leaping and stabbing their poles in the dirt to simulate skiing, and hooting to each other. "It's gonna snow!" one of them would yell, and the other team members would yell back "Yeah! Snow! Snow! Snow!" They had been doing this since November, trying to encourage the sky to let loose. "Snow!" one yelled. "Tomorrow!" They seemed more desperate than ever. Their hats, all bright blues, pinks, purples, and blacks with stripes and zigzag patterns, no two the same, stood out sharply against the yellow-brown ground and gray trees. I watched them huff around the side of the middle school and disappear, their cheering voices following like a wake. It wouldn't snow. Already the air was wet and smelled sweet like cold rain.

My father was in the math office waiting for me, clipping his fingernails. He had pudgy, muscular fingers. When I was younger he kept the fingernails on his right hand as long as a woman's to play the guitar, but he rarely played now and, when he did, he used a flat pick. He looked up when I came in the door, lowered his feet from his desk and sat forward so his desk chair creaked. There were three books in the steel shelves over his desk—a dictionary and two math texts—and a withered aloe plant, more brown than green, with crumbs of dirt around it. One other teacher was in the room, a little man with gray-blond hair, scoring tests with a red pencil. "See you," my father said. "See you, Phil," the man said, not looking up, and we left.

Walking out of the school we barely spoke. Once, leaving his office alone at this hour I had come around a corner and almost bumped into two lovers, both of them with long curly blond hair, standing against the wall with their mouths stuck together and their shirts untucked. I had hurried by and once I'd gotten a safe distance, stopped to watch a while, to see if they ever got tired or changed position. Their hands slipped in and out of each other's clothes. The boy rocked against the girl, making the locker behind her clang. Then the girl was suddenly looking right at me over the boy's shoulder. She had black eyebrows and eyelashes in spite of her blond hair. "Take a picture, it lasts longer," she said. Now, every time I walked by the spot where the lovers had been I thought of them like they were still there. I remembered the insulting, half-provocative tone of her voice and felt the same numbness, not knowing what in the world to say back to her. I tried to imagine an expression on my face that was as close to the tone of her voice as possible. Still I didn't know what I'd say to her.

"So, what's new with you?" my father asked.

"Nothing *new*," I said. "What do you think?" For a second I wondered if my thoughts about the lovers had somehow slipped up and shown themselves without my realizing it. I glanced at him and watched the way his head bobbed forward and back when he walked. We were almost the same height then. I had his hair—black and straight with a part on the side, although his was longer and mixed with silver in front. He looked back at me and smiled tightly, two patches of puffy dry skin at either end of his mouth lifting so his smile looked bracketed.

"Just asking," he said. He dropped his smile and the dry patches extended downward from the corners of his mouth again, giving him an exaggerated fish-frown.

Outside it smelled even more like rain. More rain, no snow. I ran ahead and circled our old Impala, chanting, "Snow, snow, snow," until he caught up with me. He had his keys out, ready to unlock the door. I almost knocked into him but he stepped aside at the last second.

"What the hell's the matter with you?" he asked.

"What's the matter with *you?*" I retorted, and circled the car again banging on the roof and fenders with my fist while he revved the engine.

"Come skating with me when we get home," I said, slinging my knapsack next to his on the seat between us. "May be our last chance for a while. If it rains." I didn't know why I was asking him this. All day I had looked forward to getting out there alone, seeing if I could find Lucy, tracking her as completely as possible for as long as there was light. I didn't want him along. I wanted him to know there was something hidden and not to know what it was or that I was deliberately hiding it.

"Don't think so, Jem. I have about a hundred tests to grade tonight." He put his arm across the seat and looked over his shoulder, backing out of the parking space. "And unless I'm mistaken you have a few other things to take care of yourself." As we drove out of the lot he began listing chores I'd neglected all week in order to skate—the wood, the laundry, the vacuuming, my bedroom.

"OK, OK, give it a rest," I cut in. "I get the picture."

We drove in silence. Turning off the main highway onto the long dirt road home he put his hand on my shoulder. A man who lived up the road passed us heading the other way, the hood and front grate of his pickup so skewed to one side it looked as if he was aiming to drive off the road. My father raised one finger on the steering wheel at him and the man raised his back. "You're a good kid," he said. "You know that?"

"No."

He patted me twice and withdrew his hand from my shoulder.

Coming around the last corner at the top of the ridge we could see our house for a moment below—bay green, with six windows in front and wide white window trim, the broad, peaked back of the roof almost hidden in trees. "Home sweet home!" he used to say, when I was younger, as we passed this point in the road. Now he said nothing. His face relaxed, his eyebrows leveling and stretching back, and the corners of his mouth softening. And then we were going much faster. The gravel popped under us and rocks rang against the wheel-wells and the floor. Through the side window I saw more trees and gray sky, oaks and ashes trapped in the curved, dirty window glass.

That night it rained. I kept waking up and falling asleep again. Rain rattled in the gutters and blew down through the trees and spattered against the side of our house. I thought I heard a door slam downstairs and got up to see what it was. But nothing looked out of place—the doors and windows were all shut, lights off and chairs standing empty. A faint dawn glow, barely purple, showed through the trees. I flipped on the porch light where I had always liked watching the snow come down and saw the wet porch floorboards, gleaming and bare. Then I went back upstairs and down the hall, into my father's room where it was peacefully dark still and smelled of his sleep. He was on the floor on bamboo mats next to the window where my mother's sewing machine had been, the futon they had shared folded against a wall and covered with his books and papers and opened letters and cassette tapes.

I squatted next to him and his eyes opened right away.

"What time is it?" he asked, his voice completely alert as if he hadn't been sleeping at all.

"I don't know. About five. Five or six."

He yawned and stretched. "Can't you sleep?" he asked.

I shook my head. I wished I didn't care. I wished the rain soaking through the ground outside and lighting up every surface didn't bother me. "It's *raining*," I said.

"Yes," he said. "I know." He sighed and shut his eyes.

There was a gust of wind and I smelled rain mixed with a smell of thawing earth coming through the crack in his window. I felt it in the air touching my face and bare ankles and there was nothing I could think of to console myself— no pleasing harmony between what was and what should have been; between what I imagined and what was true; between words and the things they were. The armature of my brain felt stirred or tipped upside down and everything had the look of a mathematical puzzle gone wild. It was raining when there should be snow. I didn't know why I felt this out-of-joint, or how to say anything to him about it.

"Lie down," he said. "Nothing worse than being by yourself when you can't sleep." He threw part of a blanket over me, rolled onto his side facing me and said, "Wake me up if you want to talk."

I lay there listening to his clock hum and the quiet sound of his breaths in and out, trying not to think about the rain. For a while I shut my eyes and imagined myself departing through gray water as dim as the light seeping across the ceiling. But it was no good. I rolled onto my side and saw him next to me in his V-neck T-shirt, hands folded in front of his face and his hair falling across the bridge of his nose and the crescent dent in his cheek where he'd fractured his cheekbone one night falling down stairs. More and more his skin was settling against the structure of his face, narrowing it, so I could see the shape of his bones and muscles inside. I wondered if he had looked this old for a long time and I hadn't noticed, or if his being asleep made him look older. He would be forty-eight that summer.

When his alarm went off he reached behind his pillow for it without opening his eyes. He sat up, rubbing his face and stretching. "Sleep at all?" he asked. He put his hand on my leg a moment.

"Not really," I said. "Sort of."

He grunted. His knees clicked as he drew his feet up under himself, stood and stepped over me to get to the bathroom. There were thin, burst veins in his calves and his feet were chafed, the nails on his big toes thick as shells. "You can tell me what's bothering you," he said, as he went across the room.

"Sure," I said.

He yawned. "Go get ready for school. We'll talk about it on the way." We wouldn't talk. I knew that. The bathroom door creaked open and shut and I heard the shower water come on, and suddenly I was unbelievably sleepy. I rolled into the spot where he had been, shut my eyes and fell instantly to sleep.

———

I saw Lucy Sanders on Saturday, the weekend after it rained. She was at the colder, west side of the quarry in the shadow of the mountain, hunched between the big rocks on the shore as if she'd lost something. "Lucy," I shouted. I was still closer to the middle of the quarry.

She spun around to face me and waved with both arms. "Come here! You have to see this!"

I continued at the same speed I'd been going, stretching my legs behind me and feeling the sun on my face until I entered the shadow of the mountain, and for a moment I felt plunged in darkness. I blinked hard and waited for my eyes to adjust. When they did, I saw Lucy was kneeling next to a rock, her purple coat splayed on the ice around her. Her face, in profile, was almost too square to call pretty, then she turned toward me and I was taken by her eyes again, her eyebrows and the shape of her mouth. "Come here," she repeated. "There are fossils!"

I stopped and carefully lowered myself onto my knees next to her. "What fossils?"

"Look," she said. She pointed at some faint traces in the surface of the rock before her. "See?" she asked.

I leaned closer. There were hair-fine white lines in the rock—quartz striations and a few black nubs that looked like ordinary bumps. "No," I said. "Where?"

"You have to look hard." She pointed again, her finger moving slowly over the jagged surface of the rock. "See? Trilobites—they look a little like wood bugs, a little like crabs. Can you see it now?"

I couldn't, but to please her I pretended I did. "Ah-ha," I said, and nodded a few times. I was hot from skating, but cold too, the sweat freezing all over me. Looking at the rock I worried that my fingers would begin feeling numb and bloated. This still occasionally happened—a pattern in something I saw or heard would set me off and I would feel the mild beginnings of a hallucination. "Cool." I rubbed my mittens up and down against my thighs.

"One of the first exoskeletal life-forms known. Paleozoic, I think." She leaned back on her knees and gestured to the many half submerged rocks surrounding us. "I've been finding them all over this afternoon. It's amazing. Come on. I'll show you."

I trailed behind, walking on the toes of my skates, occasionally gliding a step or two where there was enough open space between rocks. I pounded my hands together. "Is that what you're doing here?" I asked. "Looking for fossils or something?"

She glanced back at me. "I'm not doing anything. Why do I have to be *doing* anything?" She threw her arms out dramatically, let them drop at her sides and laughed. I could see she enjoyed saying this, but I wasn't sure if she meant it. She stopped next to another rock, put out a hand and leaned close to it. She had a look on her face now like she was getting ready to greet someone she hadn't seen in a long time.

Her breath frosted in the air. "Yup. This is another one," she said. "Oh! They're much more defined here. Come look."

I put my hand on her shoulder a moment to steady myself, and leaned down. This time I was pretty sure I saw them—fossilized triangular bugs like kites, some right-side up, some upside down. I bent closer, but I was still worried about hallucinating. The wind blew up the back of my sweater. She was talking about prehistoric times and the formation of sedimentary rock, but I couldn't concentrate. "Oh, look at this!" She dropped to her knees, pointing. "Look, look! Doesn't it just take you out of yourself?"

"Yes," I said.

"And look at this!" she said, running her finger over the rock. "Ferns!"

"Cool," I said. I turned around to face the quarry. A flock of finches wheeled overhead and suddenly changed direction, light turning yellow and white on their backs as they beat their wings so they looked like a place where the sky had turned solid and begun churning. I looked down at Lucy again, her dirty hair sticking under her collar and going across her shoulders, and I wanted to put my hand on her head, or under her hair, on her neck. At the same time, I wanted to get as far from her as possible. "Hey," I said. "It's freezing. Aren't you freezing? Let's go back out into the sun."

She glanced at me and blinked, her expression tightening as if she were trying to figure out who I was; then she looked back at the rock and her face relaxed again. "Aren't they nice? They don't know a thing. They just sit here eternally."

When she stood up I detected a faintly acrid smell about her, like wood smoke. I disliked it, though as soon as it had shifted away from us in the breeze I wanted it back again. A few raised white dots stood out in the skin under her eyes and along her jaw—more signs of her being unclean. She stood hunched forward with her hands in her pockets to keep her coat closed.

"Want to come?" I asked.

She looked at me a second, then away, and shrugged. "No," she said. She lifted her hands, still inside her pockets, so her coat opened and I saw she had on a worn green cardigan buttoned up wrong. "Maybe next time," she said, and lowered her hands.

"What next time?"

"Next time I see you."

I frowned and shook my head to let her know I understood there would be no next time.

She took a step forward so one of her feet was touching mine, and put her hand on my shoulder. "You look unhappy," she said. "Why so unhappy? At your age life should still be one pleasurable thing after the next." Up close she smelled more musty than smoky. Then she pulled me to her and her mouth covered the side of my mouth and part of my cheek. I breathed in and tasted her strange smell at the back of my throat. I shut my eyes and gave myself over until there was only her cold skin and spit and the smell of her to let me know I was in the world. When she released me I didn't brush her saliva from the corner of my mouth, though it burned in the cold air. She stepped back from me and I watched her face receding, our eyes still fused, and for a second I was dizzy. "I'm responding to your need—your unhappiness and need. That's all," she said.

"But I'm not unhappy." I couldn't get my eyes out of hers. She scowled. I felt like a liar though I was pretty sure I was telling the truth. "I like my life."

She shook her head and started walking away. "Tell your mother to buy you some new skates so you can give me those. Girls' skates are for girls anyway."

"Wait!" She was on the shore now, walking quickly away. I went right to the edge of the water.

"No! Don't follow," she said. "I'll see you again some-time." She continued up into the woods and in a few minutes I couldn't see her at all. I still heard her snapping sticks and breaking through underbrush every few minutes. Soon there wasn't even that. I turned back to the quarry and that flock of finches dropped down and broke open at the heart of the water, heading in two directions and then weaving back together. They went right above me and the sound of their wings beating, a familiar rushing noise, was gone in the same instant it became audible.

By the end of the day I had lost interest in skating. I could skate forward and backward. I could cross over my left skate when I was going into a turn full speed. But I couldn't leap or spin or pirouette. Worse than that, I didn't care. I was tired of the wind on my face, and the mountain, and the trees, and the Boys Club repeating themselves over and over as I circled the quarry. Now the sky was filling with clouds. When I looked up suddenly sometimes I would remember the exact feel of Lucy's lips touching the side of my mouth and the cold star-shaped mark she had left on my skin. Then as suddenly, I would forget. There was a sickle moon, bright in the pale sky between the clouds. I felt pierced through when I looked up and saw it and remembered her kissing me; already I couldn't tell what I remembered and what I was making up.

———

STONE FISH
———

217

That same winter, my father finished his sculpture of the two stone fish. They were fat, spawning she-fish fighting upstream with their tails half entwined in the same bit of rough unfinished stone. I was with him when he was finishing their heads and faces, tapping around them with a flat chisel for smooth surfaces, then the sharpest one for outlines. He kept stepping back and cocking his head to one side, then moving in quickly to change some little detail. "Pop, tell me a story," I said. I didn't care what he said as long as he spoke so I wasn't left alone, tempted to fill in the silence and then judging myself badly for what I said.

He kept on tapping, going around the fish, sending up a spray of stone, finding more and more detail for their faces. "What story?" he said.

"I don't know. Anything at all."

He hit a little harder, his strikes coming three at a time, a bright metal-on-metal sound—tink-tink-TINK, tink-tink-TINK, tink-tink-TINK-tink—with lower, bass undertones from the stone absorbing the shock. "When we lived in Italy, your mother and I, before you were born, we used to go out in a rowboat every day. Almost every day." His voice tightened as he leaned to one side to see something. "We were living in a hostel and didn't have much privacy otherwise." He stood straight, rubbed one fish's cheek with his thumb and then tapped twice lightly with the sharp chisel to make a crease in it. "She used to say that to me."

"Say what?"

"Tell me," he went to the other side of the fish to do its opposite cheek the same way, "a story."

"I'm bugging you, huh?"

"No."

"Then, what stories did you tell her?"

Tink-TINK. "I don't remember."

"You do so."

He sighed. "She liked pretending we were that couple in the movie where the young soldier rows to Switzerland with his girlfriend all night to escape the German army. I forget what it was called. She liked stories like that. People on the run. We were in Italy ourselves to avoid the draft—for me to avoid the draft, so I guess it was a parallel situation, though times were very, very different." He rubbed one fish's mouth a few times with his little finger and shook his head, then went over it again, tapping lightly. I pictured him in a white T-shirt while a woman who looked like me taunted him, leaning forward in a rowboat and asking for stories. Switzerland, I reminded myself, and added steep white-capped mountains behind them with gondolas and skiers and mountaineers.

"Tell me more," I said.

"Nothing to tell." He set down his chisels and stood back to look at the fish. "I think that's it," he said. He put both hands on the small of his back where he said he sometimes had a spasm of warm feelings, finishing one of his sculptures. "Yes, yes. I really think so. Do you think?"

"Looks good to me."

He untied his apron and went to the sink to wash his hands, still glancing over his shoulder at the fish every few seconds as if he thought he might catch them at something unexpected. They weren't really done. Tomorrow he would come down, see every last thing, and really finish them. Then he'd tell me to come look again. He would be beaming, walking around on the balls of his feet, and he might make a few strange pronouncements about how life and light and form reiterate one another in stone.

STONE FISH

"Pa, did you love her?"

He turned the spigots hard to stop the water and the pipes overhead clanged from the change in pressure. He flicked his hands dry. The water in the basement was unfiltered, gold-amber with a red sediment you could see in the bottom of a jar if you left it overnight. I imagined the drops flying from his fingers, red liquid jewels splashing the cement wall and clinging to the spigot handles in front of him. "Of course I loved her," he said. "Why do you think we were married?" The way he said this I knew it wasn't why they'd married, though I was also pretty sure he loved her. He shook his head as he went by me, touched me lightly on the shoulder with two wet fingers, and headed upstairs. "You coming?" he called from the top of the stairs.

"In a minute," I said. I wanted to be alone admiring his fish—how they curved in opposite directions like a pair of parentheses, one going high, the other low, both of their bellies half-sunk in the rock. They were not looking at each other, but from the way their heads angled I knew they wouldn't collide. They were the most real-looking fish I'd seen him make in a while, and for the first time I was noticing how much they resembled him—the dented cheek and the frown that wasn't a frown. I rubbed my finger in the groove between them to feel the unfinished stone, and tried to understand how in the world he knew what was fish and what was rock when he was carving. There was a song in my head then, one he used to sing about a pony and a girl. I hadn't heard him sing it for years. I remembered sitting in the tub as a small child, hearing them downstairs singing, their voices like the stone fish going one over the other, high and low, slipping around each other and not colliding. Tree limbs blew back and forth in the skylight above me in the tub and I felt warm and protected, though I also felt like I didn't exist. I was skylight, tiled floor, steamy walls, and the sound of their voices.

Upstairs, he was in the kitchen heating beans in the frying pan. They smelled good, sizzling as he spun them around in the butter with a metal spoon. I came up behind him and leaned my head on his shoulder a second. He lowered his head so his ear pressed against me. "Want lunch?" he asked.

"No."

I sat at the table—watched him sprinkle in salsa, cayenne, and salt, then roll the beans in a flour tortilla with grated cabbage and cheese. He ate leaning against the stove, holding the tortilla in one hand and a plate under his chin with the other. Neither of us spoke but I was pretty sure we were thinking the same thing: we were wondering what life would be like for us if she returned; maybe, for the first time, thinking of her not as someone absent but as someone truly gone.

———

Mid-March we were running low on wood. Snow had piled waist high on either side of the road and two-feet thick on the roof. The last few days had been gorgeous, fake-spring, close to fifty degrees and I was outside in the brilliant sun, knocking apart pieces of fruitwood—half a cord my father had gotten for cheap from a man up the road. I wore a bandanna around my forehead and had my T-shirt hanging from my back pocket like a tail. Now and then I'd stop splitting and go look at my reflection in the car window—my muscles stretching and distorted in the tinted glass, my thick, crow black hair, and my ribs rippling in and out with my breaths.

I had on a pair of his old ski glasses and when I leaned close to the window I could see a reflection of my reflection in them; closer still and I saw behind the glasses, my eyelids flipping up and down, the hair-rimmed pink folds of my eyelids magnified.

Around noon I hit a section of trunk that was exceptionally easy—wood dividing like butter for me. I felt powerful, bouncing up on the balls of my feet, running the maul right through and tossing split pieces aside, enveloped in the ketchup-sweet smell of burst wood fibers. I kept imagining my mother coming up the road behind me in our old car, the white station wagon, pulling herself from behind the wheel and raising her sunglasses on her forehead, then standing with one arm over the top of the door, admiring me, staring, not really smiling, half-stricken by my new appearance to her. I could see this so clearly it made my heart race and my skin prickle with anticipation. I saw her brown-gray hair and green eyes—the one lazy one that made her look almost walleyed from certain angles. Her voice would be sweet and slow when she said my name. I saw it so clearly once or twice I had to stop and turn around to convince myself she wasn't there.

Soon my father came outside in his running shorts. He stood next to me awhile watching, and didn't say anything.

"Here," I said finally, dropping the maul and stepping around him. "You do a few. I'm whipped." I leaned against the hot fender of his car to watch. He was much faster than I was and more efficient, completely focused on the wood. There were no dreamy pauses between one swing and the next. He was so fast he could hit a piece of wood that was wobbling out of balance—knock it in two pieces before it fell. Now and then he'd look up as he was throwing aside split pieces and our eyes would meet and there was a question in them I didn't understand. *What?* he seemed to be asking. *What is it?* Then before I could say anything or begin a conversation he was finding another piece of wood, moving more and more quickly, setting it up, whacking it in half.

"All yours," he said when he was done, and ran by me out to the road, one hand raised to slap mine as he passed. We were as separate and alike as his stone fish, sunk in the silence not because of my mother but because of all our likeness and because, for now, there was nothing more to say.

ZIGZAG CABINET

———

THEY PARK IN BLOND FIELDS OF STRAW STUBBLE, HALF A mile from the fairgrounds, the land here swelling and rolling like waves, and walk with dozens of other festivalgoers in the air that is thick with dust and straw particles, the sun fracturing into shafts through it. He's comfortable enough with her to slip his hand under her bare arm, up to the armpit and back; to touch his lips to her jaw every few minutes and say, "God, you're beautiful." But the comfort is at least half a lie. He has no idea what she's really thinking, or what he thinks of her. They barely know each other. "This," he says, his hand going up under her shirt, palm flat against her ribs, "is a perfect fifth." She laughs. "Right? And this," he cups his hand over her shoulder and squeezes, "is a third. No." He squeezes again. "A *minor* third." He puts his hand on top of her head, spread over her sun-hot hair. "Octave," he says. She sings the interval. He first fell for her because of her singing voice which is rich and stagy and comforting all at the same time. "The dissonant intervals," he leans closer to her ear, "are not available in public. That's why those monks in the fourteen hundreds banned them. Tritones," he whispers. "Major sevenths."

Later, they slip off behind the tents and crafts displays and vegetable stands to get high and when they come back, wandering between aisles of carnival barkers, she tells him about being a magician's assistant. "Did I ever tell you?" she begins. He feels a drop in his stomach. She's always telling him things from her past which half-stun and half-arouse him—men she's slept with, women she's slept with. "I was a magician's assistant once, for about a year and a half."

"No," he says. "Tell me." He's nervous now and has the flattened, split-apart feeling of being too high. He can see the ground and the path they're taking and he understands what she's saying—the words she's using. When he looks at her he sees the perspiration on her forehead and the colors in her eyes that he likes so much. He knows these things one at a time but not together.

"Nothing to tell. I was a kid. This old guy would pick me up at my parents' house. He gave me like twenty-five dollars a show."

He concentrates on the rocks he can feel under the soles of his boots and wills himself to come up with the next question. They are headed for the Ferris wheel which is huge and slow that year, the cars on it like oversized golf carts with roofs to protect you from the sun. "So how do they cut you in half like that, when they cut you apart?" he asks, trying to keep his voice appropriately light.

She says nothing at first. He watches her profile a few seconds, again feeling in his stomach like he's about to fall.

Then, "I can't say. I'm sworn to secrecy," she says. "Part of the trade."

"But it's story material! Think what I could do with it!" he says.

"Huh." She nods. "Yeah, that's true." She looks puzzled for a moment and they walk on in silence.

"So tell me."

"You know, I just don't think I can really. I mean, I can't demonstrate here, without lying down on the ground. It's more a three-dimensional explanation than a thing you can say. Oh, Billy, look! A Terminator!"

"A what?"

She jerks his arm and pulls him after her to a tall, octopus-looking ride with no line.

"What is this?" he asks as she hands the barker their tickets; he follows her around the blazing, tread-studded aluminum platform encircling the ride, looking for an empty car.

"Here," she says, "perfect. The outside ones give you a little more spin. You first."

He gets in and there is a moment of goofy stillness, strapped in and hanging face-up, waiting. Later he remembers it as the most purely terrifying part of the ride. "Am I going to regret this?" he asks. The machine inches upward, creaking, then stops and settles back slightly, letting more people on. He watches her—her green-yellow eyes skimming the interior of the cage-like, mesh metal enclosure they're in. There's a scraped and faded warning about heart conditions and people prone to dizziness riveted to the mesh just next to him. Someone has scratched crookedly into it, "Tanya and Tony," taking away paint and metal.

Her eyes finally meet his. "Trust me," she says. "You'll love it."

Then they're in motion, being flung end-over-end, slowly at first, then faster, their legs and shoulders mashing together so hard he can't tell where the boundary of their skin is and can't remember any sound in his ears but the wind and the machinery and her shrieks. He never loses awareness of his body's weight and physical proportions; always he feels himself moving intact through the loops and turns and sudden double-backs—every movement going painfully against gravity. The best rides, in his opinion, are ones that suck you out of yourself, gently or forcefully—ones that make your eyes swim up in your head like being asleep and your stomach float and your muscles press out against your skin. This is one long bone-jarring discomfort. The world whips by all out of joint with his perceptions, the ground where the horizon should be, the sun through his feet.

Later, on the Ferris wheel, coasting down from the sky's pure radiant heat to the ground's dust-browned one (brushed in back with the smells of popcorn and hot dogs and garlic), he remembers again to ask her about being a magician's assistant. He wonders if now would be a good time to have her demonstrate, prone on the adjacent seat there, how a man once magically chopped her in pieces. He forms some of the words for asking but he can't get to them. He thinks his curiosity is probably perverse—an illusion itself and not attachable to anything that's really her. He looks at her lips and the sunlight flickering in her eyelashes, sunlight outlining her hair. "Sasha," he says, turning her face to his, and decides it's a better thing to get lost in these kisses with the sun between them, than to ask about a magician, ten years ago, cutting her apart.

His first lover was also a musician, ten years ago. She had hair the color of sunlight on fall leaves and her wrists were thick as a boy's, with fuzz outlining the bones. After school they would go to her house—both her parents worked at the college and stayed away late, until dinner, sometimes longer, at their offices—and he would lie on her bed, listening to her practice the flute. He pictured her notes like furrows blown into the air, plowing the air into musical order, and let himself drop off, in and out of sleep. Sometimes she sputtered into the mouthpiece, straining for a high note or trying to tongue too many notes at once. It made an embarrassing sucking-spluttering noise. Then she would stop to pound the flute in her hand or slap herself viciously in the forehead saying, "No, no, stupid idiot." He'd wake up out of his music stupor to see her in the window-light, loose old jeans and the men's button-collar shirts she liked, her cheeks and neck flushed from all those long notes and suddenly expelled staccatos. Always, she looked painted, like one of Vermeer's women—no matter how angry she was—legato features and half-sad eyes, nothing unsmooth on the surface.

"Hey, you stopped. It sounded wonderful," he might say.

"You're not even listening. How can you say that?"

"You were playing the gavotte part." He'd close his eyes and wait for her to begin again—wait for her notes to plow him back under.

Afterward, making love, they barely looked at each other. She lay on top of him and they kissed, her mouth still hot from the flute, her lips pliant and dry. Sometimes she would snicker just as he slipped inside her, he was never sure why—it was the faintest laugh on the tail of an outbreath— maybe she was pleased and aroused, maybe she felt herself to be more in control now that he was inside her. He lifted her hips in his palms so her weight fell more evenly across his chest and stomach. Sometimes they rolled one way or the other, never letting go of each other, so he could be on top awhile, but it didn't work as well and they always finished with her on top. He didn't know what it was about their lovemaking that required such constant contact. He wasn't even sure what her body was like, undressed, so he couldn't visualize it. Any visualization wasn't of her, then—couldn't be—and cheapened the moment by removing him from her; so he tried to put the picture-making part of his mind to rest as best as he could. He concentrated on her breathing and timed his breaths in and out with hers to keep their stomachs flat against each other. He loved the smell of her—her hair which was like citrus and baby powder, her mint- and metal-smelling mouth, and the faint sea-smell of her crotch. Since there was no visualization, no holding himself apart against visualized details, there was hardly any damming up. He ran right out into her, more or less, never thinking about how long it was taking.

"You enjoyed that," she said afterward, still lying on him, her chin propped in her hands so her hair fell around their faces, enclosing them. It was an afternoon like any other afternoon that spring.

"What's not to enjoy?"

"Nothing, I guess." She laughed—the vaguely amused snicker that might mean arousal, might mean she felt better than him.

When he touched her he tried to stay as close as possible, both legs around one of hers, or one leg slung over her hip. Somehow he understood that if this was how she liked having him inside her then it must be how she liked being touched as well. He moved his face and lips over her chest, licking and kissing like he meant to sow her with his tongue.

Toward the end, the heat thrown off her body was almost too much to bear and there was a kind of squeezing in, her body shutting down against the last seconds of climax, which made him feel weirdly excluded. Her legs shook and her breathing became so accelerated it scared him. By then he was removed, too, absorbed in dream-like visualizations he couldn't really help—the culminating point of a church steeple, the curled edges of leaves, a slope of trees, peeling birch bark, always the edges of things against a sky. He was half-asleep over her racing heart, not really bored but not fully present either. Afterward he rocked her and held her close until her breathing steadied and she stopped shaking.

Now he was anxious to be home. He wanted to be playing the violin, walking around in his father's study and reading the spines of books as the daylight faded, playing and reading. There was nothing mechanically similar between the way his fingers worked on the violin and the way they worked touching her, yet the effect was similar—the rising emotion and the way he went off in his head into dream-like pictures. Both were a little like being asleep and awake at the same time and both gave him the feeling of being in love. She uncrossed her ankles and moved her hips against him.

"Again?" he asked.

She laughed. "Unless you don't want to."

Downstairs, the dog barked, scratched at the back door and barked again. He pictured her parents' kitchen with no one in it—the clock humming, sunlight fading across the bare floor, the crooked red countertops, and cloth-faced cupboard doors. An hour from now, she'd be down there across from them at the kitchen table eating and talking to them about her schoolwork and her music—like none of this had happened. A newspaper hit the side of the house and he heard or felt-heard in the silence after it the rush of air in the paper-boy's bicycle spokes—the hiss of wind like water redirected in a boat's wake. He pictured the boy's face too, as he struggled up the next hill, pedaling and pitching papers. He'd had part of this street on his own route years ago, in grade school.

"No," he said. "I don't care."

She pushed him over onto his back. "Well, I would think you should *care*, Billy."

"I don't mean to say I don't care. I'm just satisfied now. That's all."

She waited a second—long enough to let him know something was wrong. "'Satisfied?'" she said. "That's the best you can do?"

"Blissful. Content. Jenny, what am I supposed to say? Annihilated with pleasure?"

She rolled away from him and began pulling on her clothes at the edge of the bed—shirt, socks, underwear. He heard the different fabrics stretch and slide and snap over her skin, each one removing her further from him. He opened his eyes, rolled toward her, and put a hand on her shoulder.

"Jenny," he said.

She shrugged him away and stood to tuck in her shirt and button her pants.

"Hey," he said.

She adjusted the waist of her jeans, pulled out the tails of her shirt a little, and dug her hands into her pockets for a hair elastic, staring down at him until she'd tied her hair back. "Hey what?" she asked, when she was done. "Spit it out."

"I didn't mean to be insulting." He rolled onto his back, exasperated. "God. I swear it, sometimes I just don't know how to talk to you."

"Try words," she said. She went back to the window ledge for her flute and started playing. The whole time he was getting dressed she kept playing, her back to him at the bureau mirror. She blew long fierce notes, notes with no edge or depth. She wasn't looking at him over her shoulder in the mirror reflection, either. When he was dressed he went to her bedroom door, opened it and stood there a few seconds before saying he was leaving. He tried to make his voice as inflectionless as her playing. She faced him, her eyebrows squaring together and her lips shiny with spit, embouchure twisted slightly to the left, but she didn't stop. Her playing sounded louder to him now because she was facing him; it bit into his ears so he could hear the edges, the tiny shrill breaks in tone where her breath and spit turned to music. He held her gaze for as long as he could and then went out, down the back stairs and through the dim kitchen, out the back door, across the deck to his bicycle, and home.

It's two weeks later, and they've seen each other almost every night since the Garlic Festival. He's been at her house so often he's left a pillow, a hairbrush, some moccasins, and a few of his favorite CD's. He's in love with the drive over the Richmond Bridge from El Cerrito to her house in Marin. At sunset the sky behind Mount Tam gets so red it's like glazed ceramic. He's never seen a sky that lit up or depthless. Most of the time he arrives in a weird, spiritually-winded state, his voice shot from screaming along with the tape player and his skin numb from prickling in sympathy with so much beauty—visual, aural, and tactile, the soft sea air blowing in his side window and making him feel like nothing in the world can harm him. "What a drive," he says, and they stand at the picture window in her living room with their arms around each other, looking back at the East Bay where he just came from, and the reflected colors of the sunset fading across it. Sometimes, if it's early enough, they walk up to the end of her street to a picnic table stuck under some manzanita and poplars. They sit next to each other in silence, shoulders touching, and watch the lights—houselights, streetlights, car lights—coming on across the bay as the sky fades to amber-navy.

But tonight she's at his house, a two-room, cinder-block bungalow with green carpeting and bamboo plants growing like a curtain over the kitchen window, lying across him on the couch and eating orange chicken and sweet-and-sour pork from the take-out place two blocks south on Shattuck. Her hair is pinned at her neck and she has on jeans and a tight white tank top with string-straps for shoulders. Often, when he first sees her after a day or two apart, he has the feeling he doesn't know who she is. In part this is because she has such changeable looks and a range of facial expressions he can't predict—her skin goes from pale to ruddy in seconds, her eyes and nostrils puff up from emotional or allergic reactions, then smooth again to their original shape in minutes, and when she lets her hair down (pinned up it's chestnut, let down it's more blond) she looks as if she's lost five pounds and two inches of height and her face suddenly squares out at the cheeks so she looks slightly downcast. Mostly, he thinks, she's always surprising him because he just doesn't know her that well (it's only a month now)—or maybe it's the other way around: he doesn't know her because she's constantly surprising him.

Halfway through the movie she falls asleep. He sees her fighting it, eyes flicking open and shut. Just before the point where the main character finally finds the man who's kid-napped his girlfriend, she drops off. Her eyelids look weird to him—like shut flowers or painted seedpods—and he pauses the movie to watch her sleeping, the only light coming from the static image on-screen. He tries to imagine what's behind her breathing—what thoughts or images; the feeling of getting her lungs that full, that steadily. He shakes her leg. "Sasha," he says. "Sasha." The male lead in the movie had spent a lot of time shouting his lover's name into the night and the parity between his saying Sasha's name now and the distraught man's shouting in the movie makes him feel a little silly and self-conscious—then sad because he's alone and feeling self-conscious, which is stupid. He slips out from under her legs and stands next to the couch, hands on his knees, leaning forward. "Sasha," he whispers, then again closer to her ear.

She groans.

He slides in one arm under her neck and the other at the backs of her knees and lifts. He knows the reason she fell so soundly asleep is because they drank too much wine with dinner; he feels it too now as he stands, the blood beating at his temples, making him dizzy and slicing up his vision. She's heavier than he expected. And as soon as he turns to carry her into the bedroom she wakes up, her body stiffening in alarm. "Henry?" she asks.

"Shh, no, it's Billy," he says. "It's OK, you fell asleep."

"Put me down!" She pounds lightly on his shoulder.

He tips his arms so her feet will hit first and lets go.

"What the hell!" she says, looking around, still disconcerted and patting her hair back into place.

"What the hell, what? We were watching a movie," he says. "You fell asleep."

He watches her take things in—the stilled, flickering image of a man chasing another man across a field on the television, the kitchen table cluttered with his books and magazines, her tennis shoes by the couch, the cartons of Chinese takeout with chopsticks sticking out of them. "Oh," she says, and pats her hair once more, then sinks against him, her arms around his neck and her sleep-sour, wine-sour breath blowing across his cheek. "I'm sorry. That's so weird—I woke up and I thought you were Tommy. I must have been dreaming."

"Henry," he says after a second, when she doesn't correct herself, squeezing his hands at her waist.

"Did I say that? Henry? I meant Tommy. The feeling I had was definitely from that time in my life—like being married."

"Married?"

"You know. So to speak, not legally. I told you all about it."

"Yes, that's right."

But her past is such a jumble of commitments and half-commitments, if she told him he's not sure whether Tommy is supposed to be the folksinger with the high voice who drank too much, or the famous country-western guitarist she lived with for two years just before he made it big, or the poet from Alaska who occasionally hit her. Those are the three she talks about most.

The pause button releases and the image on the screen jumps to life, cello tremolo underscoring the action and filling the room, one man chasing the other again and shouting in French.

She turns in his arms to watch a few seconds. "Did they—" she pauses to yawn, "did they find the girl yet?"

He shakes his head. He thinks of the magician then, remembering how the movie ends (he saw it once when it first came out and was deeply impressed)—the main character waking up in a coffin, something like a magician's cabinet, to the sound of dirt being shoveled over him, rocks and clumps of earth that spray apart when they hit the coffin boards. This is how the man's girlfriend vanished and where she's been all along: buried. Finally, he knows, just as the kidnapper had promised him he would. He shouts for help and flicks his cigarette lighter to see where he is, but the space is so tight he can barely lift his head to make out the toes of his shoes. Soon his lighter dies. The sound of rocks and dirt hitting is more and more muffled and his shouts are increasingly contained, deadened by the weight of earth above. He thinks of his girlfriend buried somewhere next to him and remembers what she had shouted to him coming out of a tunnel the last day they were together, her face backlit by blinding sunshine.

"Almost," he says. "We'll watch the rest tomorrow."

She yawns again. "Come," she says, pulling him after her to the bedroom.

———

At his desk the next morning he unburies this memory (seeing it is like watching a movie, not like dreaming or remembering): Late spring, just after sunset and Jenny wasn't expecting him for another half-hour, but he'd managed to get out of his rehearsal early, faking a stomachache. He came in through the basement like she'd told him to, up the twelve plank stairs—it wasn't completely dark, but almost—and pushed on the door which she'd left unlocked and ajar.

"Jenny," he'd whispered. "Jen?" But the television was on and he didn't want to wake up the kids she was baby-sitting, being too loud. She didn't hear him. At first he couldn't tell what was going on. She was on the floor with her head against the couch, her hair spilling into the cushions, and she seemed to be bearing down on something with her hips and ass, pushing out with her legs against the seams of her lowered pants, the open flap of her fly making a faint tat-tat-tat against the back of her hand, her facial expression slack with pleasure. She kept pulling the fly back with her free hand so it wouldn't hit her wrist, but it didn't stay. When he figured out what she was doing he was stunned—couldn't move or say a word, and he couldn't look away. He felt like a bee, stoned on pollen and out of his mind with desire. After a few more minutes she sighed once heavily and opened her eyes, looked at her watch, and sat up straight. She hiked her pants and re-buttoned her fly, wiped her fingers off on the sleeve of her shirt, sniffed them and checked the time again, then went back to watching TV.

The story he's been working on has no place for this scene. It doesn't fit anywhere or mean anything, but he can't get rid of it and soon he finds himself thinking in words to describe her—bringing himself in closer to see things he didn't actually see until later. He knows it's junk, pornography almost, but he can't help himself. Her fingernails were square, like windows, and her fingers had a strange elongated flatness he could never get used to, making him think she must perceive the world of touch flatly, in a way to correspond with such a flat shape. The only sweetness was in the little muscles between her tendons and knuckles, especially between her thumb and forefinger. They were perfect for playing the flute because they were so long and flat-tipped.

He loved watching. Sometimes before she played a piece out loud she'd tap through it with the flute against her chin, the only sound the noise of the pads clicking up and down, making random hollow percussive tones, fourths and thirds, nothing corresponding to the actual music. It reminded him of beads falling and knocking against each other in a jar, or rain in a gutter, but it didn't sound like that. Really, it sounded like nothing but itself.

The story he's working on, "A View of You," is about a pregnant woman whose boyfriend kidnaps her on the way to the abortion clinic. For two months the boyfriend keeps her in a heated shed at the back of his house—brings her gourmet food, books to read, blankets, a paint set, some tropical fish. He vacuums every day, sometimes twice, to keep down the dust and cobwebs (she's allergic), and always lets her outside for the warmest hours of the day.

Billy hates the boyfriend, though he enjoys the feeling of being in his head—blunting and refiguring the world so every object is a potential comfort or hazard to the captive woman. The character can't look at a wall or a door without wondering how well it might contain the woman and muffle her voice. He can't consider warmth without putting a dollar sign next to it and making projections into the future—will he always be able to afford it?—and so on. He keeps a side-porch greenhouse, mostly rose-geraniums, and in the morning he eats apple jelly flavored with geranium petals on wheat bread, with well-milked tea. He wishes he could really taste the geranium petals on his bread but he can't, he can only imagine the smell transforming the tartness of apple jelly because the petals have no true taste. This is the point Billy's stuck on, now, and it has nothing to do with the girlfriend he had liked watching touch herself, but there she is. He realizes she's always there when he's beginning to love a new woman. His computer hums. Outside the fog whips off the bay and the bottlebrush tree growing next to his window, just in flower, bobs against the wind. The telephone is ringing.

———

The next week his story, his first ever in glossy print, hits the newsstands, and he and Sasha go into the mountains to celebrate, walking. "You stud," she says. "You're such a stud. I can't believe it." For a while she stops every second or third party of walkers they meet up with, starts a conversation and then says, "Hey! Look at this," pulling an open copy of the magazine from her knapsack pocket and pointing out his story, there amidst advertisements and pictures of naked college girls. "His first one!"

"It's embarrassing," he says, after the last party's gone on, shuffling past them over the rocks and pine cones, mumbling "Congratulations!" and "Good going!" over their shoulders.

"Why, because of the girlie pictures?"

"No. It's just ridiculous. Bragging."

"Hey. That's why *I* brag *for* you," she says, punching him lightly in the shoulder. "Someone has to."

"No," he says. Then coldly, "In fact—no, nobody has to." He looks hard at her, watching her take this in—her eyes puffing in the corners, the lids lowering like she's frustrated or about to lose her temper. They're at an open section of the trail, overlooking a dried-out slope of pine and sagebrush, pine-smelling air blowing up into their faces from the valley.

She scrapes the end of her walking stick in the dirt. "Fine," she says, facing him. "Fine. It'll never happen again." She says it matter-of-factly, but with enough resistance underlying the words to let him know she thinks he's the one being a fool. Though he can also see that she means it sincerely. Maybe too sincerely. And despite the sincerity (because of it?) finger-like red streaks flare at either side of her nose, then a smaller smear on her chin. Whatever she's thinking, he'll never know.

"No big deal," he says, and for a second, before she's in his arms, he's overwhelmed with appreciation for her—her legs which are firm and supple with light black hair coming up almost to her knees and vanishing, her thin waist and wide shoulders. Then there's only the smell of her hair, her hair tickling his nose, and the full weight of her against him.

Later, watching her walk away, up the trail, nothing between them again but the sight of her and his eyes going over her, he remembers the business about the magician who'd cut her in pieces. "A zigzag cabinet," she told him a few days ago, when he asked about it over dinner at her house. "The cabinet has extra compartments so you can turn one way and then the other to get out of the way." She tried to demonstrate in her chair, across from him. "I don't know how to explain it, really, it's just—see, it looks like you're facing forward because all the audience can see is your face and your feet." She put on a stage-smile and swiveled her shoulders to the side. "But really you're turned to the side in the cabinet and—" she shook her head. "See, I just can't really explain it. You have to be skinny so you can get your behind out of the way, all the way over to the side. I don't know how else to tell you."

So he has a general concept of the illusion, but no real

picture. He had expected something more transformational and dramatic, something magical like the way light splits through air, or total like the buried couple in the movie. Instead, it's only practical—a matter of shifting physical dimension in tight quarters. Because, of course, a woman could never be cut apart and reconstituted, magically or otherwise; anyone knew that.

———

When school ended Jenny's parents were suddenly home all the time, cooking and sitting out on the back deck with books in their laps, or crouched over piles of exams and papers in the living room. Jenny and Billy met at the art museum. They hid their bikes at the back of the museum and walked up the edges of cow pastures, slipping barbed wire fences and sidestepping bogs, to the top of Stone Hill where there was a secluded Eden of dry ground—untrampled grass and little bushes and saplings growing together in rings almost like they'd been arranged that way. Sometimes, if the weather was bad and he could persuade his father to let him borrow the car, they'd drive out on dirt roads until they found a turnout or a field with a clear easement, then park and get in back. But the car was hot and small, with plastic seats, and it smelled like dog vomit. He could never quite forget that smell, or the bits of his father's junk lying around—crumpled shopping lists, receipts, old shirts turned to oil rags, coffee cups—all reminding him that none of this was supposed to be happening.

She was so white around the hips that when the grass touched her it was like seeing something that had no place in nature. He supposed it must have been one of those times, outdoors, in the sadness after making love—because it was over, because it wasn't what he believed it should have been, because they were never careful enough, because her skin was so white and her hair was so vulnerably yellow—it must have been then that she got pregnant. He could even have known it at the time. The sky was particularly depthless one day, maybe, and he had a feeling of giant hands holding him down as he looked up, longing for escape. *Jenny, what are we doing?* he might have asked. *What happens if we get you pregnant?* Or maybe it was the weekend her parents were gone and he claimed to have taken off camping with friends so his father wouldn't know he was seven blocks away, at her house, bored and tired and elated and overwhelmed from so much time alone with her.

The day before her abortion they went to Whitingham Lake, two hours over the border into Vermont (her idea, because she was hungry for sun and water, and because she said she wanted them both not to think about tomorrow). They paddled to the far side of the lake and lay out on the rocks, their rented canoe splashing in the dead water next to them. The sunlight was so strong against the marble and granite that when he slipped into the woods to piss he could not see at all, and coming back into the light Jenny looked wiped out to him, her elastic-frayed underpants and translucently pale skin and her T-shirt knotted between her breasts to expose her rib cage—like something he'd lost the ability to perceive.

"Aren't you a little sad about it?" she asked, as he sat down next to her.

"Sad?" He drew his knees under his chin. "I don't know. I feel terrible. Guilty, mostly. Like everything's my fault." She reached for his hand. Touch was different now they weren't always thinking of sex—or, now they had to think of sex as procreation, not just pleasure. He turned her hand palm-down in his, massaged her knuckles and spun off one of her rings, then slipped it back on.

At its center the lake was stone blue. He knew it was so blue because it was dead from acid rain—no lilies, no algae, no fish to color it. You could row out there, drop a rock and watch it fall hundreds of feet, slowly flashing out of sight, never hitting bottom. At the bottom was a town: Whitingham. Rowing across he'd get so spooked at times he could barely keep going. He was sure no one had been left when the dam went up and the water rose; people must have moved their things away long ago, dug up the cemetery and probably wrecked most of the last standing structures. It was a failing mill town anyway and no one would have wanted to stay. Still, he couldn't stop himself from picturing it—people stranded down there in the weedy streets, Jenny and him floating by overhead, their canoe-bottom on the water surface like nothing at all, smaller than a plane crossing the sky, and the little eddy-trail behind them where their paddles tore in and vanished.

———

Sara is zigzag across the bed, one leg out straight, the other drawn up, knee bent like she's scaling a mountain. A year ago, when we first met, I was alarmed by the way she would fall into a stupor like this, after drinking. I'd lie awake sometimes for hours feeling cheated, wondering how she could make such a sudden, total exit from consciousness—no post-connubial wind down or reluctant last kisses—and what was wrong with me that I had such feelings of hurt and annoyance. One night she passed out upside-down in the bed, at a diagonal so her feet were on both pillows and I had nowhere to lie. I tried prodding her awake for a while, even flicked the lamp on and off and tapped her lightly on the cheeks. No help. I got out of bed and went into the living room to watch the end of a movie we'd started earlier. When I came back to bed she had shifted her position so at least I could lie down, though still I couldn't wake her.

Tonight is our last night together for the next two months and I'm awake trying to prepare myself for that, trying to convince myself it's OK, practicing being alone while she's still physically present so it won't be such a shock later. My tongue feels swollen and my mouth is paint-purple from expensive wine. I know because in the last few hours I've used the bathroom about a dozen times, each time stopping at the mirror to have a good look in my eyes and be grounded—to say things like, "Hey, I never meant to get mixed up with a musician. For God's sake, this isn't what I *wanted*." But it doesn't matter what I say or how I feel about her leaving, or how long I sit here next to the bed, not sleeping. The fact remains: as soon as it's light she will throw together a few last things she hasn't already packed in the trunk of her car, steam herself an espresso and vanish. There's a trajectory which carries her away from me. I know its geography and can name most of the places she'll be playing in the next few weeks. And I know that what she loves (being on stage: her voice, her hair, her fingers, her body, her guitar, all things to be fractured and reconfigured, lovingly or not, in the minds of her listeners)—I know this is what takes her from me and that it makes her happy. And although understanding is some relief, it never makes her disappearance anything less than total.

Later today, in my writing class, I'll have to struggle to finish sentences and not pause incongruously over every third or fourth word. My eyelids will twitch and pulse from exhaustion. My students won't notice. They'll think class is dull, maybe, but they won't know what strain I'm under to keep my senses intact. There's something I've been meaning to tell them for a while now—maybe today—something about climax and stories and the storm of sperm cells it takes to fertilize one egg. "All creative acts are alike," I'll say. "Because it takes a storm of bad ideas and images and words set adrift to find the one penetrating image, moment, what-ever—the one thing," I'll throw my hands up, "that finally gets inside your story and lights it up. Makes it live. So don't hold back." But maybe I won't bring it up at all. When I was younger, teaching the violin, I tried to make my students understand tone production by telling them to visualize male and female forces mating in the center of a note. "Tone is sexual," I'd say. "Make it yin and yang, the flower and the bee, the wind and what it goes against." None of them ever seemed helped by my crackpot metaphors and eventually I gave up—took a more purely mechanical approach.

Sara turns toward me. I see her eyes catching light from the street lamp outside the window next to me, glinting clear and vanishing again. "David?" she says. She yawns.

"Right here." I lean forward and the light goes more evenly across her face.

"Why don't you come to bed?" She reaches a hand for me. She doesn't sound sad or defeated, only welcoming. "Come," she says, flexing her hand open and shut, then letting it fall on the mattress beside her. "I have to be up soon anyway. We'll lie together." She yawns again and clears her throat. "Listen, soon you'll have so much of me around here

you won't be able to stand it. Just think about that, once."
She pauses. She has as much faith in this description of our
future together as she has in anything. Whether or not it's
true, in the end, is another story. "Now come lie down. I
have to have you next to me."

I go to her. But even enveloped in the musty-sweet smell
of her sleep and sweat, her head on my chest and our legs
crossed together, I can't let go. Her breath tickles on my collarbone, hot and cold, and I try to picture us from above,
how the blankets have slipped down to our waists and her
hair lies across the pillow behind her. I have only one trick
left to make myself relax—the memory trick. So I start from
the beginning, hoping the picked-over armature of sentences
will bring me back under, down to whatever half-conscious
music and logic and memory spawned them. I see the words
on the page and try to feel them three-dimensionally: *They
park in blond fields of straw stubble, half a mile from the
fairgrounds, the land here rolling and swelling like waves,
and walk with dozens of other festivalgoers in the air that is
thick with dust and straw particles, sunlight fracturing into
shafts through it....* Sara rolls away from me and I roll with
her, my arm across her hip. Light comes in through the
blinds now—faint green and orange first light—so it's almost
time. I close my eyes and begin again, looking for a way out
of myself: *They park in fields of blond straw stubble half a
mile from the fairgrounds ...* but it's no good. The dream
inside the words is gone. I press my nose to her spine, a hand
on her stomach and slide in one leg between hers. Her hand
closes on mine, fingers squeezing between fingers, and we lie
like that, not moving, until full light.

ACKNOWLEDGMENTS

I WOULD LIKE TO THANK THE MACDOWELL COLONY, THE Ragdale Foundation, The Corporation at Yaddo, The University of Iowa Writers' Workshop, and the Michener-Copernicus Society of America for support while writing these stories. Thanks also to Marilynne Robinson, Ann Williams, David Lavender, Deb Garrison, Devon Jersild, and Marianne Leslie Nora for reading and invaluable editorial advice. Thanks to my parents, Larry and Alice Spatz, for always being there when I needed them. Most of all, thanks to my wife, Caridwen, for her wisdom, unflagging patience, and generosity.